STOLEN
ONES

BOOKS BY ANGELA MARSONS

Angela
MARSONS
STOLEN
ONES

bookouture

Published by Bookouture in 2021

An imprint of Storyfire Ltd.
Carmelite House
50 Victoria Embankment
London EC4Y 0DZ

www.bookouture.com

Paperback ISBN: 978-1-83888-737-7
eBook ISBN: 978-1-83888-736-0

This book is dedicated to Claire Bord, the most passionate, supportive and committed editor in the world. And so much more.

PROLOGUE

The door opens and I stare at it. Why is the door opening after all this time?

I grab brown bear and hold him close.

Is someone coming in? Are they coming to get me? Where am I being taken now?

I don't know how I feel.

I've waited so long for the door to open, and now my stomach is rolling like when I had to do a sums test that I wasn't ready for.

'Oh no... oh no... oh no...' I whisper as I back away from it. I don't understand.

Brown bear's ear hovers close to my mouth. I give in to temptation and allow it into my mouth. I spit it back out again. Only little girls chew on toys.

I reach for the hairbrush on the dressing table. It sits beside the small glass jewellery box that holds my most treasured possessions: a sparkly bangle and a silver chain. They're new and I just love to take them out, touch them and put them back again.

Behind the jewellery box is my diary, covered with my favourite Barbie picture. I never had anything so lovely before in my whole life.

I turn away from the door completely and look at the other side of the dresser. The triangular sandwich packaging from lunch sits on the top. The apple core has fallen inside it. Hot meal for breakfast; sandwich, crisps and fruit for lunch; and biscuits and crackers for snacks.

Keeping my back to the door, I move to the desk in the corner. My schoolbooks are open. Double reading on Tuesday afternoon. Every Tuesday afternoon.

I remove the strawberry from the end of the pencil and replace it with a furry grape. It's purple, my favourite. Another present. I love it.

I turn back to my books but can't concentrate. Before I realise it, I am chewing on the purple grape, and strands of fur are resting on my tongue.

I scratch at my tongue to remove them and wipe my hands on my jeans.

Gross.

I step into the bathroom and swill my hands under the mixer tap. Maybe when I return the door will be closed again.

After using the towel, I fold it. I'm not sure why. No one else uses this bathroom.

It's mine. All mine.

It's my toilet, my bath, my shower, my sink. My wardrobe filled with new clothes. My bed that's bigger than a single but not as big as Mummy's bed.

My very own television is fixed to the wall above my desk. I can see it from my bed or from the soft cushioned single chair beside the door.

I still don't understand what's going on.

I look to the single camera nestled in the far corner of the room. I stare at it waiting for an answer.

It doesn't answer me.

Beyond the door is grass, bushes, trees. I strain my neck to get a better look, to see what else is beyond.

Nothing happens.

I take a step, making sure I take brown bear with me.

Another step.

And then suddenly I am there. I am at the open door.

I have only one question.

What am I supposed to do now?

ONE

'So, where were you when Melody Jones was abducted?' Kim asked, turning off Bryant's car radio. She'd already heard the mother's plea for new information on breakfast news earlier that day. It was the twenty-five-year anniversary of the seven-year-old's abduction, and Kim had every sympathy for a family that was still waiting for closure.

'Hmm... twenty-five years ago I was a young, good-looking police officer in my late-twenties. Had myself a gorgeous fiancée and was pretty happy with life.'

'And I'd just left foster family number five,' Kim said.

'Bloody hell, guv, way to make me feel old,' he grumbled, pulling into Halesowen police station car park.

He didn't ask questions about any of her seven foster homes, knowing she was unlikely to share.

She got out of the car and didn't rush into the building as she normally did.

Bryant eyed her questioningly.

'You carry on up – I'll be with you in a minute.'

He shrugged and headed into the building.

She leaned against the wall and took out her phone. She'd set it on silent first thing, not because of the statement they'd been to take for an assault, but because unwanted calls were blowing up her phone twice a day, every day. Although she hated keeping anything from her team, Bryant in particular would be most concerned about any contact from the sociopathic psychiatrist. It had been almost a week since Alexandra Thorne had first tried to call her from prison, and she had rejected every call. So far.

Her sensible brain wondered which part of her psyche had added those two words to the end of the thought. Without those two words the thought was decisive, definite, resolute. Those two words left a question in her mind.

She was sure there was nothing the woman had to say that she wanted to hear. And yet.

God damn those two-word hecklers that insisted on inserting themselves into her musings.

Anyone who knew her could testify that contact of any kind with the sociopathic psychiatrist was detrimental to her well-being. Doctor Alexandra Thorne was the most intelligent person Kim had ever known. She was also the most evil, ruthless, amoral, despicable excuse for a human being that she'd ever had the misfortune to meet.

Despite Kim's enviable defences, Alex had the ability to see right inside her, as though looking at an X-ray. She had the skill, like a cadaver dog, to sniff out every weakness that Kim was able to hide from everyone else. And Alex had made it her mission in life to seek out those vulnerabilities and expose every one.

Yes, the fascination had run both ways between them, Kim admitted. She had been equally repulsed and intrigued by the cold detachment with which the woman had played with people's lives and emotions for her own sick game.

So far, after both encounters with the woman, Kim had walked away intact.

She was willing to bet that a third time she would not be quite so lucky.

TWO

'Okay, kiddies, what's cooking?' Kim asked, entering the squad room. She was pleased to see that a fresh pot of coffee was already brewing. Bryant had put his head start up the stairs to good use.

'Got CPS approval for a charge on Lester Baggot,' Stacey said, fist pumping the air.

'Great news,' Kim said, sitting on the edge of the spare desk.

Lester Baggot had been abusing his wife, to their knowledge, for the last five years. A routine had developed. They received the call of a disturbance at the address. They attended, separated the couple, begged Louise to press charges, she'd refuse and a few weeks later they'd be back again and the whole process would be repeated.

Four nights ago, Louise had been taken to hospital with two broken bones and a serious concussion. The decision to charge had been taken out of her hands. Kim just hoped the woman took the opportunity to make a fresh start away from her abusive husband.

'Penn?'

'Hard act to follow,' he said, smiling at his colleague. 'No such luck for me. Still can't find anyone matching the description of Casper.'

The DS had been investigating a string of car thefts on the Blakemore Estate. As far as crooks went, this one was a bit of a gentleman. Broke in during the night, found the car keys, stole the car, left nothing disturbed, woke no one and then managed to disappear, avoiding camera detection. Penn had nicknamed him the friendly ghost.

'Got one hit of the stolen Toyota passing by a front garden at 3.15 a.m., but then nothing.'

It was the fifth car to go missing from the same estate in a month.

'I've put in a request for some mobile CCTV units to be positioned on the entry and exit points of the estate.'

Kim nodded her agreement and wondered, for the hundredth time, what kind of world they'd live in if the criminals used their intelligence and skills to do good.

'Okay, make sure you get one placed at—'

Kim stopped speaking as Bryant's phone rang.

He listened and then pushed the receiver towards her.

'It's Jack for you.'

Did no one ring her own phone anymore? Was all communication filtered through her colleague?

She reached across and hit the loudspeaker.

'Go ahead, Jack,' she said to the desk sergeant.

'I've got another one, marm,' he offered wearily.

Kim groaned. She didn't need any explanation. Anniversaries brought out the weirdos. The more the media coverage, the more confessions they received, and in the last two days, three men and one woman had come in to confess to the abduction of Melody Jones. The last one hadn't done his sums right and had no answer when Penn had asked how he'd managed to pull it off when he'd only been two and a half years old himself.

Kim looked around the room. 'Okay, by my count it's Stacey's turn to...'

'Only wants you, marm. He really insists you're going to want to hear him out.'

Kim felt herself stiffen. If there was one thing she hated more than weirdos wasting their time, it was the ones who insisted on wasting hers.

'Okay, Jack, put him in interview room one. I'll be down shortly.'

Bryant filled her mug with strong black coffee. 'Keeps her calm,' he said to the others.

'You wish,' Kim said, taking the drink from him.

She had a mind to make their visitor wait, but she couldn't get on with her day until she'd listened and discredited confessor number five.

As she headed down the stairs, coffee in hand, she considered just how many pieces of her mind she was going to give him for wasting their time.

She opened the door and stepped in, immediately hiding her surprise.

It wasn't news to her that you couldn't deduce anything by appearance. There was no photofit for a criminal, a murderer, a paedophile or someone suffering from mental illness. She knew that, but the man standing before her appeared to be none of the above.

She guessed him to be mid-fifties. He had salt-and-pepper hair cut tidily around an attractive, tanned face.

His light-blue shirt was a quality brand that fitted him perfectly and was tucked into belted black trousers. He stood a couple of inches higher than her own five foot nine, and he appeared to have an athletic build.

'Steven Harte,' he said, thrusting out his hand as though they were meeting at some kind of conference.

She ignored the hand and sat down.

'Please take a seat, Mr Harte, and tell me what you profess to know about the abduction of Melody Jones.'

'Profess?' he asked, frowning, as he took a seat.

'You're our fifth this week, so please forgive my suspicion.'

The frown remained.

'But why would someone confess to something they didn't do?'

'Yes quite, Mr Harte, why would they?'

'I'm not here with any kind of false confession, DI Stone. I have information that will lead you straight to her.'

His voice was calm and measured if a little surprised that he was being doubted.

Kim liked to understand the motivation of people's actions. Common sense told her the man before her was a liar, just like the four previous confessors, although he wasn't claiming to have actually abducted her.

So far, they'd had a sixty-five-year-old male who came in and confessed to every major crime. The next one had been a confirmed delusional; the third one, a female, had been a reporter from Berkshire trying to learn more about the case for a feature she was writing; and the fourth had been Penn's maths genius who had pissed off someone from a rival gang and thought the police station was the safest place for him until it died down.

Their confessions had all been debunked, and they'd been asked to leave once she'd understood their motives for lying.

And that was all she wanted from this guy before she showed him the door.

'So, what date was Melody Jones taken?'

'Sixteenth of August in 1996.'

'What time?'

'Three o'clock.'

'From where?' Kim asked.

She didn't need any paperwork to check his answers. She now knew them by heart.

'The playground at the edge of Hollytree Estate.'

'And what was she wearing?'

The man closed his eyes. A little smile tugged at his lips as though recalling a fond memory. Kim felt nausea swirl in her stomach.

'Little pink leggings. I think they were called pedal pushers. They had blue spots on. Her vest top was rainbow stripes. It was a hot day.' He frowned. 'She didn't have any lotion on.'

Kim ignored the disapproval in his voice and focused on his answers. Everything he'd answered so far was correct. It was also public record. There was no mention of the silver chain with a heart that had been on her wrist. A present from her grandmother with her initials engraved on the heart. That detail had never been released.

'Tell me something that you couldn't have found out by reading the thousands of news reports available.'

He smiled and traced imaginary circles on the table.

'And where would be the fun in that?'

Evasion.

Kim's heart rate began to slow as his motivations became clear. For a minute, he'd had her going with his easy and accurate recall of the details, but his failure to offer anything extra demonstrated he was just another crackpot. A well-dressed, presentable crackpot but not all crackpots came from Hollytree. She had spent the first six years of her life in that place.

'You will find out everything eventually, Inspector, but it'll be on my terms.'

'There are no terms, Mr Harte, unless you want to take me to the body. You drive, I'll dig.'

He smiled. 'All in good time, but you're about to be faced with a more urgent problem and—'

'I think you've taken enough of my time already, Mr Harte,' she said, pushing back her chair. 'I now understand your motivation for this confession. You want to play games with the police. You want some kind of fame off the back of a family's misery, and you expect us to play along with the false hope that we'll recover Melody's body.'

Again, that tolerant smile but no words.

'I don't know why you need this kind of attention, Mr Harte, but you're not going to get it here.'

She headed to the door, opened it and turned back.

'The desk sergeant will show you out.'

She stormed back up the stairs, even more annoyed with this waster than the others. This one had wanted nothing more than to get the attention of the police and engage them in some sort of twisted game.

'I swear, Bryant, you're taking the next one,' she growled, entering the squad room.

'Sshh...' Bryant said, turning up his police radio.

All three heads were turned towards it.

'Another one gone, boss,' Penn said.

'Another...?'

'Little girl, guv,' Bryant answered. 'Taken from a kiddie's day centre in Netherton. Eight years old.'

Kim stopped dead. Every cell in her body turned to ice.

You're about to be faced with a more urgent problem.

'Oh, shit,' she said, running out of the office.

Was that what Steven Harte had been talking about? And how the hell had he known?

'Fuck,' she cursed as she ran down the stairs as quickly as she could.

She key coded herself out of the corridor and fled past a surprised-looking Jack as she almost ran into the automatic doors instead of waiting for them to open.

He couldn't have gone far. She'd left him only minutes ago.

She scanned the car park. There was no one getting into a car and no car waiting to exit.

Damn. She didn't even know if he'd come on foot.

Right now, Kim didn't know if she'd just been speaking with a killer or not, but she wanted to know how he'd foreseen the disappearance of another little girl, or what he'd meant by his prophetic comment.

She ran back inside.

'Jack, did you see which way he went?'

'Who?'

'The guy you showed into the interview room earlier. Which way did he go?'

'He didn't.'

'Didn't what?' she snapped.

'Leave.'

'Jack, you're testing my...'

He nodded towards the corridor. 'He's still in there. He said you'd be back in a minute.'

Kim's relief quickly turned to annoyance. What game was this guy playing? How the hell had he known?

She steadied her breathing before re-entering the interview room. Right now, her instinct was telling her to barge in there and pin him up against the wall. She took a moment to calm down. Before she set any wheels in motion, she had to get her thinking head on. Up to this point he had admitted nothing. His carefully worded statements were nowhere near a confession to any crime.

She couldn't even call him a suspect or a witness. At best he was a member of the public who wanted to assist them with their enquiries.

She kept that thought in her head as she re-entered the room.

'So, you appear to be psychic, Mr Harte. Either that or you had some involvement in the abduction of a little girl earlier today.'

He shrugged and offered that half-smile she wanted to smack from his face.

'Would you like to share where she is?' Kim asked, fixing him with a hard stare.

'I'm more than happy to tell you everything I know. On my terms.'

'And what are they?' Kim asked, trying to keep her tone in check. She still had no clue as to what she was dealing with. A lucky prankster or a kidnapper and murderer.

'I'll let you know later, once you get back.'

'From where?' Kim asked.

'Well, I'd imagine you need to be present at the scene of the crime. Take some statements, question the witnesses, do police things. You can go,' he said dismissively.

Kim kept the rage inside her mouth at his superior attitude. Damn it. That was exactly where she needed to be.

'Don't worry, I'm not going anywhere,' he said, leaning back in his seat. 'I'm sure you can keep an eye on me,' he added, nodding towards the CCTV camera nestled in the corner.

'What the hell are you playing at, Mr Harte?' she asked, already feeling the pull towards the site of the disappearance.

He linked his hands behind his head. 'I'll be perfectly fine while you're gone. If Jack could just get me a strong cup of tea, one sugar.'

Kim rarely, if ever, felt at a complete loss with how to handle someone but right now she had to err on the side of caution. If he did have information on the disappearance of either Melody Jones or the girl she'd just heard about, she had to tread carefully.

She pushed the chair back.

'Mr Harte, I'm leaving now. If you know something about this abduction and you leave, I will find you and charge you with withholding evidence. If you have no wish to help the investigation or if you hinder it, I will ensure that you are punished to the full extent of the law.'

'Dramatic words, Inspector, but totally unnecessary. I'll be here when you get back. I'm looking forward to it.'

Kim offered him one last look before leaving with her fists buried deeply in her pockets.

He hadn't said enough of anything to warrant an arrest. If the PACE regulations listed being a superior, annoying knob as an offence, he'd already be in a cell but, unfortunately, she didn't have that power.

'Fire up that computer,' Kim said, pointing to the PC that occupied the spare desk in the squad room.

Three pairs of eyes questioned her. She guessed they were all wondering why she wasn't already on her way to Netherton.

Bryant stood. 'Guv, do you not think we should be on our way to—'

'I'm aware of where we need to be,' she snapped, nodding towards Stacey to do what she'd asked.

Stacey rose from her own desk and logged in to the computer.

'Interview room one,' she said.

A few keystrokes later she was looking at the man himself.

'Meet Steven Harte,' Kim said to the rest of her team, who all moved forward to take a closer look. 'Our latest weirdo who might not be so weird after all.'

'You think he knows something about Melody Jones?' Penn asked.

'Says he does and also alluded to knowing about our missing girl today.'

'And he's here voluntarily?' Stacey asked doubtfully.

'Not only is he here but he's in no great hurry to leave,' she said as Jack entered the room and placed a cup of tea on the table.

'But why?' Bryant asked.

'Exactly what I want to know,' Kim said, turning to her team.

'Stace, I want to know everything about Steven Harte, and Penn, I want you to record him and watch him until your eyes bleed. If he makes one move to leave, you delay him or stick with him. Got it?'

'Got it, boss,' he said, taking a seat.

'Bryant, we're now off to Netherton,' she said, reaching for her jacket.

She took one last look at the figure on the computer screen.

As if sensing her attention, he raised his hand to the camera and gave her a little wave.

THREE

Alexandra Thorne replaced the receiver for the second time that day and tried not to show her annoyance. Any kind of strong emotion would not serve her well this week.

To get what she wanted she had no choice but to maintain the charade that had been exhausting her for the last four and a half years.

But why wouldn't the damn woman take her call? she seethed, heading back to her cell.

No matter how diligently she planned her next move, DI Stone always managed to be the fly in the ointment.

She'd timed her approach to the detective perfectly, to coincide with her plan. She'd also bargained on the woman's curiosity getting the better of her and taking the call, but it appeared that this time DI Stone was playing hard to get.

The police officer had no idea what information Alexandra was now holding. The thought put a smile back on her face. She had knowledge that could change the woman's whole life. And she would share it. For a price.

The time that she'd invested in the scheme had yielded better results than she could ever have imagined. She had learned more than she'd ever hoped for, and the time had come for her to use the leverage. All she needed now was to get Stone on the phone and the rest would fall into place.

'Damn you for making this harder than it need be,' she whispered to herself as she entered her cell.

Her loyal and obliging cellmate lay on the bed reading a battered Jackie Collins novel.

Emma Mitchell had been an invaluable source of information to her for the last eighteen months.

Emma was what Alex liked to call one of life's 'likeables'. Slim and attractive, her physical appearance was non-threatening and non-confrontational. She had a ready smile and a pleasant demeanour that allowed her to fade. Whether intentional or not, it afforded her the luxury of being ignored most of the time, which kept her out of trouble and enabled her to float around listening to conversations and gaining intelligence. Most of which Alex had stored for future use.

'Out,' Alex instructed, sitting on her own bed. For her next move, she wanted privacy.

'Aww... come on – this is just getting juicy,' she said, waving the book about.

'Save it for bedtime then,' Alex said, offering her non-negotiable look.

Emma rolled her eyes, closed the book and sloped off the bed.

Alex waited until she was out of the room before she retrieved the A4 exercise book and pen from beneath her pillow.

For the hundredth time, Alex marvelled at the irony of the life she'd had on the outside: a flourishing career as a respected psychiatrist, a full appointment book, a nice house, a flashy car and more money than she knew what to do with. She had been able to buy anything she wanted, whenever she wanted. And now she had to beg for the most basic of necessities like a notebook and pen.

The book was allegedly her journal, her reflection of events that had led to her incarceration. A necessary part of her rehabilitation. It was nothing of the sort. It was a record of every detail she'd learned over the years about inmates and officers alike. It was her power. It held names, dates, events and most likely her ticket to freedom. It was like currency she'd been saving for a rainy day, and that storm was due to hit later this week.

She shouldn't be surprised that Stone was getting in her way again. It was all she'd done since the minute they'd met. And for that she deserved every minute of the torture she'd inflicted and intended to continue inflicting. The fact that the woman's psyche was battered and covered with scar tissue only added to her enjoyment. She knew she had the power to break the detective apart; it was just knowing which particular vulnerability would seal the deal. She looked forward to that day, but for now she just needed to get her to take her call.

And this book was going to help her do just that. Now, which of her assets was she willing to sacrifice to execute the next part of her plan?

She flicked the pages until she was five sheets in and found what she was looking for.

She smiled as a plan began to form in her mind.

Officer Barry Adams always did a cell check at 2.30 p.m., which gave her just ten minutes. Plenty of time.

She retrieved the hairbrush from the table that separated the two beds and placed it on her own bed with the thin metal teeth facing up. She rolled her T-shirt up to her breasts and tucked the fabric under her bra, then lay down on the brush using her own body weight to force the teeth against her skin. She moved around every couple of minutes and repeated the process until her abdomen was sore.

She was finished just in time as she heard Officer Adams call something into the next cell.

She put the brush aside as he appeared at her doorway.

'Everything okay, Thorne?'

'Actually, no,' she said, rising from the bed and moving unsteadily towards him.

'I don't feel well. I'm hot and light-headed. I've got some kind of rash.'

She stood in the doorway, in full view of ten or more inmates.

'Here,' she said, lifting up her top.

Officer Adams moved closer to take a look at the dozens of red spots marking her skin. He put a hand at her waist to steady her.

Three. Two. One.

'Officer Adams, what the hell are you doing?' she cried out.

Every head turned their way to see her with her T-shirt lifted up and Officer Adams standing way too close to her with his hand on her waist.

His face reddened immediately as he stepped away from her.

She moved out of sight and spoke quietly.

'I want a smartphone by six o'clock; otherwise, your attempt to touch me will be a written complaint to Warden Siviter.'

'B-But I didn't. I wouldn't...'

'Yes, but you've already had one report against you. One more and you're out of a job.'

His face turned thunderous.

A new inmate had accused him of touching her inappropriately during the body search. The complaint had gone nowhere, but a second incident would prompt a thorough investigation. And she had witnesses.

'Don't argue, Adams, because you know I'll do it. A phone by six o'clock.'

She turned and headed back into her cell.

A shiver of anticipation ran through her.

She would be speaking to DI Stone tonight.

FOUR

Little Peeps was a day-care centre situated just outside Netherton on the road to Dudley. A short walk from Hillcrest School, it served working parents for a pick-up and drop-off service outside of school hours. Throughout the school holidays it remained open for working parents who didn't have the luxury of grandparents or a family support network.

Bryant drove slowly through the groups congregating close to the premises. Vehicles were parking haphazardly all over the place as uniformed officers struggled to keep order.

'It's bloody bedlam,' Bryant observed, pulling in behind a hastily parked Citroën. The woman gave a half-apologetic wave before hurrying towards the entrance.

'You wouldn't have done the same thing with Laura when she was a kid?' she asked of his only daughter.

'She's here for the week, and if you want the truth, I don't want to let her go back,' he said, proving her point. Laura had been working away, putting her midwifery degree to good use, for almost eighteen months, and Bryant still felt safer when she was under his roof.

It was a natural reaction, and she couldn't blame them for

rushing to ensure their children's safety. The shit parking was another matter. Cars had pulled up onto the pavement and were spilling out onto the main road.

The two of them wound their way on foot to the front door, which was opened by a harassed-looking girl in her late teens. Uniformed officers were trying to keep order, but they were dealing with parents who wanted access to their children.

After checking their IDs, the girl guided them through a warren of rooms, all filled with parents exchanging anxious looks while holding tightly to their children.

Kim noted that the age range seemed to span pre-school toddlers to pre-teens.

'They're all in here,' the girl said, opening the door marked 'Office'.

Inside was Inspector Plant, a woman in her early fifties and a younger woman wearing a nurse's uniform beneath a light summer jacket. Her expression and pallor needed no introduction.

Kim introduced herself and her partner just as Inspector Plant began edging towards the door. He looked to her for confirmation. She nodded. He was eager to go and check on his team, who would be conducting the initial search of the area and carrying out door-to-door checks.

'Andrea Newhouse, owner,' said the woman from behind the desk. 'And this is Claire Lennard, Grace's mother.'

Kim nodded at them both as she took a seat. She could feel the trembling of the woman beside her. Kim guessed she was feeling a mixture of despair, anguish but also hope that Grace was going to turn up safe and sound any minute now. Kim had that same hope, but after her earlier exchange with Steven Harte the hope was diminishing with every passing minute.

'Can you tell us exactly what happened, Ms Newhouse?'

'Yes, it was just after lunch. Around two o'clock some of the staff were settling the little ones down for a nap. The older ones were making their way outside. They're planting a herb garden at the top of the yard. The fire alarm went off. Everyone headed for the designated meeting point: the shed by the back fence, away from the building. There was a roll call. Everyone was present and accounted for. We did a search of the premises. The fire service attended to do a check. They put it down to a blip in the app we all have on our phones that control the intruder and smoke alarms. They reset the system, declared us safe and left. The kids were all milling around, chatting about all the excitement, when Deana noticed the back gate had been left open by the firefighters. She alerted all staff and took another roll call and that's when we found that Grace was missing.'

'Did you check the immediate area?'

The woman nodded. Of course she had. Any decent day-care business had procedures in place.

'Myself and two colleagues searched the streets behind the property while another staff member called the police.'

'What was the exact time of the second roll call?' Kim asked.

'Two thirty-eight,' she said as Bryant noted the times in his notebook.

Grace had been gone for almost three hours.

'So, she might still be wandering around, lost, might she?' Claire Lennard asked hopefully. She stood. 'I should be out looking...'

'Please sit down, Ms Lennard,' Kim said, placing a steadying hand on the woman's arm. 'There are officers out searching for Grace right now.'

Kim knew that every available officer had been called to the area. They would already be knocking doors and checking gardens.

'I know you want to be out there trying to find her, but we need you here right now.'

She nodded and sat back down.

'Is there anyone at home?'

Claire shook her head.

'How far is it and could Grace make her way back?'

'It's about four miles away, in Sedgley, but I don't think...'

'Kids are cleverer than we think. Can you call a neighbour and ask them to keep watch on the house until we get someone there to check properly?'

'Yes, yes, of course,' she said, taking out her phone.

Kim wasn't hopeful but she had to cover all bases and treat it like every other missing child case. She had to put the conversation with Steven Harte out of her mind.

'Have you noticed anything suspicious around the property?' Kim asked the nursery owner as Claire ended her call. Kim caught the look of horror that crossed Andrea Newhouse's face.

'You don't think she's been taken?' Claire asked.

'We have to consider every possibility,' Kim offered gently.

She knew full well that the thought would already have crossed the woman's mind. But it didn't have legs until it came out of someone else's mouth.

'We're doing everything we can to find her, Ms Lennard. I promise you,' Kim assured her, turning back to the business owner as she spoke.

'Nothing suspicious that I'm aware of, Officer, but the girls are talking to all the children to see if they've noticed anything untoward.'

Kim turned again to Claire. 'Has there been anything strange at home? Weird phone calls? Unusual comments from Grace?'

Claire shook her head as the tears began to gather in her eyes.

'Grace's father?'

Claire shook her head.

'Are you sure he couldn't have...?'

'He's dead,' she offered, severing the tie on one of the last balloons of hope Kim had.

'Sorry. I didn't mean...'

Claire waved away her apology.

'CCTV?' she asked Ms Newhouse.

She nodded and stood. 'I have the app on my phone, but the full system is next door.'

Kim stood. Their interrogation of the system would take more than a mobile-phone app.

'I'll be back in a sec, Claire,' the woman said before leaving the room.

Kim noted the business owner's hunched apologetic demeanour as it finally hit her that she'd lost someone else's child.

She followed the woman past a kitchen/break room to a door marked 'Private' at the end of the corridor. She key coded the door and pushed it open.

'Do you need me to...?'

'Just the password,' Kim said, expecting the woman to move ahead and log them into the system.

'Top drawer, yellow Post-it notes and yes, I know what you're going to say, but I can't remember them all.'

Oh, if only it was one of their priorities to police password security instead of dead bodies and missing children.

'Thanks, we'll be fine.'

Bryant took the seat closest to the keyboard and mouse. Although not technically minded like Stacey or Penn, he was adept at navigating his way around most CCTV systems, and this looked like a decent set-up.

Bryant logged in using the password from the Post-it note.

The screen filled with mini screens, sixteen in total. In the bottom left-hand corner was a label for each location.

'Where to start?' Bryant asked.

'Confirm the timeline,' Kim said.

Bryant clicked on the screen for the kitchen and set the clock for two o'clock. She could see three adults and two older kids tidying around the area. At exactly five minutes past the hour they all froze and looked at each other. Okay, the owner was bang on with that.

'Okay, go outside,' Kim said.

'Which one?'

There were four external cameras. One on the front door, one on the back door, a wide lens that covered almost all of the outside space and a fixed camera on the back gate.

'The wide view,' she said, poking the screen.

He adjusted the time to catch the mass exodus of kids and adults as they streamed out of the back door and headed towards the shed at the edge of the property.

Last to leave was the owner, carrying a clipboard, behind two women each carrying a young child.

'There she is,' Bryant said as Grace Lennard entered the screen from the other side of the garden, matching the description they'd been given while they'd been travelling towards the day centre.

Kim heard the emotion in his voice.

'She has the exact same colour hair that Laura had at that age.'

Kim couldn't help the feeling of sickness that stole over her as she watched the little girl dust off her dirty hands and then wipe them on her purple trousers. Blonde curls tumbled around her face, and one of the Bratz characters was visible on her white T-shirt.

Kim watched as she became part of the crowd. She started talking to the other kids, acting naturally, enjoying all of the excitement of the incident while seeing none of the danger.

Kim wanted to pause the recording, run outside and grab her to stop what was about to happen. A part of her brain fooled her that she was watching events in real time, which happened when you could see the object of your attention talking and moving before your very eyes.

Bryant's silence told her he was thinking the exact same thing.

Everyone stayed together as Ms Newhouse took a roll call. The kids raised their hands and shouted out when their name was called.

Within minutes the owner opened the back gate and two fire officers entered.

Lock the gate, Kim screamed inside as a young girl just pushed it back into place.

Ms Newhouse accompanied the fire officers into the building.

The camera continued to record the staff and children outside. The groups moved and changed as kids joined other groups and carried on talking.

Kim kept her gaze on Grace Lennard, looking for anything out of the ordinary. There was nothing. She moved amongst her friends, chattering and laughing, secure in the knowledge that the incident was being handled by the adults.

Fifteen minutes elapsed before Newhouse returned to the group and everyone began to filter back towards the building.

Kim guessed they'd been given the all-clear by the fire service to return.

The nausea in Kim's stomach increased as she saw Grace hanging back. She approached the last adult and pointed in the direction from which she'd come when the fire alarm had sounded. The adult nodded, and Grace left the scope of the camera. Alone.

Lock the bloody gate, she wanted to scream at the camera.

'You want me to switch to another...?'

'Not yet,' Kim said. She wanted to see this camera through.

They watched an empty screen in silence until there was a movement of the gate. It opened halfway for just a few seconds before closing again.

'Not yet,' she said, knowing that Bryant wanted to switch cameras.

Three minutes after the gate had moved, the staff member last seen by Grace appeared on screen. It was clear she was looking and calling. Her movements became more frantic and urgent as she opened the shed door and then searched all around it. She moved out of shot, Kim guessed, to check the area Grace had been working.

Once back in shot she stopped dead at the unlocked gate. She took a quick look outside the gate before sprinting back into the building.

Within a minute three women charged through the screen and headed out of the back gate.

'Okay, switch to the gate camera,' Kim instructed.

She had wanted to check the timeline as well as gauge the initial response from the staff members. At this stage it was impossible to rule out inside involvement, but as yet she'd seen nothing to suggest anything untoward.

Minutes – it was literally a couple of minutes that Grace Lennard had been outside alone.

Bryant set the footage of the fixed camera on the gate to when Newhouse had returned to give the all-clear. Every bit of footage would be examined forensically later, but right now they needed a timeline and a sequence of events.

'Damn,' Kim said. It was immediately clear from the placement of the camera they would not see anything on the other side of the gate.

The minutes ticked by until they saw Grace approach the gate and stand in the gateway. She appeared to be looking at something on the ground. She then raised her head. Just one second of hesitation before she stepped through the gate and out of shot.

No person was visible on the other side. And somehow the person knew it.

'Jesus,' Bryant sighed. They were both aware that they may have been looking at Grace's last moments alive.

'Come on,' she said, pushing back her chair.

The action broke the cloud of impending despair that was trying to settle above them.

'Go tell Ms Newhouse that we're off to take a look outside,' she said, heading towards the back of the building. She passed groups of kids and adults. There was no point questioning them at this stage. It was clear that Grace had been alone.

She stepped out of a long set of bifold doors into a space that was actually bigger than it appeared on the camera.

She instantly saw the blind spot where Grace had been working at a raised planter in the far-right corner.

She headed towards it and was viewing the abandoned mini garden tools when Bryant joined her.

'A relative has just arrived to take Claire home. I assured her we'd speak to her soon.'

Kim nodded. A liaison officer would already have been appointed and would travel straight to Claire Lennard's home.

'Okay,' Kim said, turning away from the planting area but staying where Grace had been working, guided by the placement of the mini tools.

'Go to the other side of the gate,' she instructed her colleague.

Bryant did so and pushed the gate so that it was open just a fraction like they'd seen on the video.

Kim looked down at the planter. Any movement outside of the gate would have caught Grace's attention from the corner of her eye.

She stepped through the gate to where Bryant was already appraising the area.

It was an open space where a small fastener warehouse had once stood. It was accessible from the road, and there was no CCTV coverage that she could see.

'He could have been parked right by the gate,' Kim said. He would have had her away in seconds.

'Shit, Bryant, where do we even— Hang on, what's that?' she asked as something on the ground sparkled at her in the sunlight.

They both leaned down to take a closer look.

'It's a silver chain. Must have come off Grace's wrist in the struggle.'

She held out her hand palm up. Like a well-trained theatre nurse, Bryant placed a biro in her hand. She nudged the piece of jewellery so the whole thing was visible. The movement uncovered a solid silver heart. Engraved on the back were the initials 'MJ'.

'Aaaah, shit. It isn't Grace's bracelet,' she said as Bryant produced an evidence bag from his pocket. 'I think this is the bracelet that belonged to Melody Jones. It was the piece of evidence withheld from the public twenty-five years ago.'

'But why is it...?'

'It's a message, Bryant. To us. He's telling us these abductions are linked.'

She knew she didn't need to remind him that Melody Jones never came home.

FIVE

'He looks harmless enough,' Stacey said, glancing over at the computer screen. 'He's even quite good-looking. Reminds me a bit of that actor Nigel Havers.'

Her colleague had taken the boss's instruction seriously and had been watching him like a hawk.

'That's what they said about Ted Bundy,' Penn said without turning.

Stacey opened her mouth, hoping some smart retort would place itself there, until she realised he was right. The serial killer had admitted to murdering thirty women, though most experts estimated the real number to be much higher. With his good looks and personable manner, both women and men had succumbed to the serial killer's charms.

'I just don't get it,' Penn said. 'He's shown no signs of discomfort or anxiety. He's recrossed his legs once or twice, checked his watch once and looked at his mobile phone once.'

'Should we have taken his phone away?' Stacey asked.

'For what reason? He's here voluntarily, assisting us with our enquiries. If he'd said anything incriminating to the boss, he'd already be in a cell.'

'He likes his cuppa,' Stacey observed as Jack entered the room with a second plastic cup from the machine.

'Yes, all accounts and interviews claim he's teetotal,' she said, returning to her notes.

'Interviews?' Penn asked, turning away for a second and glancing her way.

'Oh yes, we have ourselves a real-life, bona fide millionaire down there.'

'You're kidding?'

'Nope. Steven Harte came out of Keele University aged twenty-two in 1989. Within two years he'd cottoned on to the personal computer in every home theory and had invented a micro-processor that sold in the millions. He had the good sense to sell the company before the big boys realised how quickly these proces-sors would need to update. That was his first few million. Next was a software program that could store thousands of bits of info and link them at the press of a button. What we'd now call a database. He actually did sell this to one of the big boys. Next he started developing mini software programs.'

'Like apps?'

Stacey nodded. 'Looks like his inventions were always ahead of the times.'

'So he'd have no trouble accessing the network for the day-care centre to trigger a fire alarm?'

'Child's play to this guy. He developed, created and then sold programs strategically, always aware of market demand.'

'You mean he always knew when to get in and when to get out?'

'Oh yeah, it's like he had some kind of sixth sense about things.'

'What's he worth now?' Penn asked.

'His millions are in the double figures, but by the looks of it he gives away as much as he makes.'

'Hang on,' Penn said, turning the screen slightly so he could give her his attention and keep an eye on their visitor. 'You're saying this guy is filthy rich and a philanthropist to boot?'

'That's exactly what I'm saying. If there's a good cause going somewhere, you can bet he's donated to it or been on the fundraising committee. He's bought acres of green belt land and done nothing with it, just to stop housing developments. He advises charities for wildlife causes free of charge and contributes heavily to the preservation and improvement of local beauty spots.'

'So why have I never heard about him?'

'Because he doesn't make a song and dance about it. His interviews focus on how he made his money more than what he does with it now.'

'Okay, I'm starting to get the Bundy Paradox thing as well. This guy does not seem the type to go abducting and murdering young girls.'

'Exactly my point,' Stacey said. 'But then what's his motivation for coming in and claiming he knows about the disappearance of Melody Jones, which happened twenty-five years ago, on the exact day that another girl goes missing?'

'Maybe he's psychic and he's here to help.'

'Penn, are you high?'

'It was a joke, Stace, although it's the only thing that makes sense. If he took Melody all those years ago, why come forward now? What does he have to gain? And if he didn't take her then why is he here at all?' Penn scratched his head. 'Any work with prisons or time served?'

Stacey shook her head. She too had wondered if he'd somehow been in contact with the real killer of Melody Jones and had information to share. But if that was the case, why not just give the information and go? Why claim to know about the disappearance of Grace Lennard?

'Doesn't make sense,' Penn said, echoing her thoughts and turning back to his screen.

She had the feeling that in the coming days they were going to say that a lot.

SIX

'Bloody hell, Stone, you didn't tell me the man in interview room one was *the* Steven Harte,' Woody said, shaking his head.

Her boss, DCI Woodward, was not normally a head shaker. He gave little away with expression or demeanour to the untrained eye. Luckily for her, she'd been pissing him off for years and knew the signs well.

'Sir, I didn't realise that there was any *the* about him until Stacey called me ten minutes ago.' She frowned. 'But I wouldn't have done anything different if I had known. I don't really care what he invented, how much money he has or how he spends it. If he has information about our missing girl, he'll be treated accordingly.'

'I wasn't suggesting you treat him any differently,' Woody snapped. 'But it helps to know who you're talking to.'

'Agreed, so do I have your permission to charge him?'

'With what?'

'Haven't decided yet but I don't like the fact he could leave at any minute.'

It was the only thing that had been on Kim's mind on the journey back from the day centre. She had left the ground operations in the capable hands of Inspector Plant and had fully expected Steven Harte to be gone upon her return.

'Has he admitted anything yet?'

She shook her head.

'Has he implicated himself in any way?'

She shook her head again.

'Then you know what you need to do.'

'Take his phone and search his house?' she asked hopefully.

Woody raised an eyebrow. 'Good luck with getting a judge to sign off on that one.'

'But what if he's wasting my time?' she asked. 'Grace Lennard is out there somewhere, and I feel like I'm chasing someone else's tail.'

'That may be true, Stone, in which case I trust you to go in there and rule out his involvement or get something concrete out of him.'

'And what if he won't budge?'

'Oh, I'm sure you can make him budge,' Woody said, returning her gaze. 'You like no better challenge than moving an immovable object.'

She turned and left the room, and for the sake of Grace Lennard, she hoped her boss was right.

SEVEN

It was just after six when Kim re-entered the interview room. She hoped that the tea in the three empty cups had loosened Steven Harte's tongue.

If he had abducted Grace, and she played her cards right, they could have the child home by supper time.

'Okay, Mr Harte, is there anything you'd like to say to me?' she asked, taking a seat.

It was not a formal interview, so she had no requirement for anyone else to be in the room. The camera in the corner was her witness, and if he was wasting police time, better that it was only hers.

'Please call me Steven, and I'd return the question to you, Inspector.'

'Where is Grace Lennard?'

He shrugged as if he had no idea what she was talking about. 'I thought we were going to talk about Melody Jones.'

'Did you leave Melody's bracelet at the day centre?'

'What bracelet? Did Melody Jones have a bracelet? There was no mention in the press of any missing jewellery.'

'Mr Harte...'

'Steven...'

'Mr Harte...'

'Steven, I insist,' he said, pushing back his chair.

'Okay, Steven,' she said, gritting her teeth. 'I repeat the question: did you abduct Grace Lennard and leave Melody Jones's silver bracelet at the scene earlier today?'

'Another girl has been abducted?' he asked with surprise.

'You already knew that.'

'How would I have known that?'

'You told me earlier that I was about to become very busy.'

'You're a detective inspector – I would imagine you're very busy most days.'

Kim had the sudden feeling she was a piece of meat being mauled by a lion. It was not a sensation she relished.

'Mr Harte... Steven, this is becoming tiresome. I'm not sure exactly what game you're trying to play with us but—'

'Have you spoken to Melody's family?' he asked, tipping his head.

'Why would I do that?'

'You should do a follow-up. Talk to them, understand her life. I think you'll be surprised.'

'Are you saying that Melody's family were involved in her disappearance?'

'I'm telling you that you should peel back a layer or two of that particular onion so that you understand.'

'How does that affect Grace Lennard?'

Her focus had to remain on the child who was missing now.

'Most lost children turn up eventually, unharmed, don't they?'

'Are you saying...?'

'I'm simply stating a statistical fact.'

'Look, Mr Harte, I am not going to be led a merry dance. If you have Grace Lennard, I will find her and—'

'Your voice is rising, Inspector. You're losing control. That won't help anyone. Your stress level appears to be high. I think we should resume first thing in the morning.'

He pushed back his chair again, but this time he stood. Her hand itched to slap a pair of cuffs on his wrist and drop-kick him into a cell until he gave her a straight answer, but he had said nothing she could hang an arrest warrant on.

'Thank you for the tea, and I look forward to speaking to you again at 9 a.m. tomorrow.'

Kim replayed both conversations in her head, desperate for any reason to detain him.

He paused and regarded her for a minute.

'I'm guessing you're used to being the one in control, Inspector, but for now you're going to have to accept that's not the case. I have a great deal to share with you, but we'll do this my way or not at all. I've proven my good faith and patience by staying here while you attend to other matters. I understand your focus is on Grace Lennard, and I'm sure we'll talk about her at some stage.'

He paused at the door. 'But tomorrow we'll talk about the others.'

EIGHT

Kim tore back into the squad room.

'Can someone find some charge in the damn PACE manual that I can throw at this bastard? I don't care what it is. Go medieval if you need to. Tell me he walked his ducks through the village on the wrong day of the week or that he was once drunk in charge of cattle. I don't fucking care, just get me something.'

'Boss, he hasn't admitted—'

'I damned well know that, Stace, and I also know I've got to let him just walk out of here when my gut tells me he's done something bloody wrong.'

The room was silent.

'Sorry, Stace, but the man is infuriating.'

Bryant handed her a black coffee.

'Keep it on tap,' she said, taking a swig and a good deep breath.

'Okay, guys, given that we couldn't prevent him from walking out the door, we need to keep him under watch. If we ask for a surveillance operation, it'll take days to arrange, as all available resources will be directed to the search for Grace. But we still need to follow him wherever he goes. He might just lead us to her.'

Penn stood. 'I'll take first shift. Jasper's over at Billy's.'

Kim knew that Penn's teenage brother spent many nights over at his friend's house. Billy's mum was a registered carer and was well read on Down's syndrome. 'Okay, I'll take the middle shift and relieve you at midnight.'

'And I'll be there at five,' Bryant added.

'You'll be following him in when he returns at nine in the morning,' Kim advised.

'He's coming back?' Penn asked as he reached the door.

'Oh yeah, now get after him. I don't want him without cover for even a minute.'

Penn nodded and left. She'd check in with him later.

'Boss, I could get someone to drop me—'

'No, Stace, we need someone to be fully functional.'

As she had no car due to not having passed her driving test, Kim couldn't consider her for a shift.

'What was that about Melody's family?' Bryant asked, reminding her that the rest of the team had been watching and listening.

'I don't know but it's hard to know what to take seriously and what to disregard, especially that last crack about "the others".'

'Boss, for what it's worth, this guy has done so much for good causes. He supports all kinds of charities, small ones that can't get much funding as well as major projects in the local area. He sponsors wildlife programmes, donkey sanctuaries, nature reserves, and apparently Hawne Park would have closed decades ago if he hadn't stepped in and saved it.'

Kim knew Hawne Park well. It was located just one mile out of Halesowen town centre.

'Doesn't mean he's not a killer, Stace,' she said.

They all knew that murderers came in all shapes and sizes and from every point on the socio-economic spectrum.

Yes, he was good-looking. Yes, he was rich, and yes, he was a generous benefactor, but none of the above precluded him from being a murderer. It just offered him more opportunity.

'We should go and see them,' Bryant said thoughtfully.

'Who?'

'Melody's family.'

'Bryant, the case is twenty-five years old. I'd love to know what happened to Melody Jones but I'm more concerned about Grace Lennard, and I'm not sure how Melody's family can help.'

'There's a reason Harte mentioned Melody specifically.'

'And if he told us to dress up in costume and dance the funky chicken, would we do that too?'

Stacey raised an eyebrow. 'Boss, what's the funk—'

'Doesn't matter. He's not going to pull our strings, Bryant.'

'We should still go,' he pushed.

'Why?'

'There was talk. Nothing concrete but locker-room stuff. I had no involvement but apparently there was something about the family that was a bit... off.'

It was a term not contained in the police manual, but every officer knew what it meant. She interviewed people herself every day who either showed too much emotion or not enough. Some people asked relevant questions too soon and some not at all. Knowing if the reactions were genuine was not something that could be taught. There was no checklist and no blueprint for people's emotional responses, and she'd never felt enough authority on the matter to judge.

If an officer felt that something was 'off' there was normally a pretty good reason for it.

She wondered if Melody's family would have anything new to offer after twenty-five years, but it didn't hurt to have a quick word.

NINE

'I thought the family lived on Hollytree,' Kim said as Bryant headed towards the Joneses' current address in Hayley Green. The area sat on the West Midlands side of the border with West Mercia Police Force. Houses ranged from half a million down to a hundred thousand in some areas, and around two hundred thousand for the terraced property on Chiltern Road where they were heading.

'They did when Melody disappeared, but they appear to have traded up a bit in the years since.'

'Come on then – what was the talk in the locker room?'

'Like I said, nothing concrete, but from what I remember, Melody was the youngest of six or seven kids, all pretty close in age with barely a year between some of them. By the time Melody disappeared, her dad was already dead, and the eldest boy appeared to have taken on the role.'

'Not unusual in that kind of situation,' Kim replied as they moved slowly along Chiltern Road. Older siblings often took a hand in rearing the youngsters in big families.

He stopped at a house with a small driveway and a garage that sat at the front of the house. To the right was a front door and a single window. It looked like a decent area, where folks mowed their lawns and tried to obscure the different wheelie bins forced to sit out front. It was a house that most of the folks on Hollytree would have sold a relative to own.

A Renault Clio was inside the open garage and an Escort van was parked on the drive.

'Not sure they're gonna appreciate seeing us after all this time,' Kim said, getting out of the car.

'Yeah, but just imagine if we can give them some closure after all these years,' Bryant answered as they knocked on the door.

By closure Kim knew he meant body.

The door was opened by an overweight male with thinning dark hair and a couple of days' growth of facial hair.

He eyed them suspiciously as he continued to chew the food in his mouth.

They both produced their ID, and Kim introduced them.

'Whaddya want?' he asked, swallowing his last mouthful of food.

Kim swallowed with him but in her mouth was a generous portion of distaste.

'To speak to Lyla Jones. She does live here, right?'

'Whatabout?' he asked as one word, which did confirm that they were in the right place. His tongue was darting around his mouth as though searching out morsels that had got lost.

'May we speak with Lyla?' Kim asked. 'It's about Melody.'

He stopped chewing to step aside and point to an open door.

Kim stepped around two bulging bin liners to enter a cramped and over-furnished lounge.

In stark comparison to her son, Lyla Jones was stick thin. She sat in a single easy chair directly in front of a large-screen TV that was out of proportion with the size of the room.

To her left was a side table holding a plate with crusty, dried-on gravy and food scraps.

Bryant offered his hand and an introduction as Kim looked around for somewhere to sit.

'Robbie, get Bess in,' Lyla said, taking her plate from the side table and lowering it to the floor.

Robbie disappeared only to be replaced by a bounding cream Labrador, who paid no attention to them and headed straight for the plate on the floor.

'Mrs Jones, we're here to talk about Melody.'

'You found her?' she asked automatically. Her tone held neither hope nor expectation.

Kim reminded herself that it had been twenty-five years and it was a relief that she wasn't having to manage expectations. Just because it was the twenty-fifth anniversary of Melody's disappearance didn't mean her body was suddenly going to come to light, as though it had been on a timer. The woman had been forced to face reality with every passing year.

'We just wanted to assure you that we're still looking and that we haven't given up on trying to bring closure to you and your family. We know you've appealed for information about her disappearance on a regular basis over the years.'

Lyla reached down and retrieved the dinner plate that had been licked clean by the dog that now lay at her feet.

'Well, they ask every now and then to do reports on our Melody, the papers, magazines, TV shows, and they pay expenses and stuff. It all helps out, you know. But I hope you ain't here to quiz me about it again. I can barely remember what I had for me tea last night, never mind all that time ago.'

Kim wasn't sure she'd ever heard a missing child compared to a plate of food before. It had been over thirty years since her brother had died of starvation in her arms, but she hadn't forgotten a minute of that day.

'Can you tell us what you do remember, Mrs Jones?' Kim asked. The detail, if she wanted it, could be gained from the files but she was interested in the memory Lyla had. She was feeling the 'offness' in waves. It was as though they were talking about a lost dog.

'It was like any other school holiday day: too many kids and not enough space in a three-bed maisonette. When one kid or another asked if they could go out and play, the answer was yes. It wore like it is today. Kids went and called for each other. They got up to mischief and came back dirty and ready for their tea.'

Kim could better understand the woman's words if they'd been talking about a teenager, but Melody had been seven years old.

'I can see the judgement in the expression you're trying to keep off your face, and I ay bothered by it. I day do nothing wrong in letting me kid go out and play.'

Kim tried to rearrange her expression. This woman needed no condemnation from her. She'd had twenty-five years to consider her parenting style, and she would live with the consequences until she died.

'Was there anything strange that you recall from that day?'

She shook her head. 'Nothing any different to washing, cooking and cleaning for a bloody houseful. Kids were coming and going, fighting and playing, and when tea time came I was one short. Didn't think much of it at first. Thought she'd found a group to play with and lost track of time. Went looking for her about seven, and no one had seen her for hours. Called the police and the rest is in your records.'

'Why are you so interested now?' Robbie asked from the doorway. Kim hadn't realised he was there. For a big man he moved with surprising stealth. 'She's dead, so what's the point?'

Kim didn't disagree with them.

'We'd still like to catch and punish the person who abducted her,' Bryant answered.

'Well, good luck with that after all these years,' Lyla said, picking up the remote control.

Kim would have liked to stay just a little longer to capture the reason that this family caused a sense of unease in her stomach but she knew a dismissal when she saw one.

TEN

Alex pushed the phone deep into her pillowcase, enjoying the warm flush of anticipation that stole over her. She would be speaking to DI Kimberly Stone later this evening, and she could barely wait, but for now she had other things to attend to.

The most important meeting of her life was due to take place at the end of the week, and she had both a plan A and a plan B running concurrently.

Warden Siviter's input and recommendation at her parole hearing was crucial to a favourable decision, and she was determined to get it by using either one of her plans.

'You ready?' she asked her cellmate.

'Yep, I'm starving Marvin,' Emma said, putting her book aside.

They headed out of the cell and towards the dinner hall – if you could call the impersonal, functional space something that sounded so grand.

During her time she'd suffered every indignity this place had to offer: the loss of liberty, the rules, the lack of control over her own life, the absence of privacy and above all the disgusting, tasteless food. Everything was boiled and seasoned as though salt was on

ration, and she was guessing the kitchen crew had never used a
herb or spice in their lives.

She could almost taste freedom and a return to her former life,
which made these last few days almost intolerable. But she had to
keep her cool. If even one thing went wrong now, she'd be looking
at another six months at least to get another hearing.

She'd been a decent prisoner for almost five years. Yes, there'd
been one or two hiccups when she hadn't got her own way, but
that was less important than the next few days. It was how you
finished and the most recent memories that stayed in someone's
head.

She was banking on it.

'You know what to do, don't you?' she asked Emma.

'Errr... yeah, it ain't rocket science.'

'Wait for my signal,' Alex said, joining the food line.

For her plan to work, she was reliant on everything happening
as it always did on a Monday night.

She followed everyone else in, pushing the newbie out of the
food line. The kid was barely out of her teens. She'd been brought
in a few hours ago and had already earned the nickname Bambi
due to her wide, terrified eyes. So far, she'd been robbed of her
phone card and smokes, and her toiletries had been taken from her
cell. Every possession was fair game in prison, and she was being
shown her order in the hierarchy. Her day wasn't going to get any
better now. Bambi was a nothing, a nobody, one of life's losers who
mattered to no one. But she mattered to Alex and was integral to
her plan.

By the time Alex sat with her food, the line was thinning and
Bambi was eyeing up opportunities to jump in. Emma hung about
in the doorway.

Right on cue, Warden Siviter entered the hall and wandered
over to the prison officer at the far end. Every night she did the
same thing before leaving. A final check that her charges were in
order.

Alex waited for just a few seconds before giving Emma the nod.

Emma strode up to Bambi and shoved her out of the way.

'Fuck off, newbie bitch, I'm first,' Emma shouted at the top of her voice. The girl fell to the ground.

'What the fuck you just call me?' Emma shouted, pouncing on her. The girl hadn't said a word.

The officers started moving towards the scuffle, but Alex got there first.

Prisoners began to chant 'fight, fight, fight' as they closed in around the skirmish.

Bambi was covering her head with her forearm as the punches continued to rain down on her.

'Emma, stop it,' Alex called out loud enough for everyone to hear. The guards were moving inmates aside, trying to get to the centre. 'The girl only wanted something to eat.'

On cue, Emma stopped punching, and Alex grabbed Bambi by the hair, lifting her to her feet.

She immediately moved her grip to the bony arm, so that when the circle opened, Alex was standing between the two parties, holding them away from each other.

Two officers quickly grabbed Emma and moved her away. She'd receive some kind of punishment, but Alex didn't care. The newbie was covered in red marks and clutches of her hair littered the floor. Emma had done a thorough job in a couple of short minutes.

But it could all have been so much worse if Alex hadn't stepped in and stopped the fight. Someone could have been seriously hurt. The whole incident could have turned into a riot if handled incorrectly, and Warden Siviter certainly didn't want that on her watch.

Alex's selfless action and disregard for her own safety had averted disaster. All worth it if the warden had seen what just happened.

Alex glanced her way. The woman's hand was hovering near her throat, twisting the simple chain around her neck anxiously, an expression of concern on her face, but the slight nod of acknowledgement that travelled the space between them confirmed Alex's hope.

She had seen.

ELEVEN

'Okay, Bryant, get off home,' Kim instructed as he pulled into the station car park. He'd need some rest before taking her off watch duty in the morning.

'Yeah, thanks, guv. I've got an evening of any film with Tom Brady in it apparently.'

Kim smiled at his defeated tone, knowing he wouldn't change it for the world. Laura was home and his pack was safe for a few days.

'Hardy,' she corrected.

'You know who he is?'

'As does most of the world. Now get lost.'

He gave her a small wave as he turned and drove away.

She took the stairs quickly, having already called ahead to brief Stacey on what she wanted.

'It's all a bit of a mess, boss,' Stacey said as she entered the office.

Kim removed her jacket and poured the dregs of the day's coffee pot. 'How so?'

'Well, the original files are partly electronic and partly hard copy.'

Kim groaned. Because there had been no charges brought in the case of Melody Jones, the evidence and statements had never been put together in one cohesive package to present to the CPS. It was like a meal that had been cooked but never plated up.

'It gets worse,' Stacey said, offering her a look that said she was bracing for impact.

'Go on.'

'It's been twenty-five years, boss. Other folks have dabbled.'

'Dabbled?' Kim asked, raising an eyebrow.

'The case has been looked at three times since the initial investigation. New notes have got mixed up with old notes and, as I said, it's all a bit of a mess really.'

'Anything that strikes you?'

'Not had much chance for a good look yet, but two of the three detectives who have picked it up as a cold case noted, for different reasons, that the family's reaction and behaviour was odd.'

Kim sipped at the tepid liquid before pushing the coffee away. None of Stacey's words were helping the unease in her stomach.

'Twelve years after Melody went missing, a new team came in. They focused all their effort on trying to account for the movements of every family member for the twenty-four hours prior to Melody's disappearance.'

'They thought a family member was involved?'

'Of course it was too late to get that kind of timeline so long after the event, but the case was reopened after Shannon Matthews.'

'They thought the family had done it for money?'

Stacey nodded. 'There was a willingness, almost an eagerness, from Lyla Jones to get on the telly and make appeals, so the new investigating team thought maybe Melody had been hidden by the family to make some money before they'd then produce her all safe and sound like Shannon Matthews, but that something went wrong.'

'Did the initial investigating team suspect the same?' Kim asked.

'If they did it wasn't noted, but that team also paid a lot of attention to family members of Melody. Whether it was just to rule them out I don't know.'

Kim knew she was never going to get anywhere with this bits-and-pieces approach. There had been too many fingers in the pie since Melody had gone missing.

She fought down her annoyance that Steven Harte's words had sent her in a direction where there appeared to be something to find. She would have been happier to find a cut-and-dried case of outside interference. She had wanted to find a believable and credible family who had alerted no suspicion. She had wanted to focus her entire attention on Steven Harte and his involvement; find proof and search his house, find Grace Lennard and return her home in time for bed.

She hadn't wanted to find the 'offness' about the family, but she had. She was now filled with more questions than answers, and she knew she had to dig deeper. The only way to do that was to go right to the source.

'Who was the first SIO?'

Stacey's face crunched with dread. 'DI Wrigley.'

Kim groaned again. Nicknamed Gum, for obvious reasons, there was no worse name Stacey could have said.

'Okay, Stace, that's enough for today. Get off home now.'

'Do you want me to try and track down…?'

'Nah, it's fine,' Kim said, getting her coat.

She knew of Gum, and at eight o'clock at night she knew exactly where she'd find him.

TWELVE

It was almost nine by the time she pulled into the car park of The Dog in Tipton. It was a double-fronted establishment sandwiched between Midland Tool and Design and a chippy. She'd had just enough time to get home, shower, change, walk and feed Barney and throw a couple of essentials into the boot for her shift of the stakeout.

'Okay, let's do a check call before I go in,' Kim said, turning towards Barney, who was seat belted into the back seat.

She pressed on Penn's number, and he answered immediately.

'Thank God,' he said.

'Problem?'

'Nope, just someone to talk to.'

Well, that answered her first question.

'No movement at all?'

'Not a thing. Gates closed behind him at five thirty, and there's been nothing in or out since.'

'Can you see anything?'

'Stretched my legs about an hour ago, but didn't go out of sight of the gate in case I missed him leaving the property.'

'Okay, Penn, if I can get to you any earlier I will.'

The guy had to be tired and starving.

'I'm all right, boss. I found a six-month-old protein bar in the back of the glovebox.'

Kim had been in his car and was surprised he'd managed to find anything in that mess.

'Okay, just stay—'

'Hang on, boss, there's a vehicle coming from...'

His words trailed away as he placed his phone face down. She could hear muffled voices but not what was being said. Had Steven Harte come out to complain about his presence? Had he called the police about a suspicious vehicle parked in front of his property? This was not an official stakeout operation, so a squad car would have attended to check out any reports. Had he sent someone to scare Penn off?

The voices continued. Her heart rate increased. Penn was there alone. If someone was threatening him, she had no way to get to...

'Sorry about that, boss,' Penn said clearly into the phone. 'It was a delivery guy.'

'Okay, what's the sneaky bastard up to?'

'Er... the sneaky bastard just sent me fish and chips.'

'He what?'

'Yeah, delivery guy insisted. Said they'd been paid for, so he was just gonna throw 'em away if I didn't take them.'

Kim could hear the longing in his voice.

'What shall I do, boss?'

Penn knew the rules about how accepting any kind of gift could be construed in court as a bribe, but the guy hadn't eaten for hours and she was nowhere near taking him off his watch shift.

'Get 'em down you, Penn, and I'll see you in a bit.'

She ended the call. She'd sort it tomorrow. Right now, she had to try and get an accurate picture of a twenty-five-year-old case from someone well known in the police force. A man used often as a cautionary tale.

'Okay, boy, I can't take you in there so sit tight,' she said, rubbing Barney's head.

She lowered her own window just an inch to let some cool air into the car. The day temperature had dropped from twenty-one to eleven degrees, but you couldn't be too cautious.

She entered the pub and stood in the doorway for just a second.

It was a typical local pub, serving their regulars for decades and serving Gum for most of them. A couple of guys were throwing darts, and a group of four were playing a game of pool at the far side of the pub. Two larger groups were gathered around tables: one group playing dominoes and the other group playing cards. One man sat on his own in the corner. Despite a couple of curious glances in her direction, the atmosphere was light and jovial.

By her count, DI Martyn Wrigley was in his early seventies and had headed the Melody Jones investigation in his late forties. She hadn't known that, but what she had known was that the man in the corner had become the stereotype. He had worked long hours, lost his family and turned to alcohol. A fact he'd managed to hide from his superiors until a heart attack on the job had revealed his poor health and alcoholism. After losing everything, he was medically retired prematurely, and the years since had turned him into a lonely, bitter old man.

'Got a minute, DI Wrigley?' she asked, approaching the table.

'For a fellow copper the answer is no. For a fellow copper with no drink in her hand the answer is fuck off.'

Kim questioned the ethics of encouraging the man's drinking habits, but he'd made his life choices way before she'd ever heard his name.

She headed to the bar, returned to the table and placed a pint of beer beside the half-full one on the table. The colour match told her she'd got it right.

'Cheapskate,' he said, nodding towards the couple of shot glasses that had been emptied and pushed to the side.

He nodded for her to sit. She did so wondering how much time that one drink had bought her.

'I'm here to ask about the Melody Jones case.'

He showed no surprise. 'Of course you are. One of you lot comes and finds me every year around the anniversary. Still haven't found her though, have you?' he asked, taking a sip of his beer.

Kim tried to keep the sadness out of her mind. Sadness that by all accounts this man had been one of the best detectives on the force. He'd been dogged and determined, and he'd met every case with the same level of passion, commitment and effort. But his energy had been like a dial he had not known how to turn off. At home, she had a dodgy gas ring on her hob. It worked perfectly at full power, but the second you tried to turn it down the thing went off. She tried not to be saddened further by the fact that despite the people he'd helped during his career, he was now without family, and his crusty manner appeared to have left him also without friends. Even sadder was the fact the man still dressed in a suit and tie as though ready to go to work.

'Yeah, we've been asked to take another look at it,' she answered.

'Take my advice: save yourself the time and work on something you've got a chance of solving.'

'You don't think we'll ever find Melody Jones?'

'Nope cos she's my punishment and—'

'Punishment for what?' Kim asked, pulling her stool closer to the table.

'Forget it. Those thoughts are best left in my head to fester. Ask your questions and then fuck off and leave me alone.'

He took a good long drink of his old pint, finishing off half the glass. He moved the new one to an easy reach spot in front of him.

Kim decided to take his advice before he had much more to drink.

'Talk to me about Melody's family.'

'Jesus, there's no foreplay with you, is there? You must be a right—'

'Did you suspect any of them of being involved in her disappearance?'

'Not at first, cos you don't really, do you? The mother seemed concerned, a couple of the younger siblings were a bit tearful, and the older ones were rallying around, except one who kept his distance, almost like he didn't want us getting too close and asking him questions.'

'Did you try?'

'No, we fucking didn't, so let's just leave it at that, eh?' he spat.

'Okay,' she said, wondering why that had hit a sore nerve. She backed off, unwilling to piss him off to the stage of non-cooperation until she'd asked all her questions. 'You said you didn't suspect the family at first but what changed?'

'Over time, and I'm talking just weeks, Lyla became very keen on doing TV, radio, magazine and newspaper interviews. It got so we could barely get near her for questioning cos someone or other was in the house or she was going to them. At first, we appreciated her efforts to keep Melody's name out there as the few leads we had dried up, but there was something not right. It was like she was enjoying the attention. For years she'd been Lyla Jones, mother of seven off Hollytree, and then she was Lyla Jones, mother of missing girl, Melody. It's like she was somebody finally. Robbie Jones still wouldn't talk to us about anything, and then the parcels and envelopes began to arrive. Money, presents, all kinds of stuff turning up by the bag load. The more Lyla appeared, the more stuff turned up.'

Kim thought about the woman's most recent appeals and the bin liners in the living room.

'You think they were using Melody's disappearance to make money?'

He shrugged. 'One of my team caught Robbie flogging the stuff on a car boot. Nothing we could do cos the stuff wasn't solicited. It was all gifts.'

There was no law against it, but Kim felt that familiar distaste rise in her mouth. Most families might have donated the gifts and money to charity.

'You wanna just tell me what you think?' Kim asked candidly.

He took another long swig. 'Why not? It's not like I think about anything else. This bloody case is stuck in my teeth like a piece of dry pork. Never stopped imagining the suffering that little girl went through just because I couldn't bring her home. What she must have gone through.'

He took another drink, prompting Kim to wonder how long after the Jones case his drinking had intensified. Was this the case that had pushed him over the edge?

'If I'd have only pushed the boss harder, we might have found her, brought her home, given the family members that cared closure and a body to bury.'

Kim pushed away thoughts of another little girl, taken that day, frightened and alone, or worse.

'Pushed the boss harder on what?'

It was clear that it was self-blame that had haunted this guy for a quarter of a century. The case had become his personal failure and he beat himself with it every day.

'I wanted him, begged him to let us go in harder on the family, make them sweat a bit, but the boss wouldn't hear of it. Back then it was okay to suspect the family members quietly, but it wasn't acceptable to go hard, cos if you were wrong and it got out... Well, let's just say that careers never recovered from that kind of exposure if it was made public, and my DCI wasn't going to allow that to happen to him. Ironically, he had no such compunction when it came to shagging the wife of a prime suspect in a double murder, which cost him his job, but no, we couldn't put a family under pressure to find a missing kid.'

'You really think they were involved?'

'Look, it's been so long now I'm not even sure what I think anymore, but I'll tell you this. Melody Jones had a miserable life, but it was a life she knew. She was pretty much ignored as the youngest, didn't have many friends and then she disappears and not one person saw a thing. Not one. How does that happen on an estate of four thousand people?'

Kim shook her head and waited for him to continue.

'Until Karen Matthews came along and did the unthinkable with her own daughter, we weren't allowed to suspect family members to that degree.'

'But surely if that was the case Melody would have been miraculously found not long after.'

He shrugged, and his face seemed to crumple.

'I still look for her, you know. Her little face is never far from my mind. Sometimes I think I see her in a shop, or in a playground. In some part of my mind she's still that little girl that went missing twenty-five years ago, but the good sense I've got left knows that she's been dead for years.'

'You think something went wrong and she died at the hands of her family?'

He looked at her for a full minute before opening his mouth again.

'Or maybe they realised she was more valuable to them dead.'

THIRTEEN

Kim had already worked out that by taking the back roads and with a good wind, she could take a quick detour and still get to Wombourne to take Penn off Harte watch at around eleven.

Kates Hill was an area that had reportedly been the scene of chaos in the 1600s when parliamentarians used it as their base in the civil war against King Charles I. Many of the roads were named in honour of parliamentary figures, and it was on Cromwell Street that she was parking now.

'Okay, boy, be good,' she said to Barney as she got out the car. She'd make sure he got some good exercise and a few dog treats once they got to Harte's house.

She took a quick look around as she walked up the path. The area had not been developed residentially until the 1830s when large numbers of houses were built to accommodate people moving to the Black Country to work in the ever-growing number of factories and coal pits.

The door to Claire Lennard's house was opened by Bernadette Jackson, a family liaison officer Kim had dealt with in the past. The woman was mid-thirties with a daughter of her own not much older than Grace. She was efficient, intuitive and empathetic. Perfect fit for this family.

'How is she?' Kim asked in the hallway.

'Tired but won't allow herself to sleep. I've not had to talk her away from the door for the last half an hour, so I'm hoping she'll get some rest soon. She's had a few calls but cuts them off quickly in case anyone needs to reach her, and by anyone, I mean you.'

Kim understood that Claire's natural reaction would be to go out and search on foot for her child, walk the streets, knock on doors, anything to feel as though she was doing something.

'Any visitors?'

Bernadette shook her head. 'A few have offered but she's refused.'

Kim's toe nudged a duffel bag in the hallway. 'You staying over?'

'Oh yeah and happy to do so. It's a decent sofa and my angelic twelve-year-old is currently hovering between sweet child and teenage spawn of Satan. It changes by the hour and could go either way, so her dad can deal with her for a bit.'

Kim smiled. She felt reassured that Bernadette would be around.

'She's in the lounge. I'll make tea that no one will drink.'

'Actually, black coffee would be great,' Kim said. It was going to be a long night.

She stepped into the lounge, and Claire Lennard's face was a mixture of hope and dread.

Kim shook her head. 'No news yet,' she said, taking a seat on the sofa. 'I just wanted to check in with you. We didn't get much chance to talk earlier.'

Her explanation for the visit was partly true. She did want to reassure Claire that everything possible was being done, but she also wanted to suss out Grace's home and family life. Gum's words had reminded her that the family had to be under suspicion. She knew that Bernadette would be attuned to anything out of the ordinary with either Claire or other family members, but she'd wanted to take a look for herself.

She'd sensed nothing untoward at the day centre from Claire whose nurse's uniform had been replaced with casual trousers and a V-neck T-shirt. An untouched sandwich with curled-up corners sat on the coffee table.

'It's all over the news. Her face is everywhere. That's good, isn't it?' she asked hopefully.

'Absolutely. The more people that see her photo the better. Our liaison team will be giving regular updates to the press to keep Grace's face on everyone's mind.' She paused. 'Tell me about her,' she said, glancing round the room. Photos of all stages of Grace's life covered the walls.

Claire's eyes lit up. 'She's a joy. She's an exceptional little girl, and of course I'm going to say that, aren't I, but she really is. She's fearless and determined, studious but fun. She loves to play Twister but also loves to lie on her bed reading. She's a typical eight-year-old girl who hasn't yet discovered the joy of electronic gadgets, although I'm sure that's just moments away.'

Claire followed Kim's gaze to the photo above the fireplace. It wasn't a professional shot. It looked like a selfie of the three of them that had been enlarged. Claire was in the foreground beaming. Her late husband had been totally buried in the sand up to the neck, and Grace was sitting on his sandy stomach, laughing.

'Our last day of innocence,' she said, smiling at the image. 'That was taken three days before we found out that Richard's headaches were due to an inoperable tumour on his brain. They gave him seven months, and he managed nine. Every single day of those months was precious.'

'I'm so sorry,' Kim said, feeing the emotion gathering in her throat.

'We knew it was coming but it didn't make our loss any easier. When Richard died, I lost the house that we'd bought when we both had reasonable careers and a bit of spare cash in the bank.

Richard wasn't insured, so together with my leave of absence from work and funeral costs, the house had to go. We were left with nothing and were homed here by the council. We fell lucky. It's a decent area, and Grace has more friends than she had at the old house. It was all very difficult at first, dealing with the hole in our lives and moving here. Those early days were indescribable. Battling through the physical pain that comes from loss. The relentless ache that suffocates your torso, the feeling that you can't go through another hour without breaking down, but Grace's courage got me out of bed every morning with the hope that maybe today would be just that little bit easier. I remember a turning point for us both.'

Kim said nothing and took the time to just listen to how this small family had regrouped after their tragic loss.

'Grace asked me when it would be okay for her to laugh again. A young boy had been making silly faces in the classroom to cheer her up and it had made her chuckle, and then she'd felt bad about it. We made a pact that day that we would never hide our feelings from each other. If we wanted to laugh, we would laugh, and if we wanted to cry, we would cry. We gave each other permission to smile again and to remember all the good times we'd had. We talk about him every day, and we keep his memory alive for each other.'

Kim swallowed down the aching in her throat. This family had been through enough. They had faced the worst possible tragedy and had come out of it a team, mother and daughter supporting each other in their own way. They had been ripped apart at a time when they needed each other more than ever.

Kim couldn't help thinking of her relationship with her own mother. A woman who had tried to kill both her and her twin brother almost from the moment they'd been born. Her most vivid memories entailed trying to keep her mother's hands off Mikey – in her worst psychotic hallucinations, she'd thought he was the reincarnation of the devil. A woman now living out the remainder of her years at a home for the criminally insane.

She couldn't think of her birth mother without also thinking of Erica though, the woman who had fostered her from age ten to thirteen. A truly selfless woman who had given her everything and expected nothing.

She had known that bond, had felt that love, however briefly.

The visit with Claire had made her even more determined than before that she would return Grace to her mother.

She had to.

FOURTEEN

'Enjoy your supper?' Kim asked, pulling alongside Penn's vehicle outside the Wombourne home of Steven Harte.

The village was known as a peaceful environment with a population of 14,000. The green space at the centre of the area was surrounded by independent shops and was the hub of the village. Although a part of South Staffordshire, many of its population travelled the few miles into the Black Country and Wolverhampton for work.

Penn smiled and patted his stomach. 'No movement from inside the house, boss. Should be a quiet night.'

'Okay, get off home.'

She waited for Penn to pull away before sliding into his position. She thought better of it and pulled forward, blocking the gate. If he wanted to leave his home in the dead of night, he'd have to ram her out of the way to do it.

'Come on, boy,' she said, undoing Barney's seat belt. He squeezed through the gap and plonked himself on the passenger seat, then looked forward, as if to say, 'What now?'

'This is it for the next few hours, matey. We just gotta sit and watch.'

She took a moment to assess the property. She'd passed through the village a mile before turning off the main road and onto a single-track lane that wound and turned for a good half mile. She'd passed one other property close to the other end of the lane, and there was no further road beyond this house. It was a dead end. It was isolated, remote and there was no risk of through traffic. There were no close neighbours to hear any noise and little chance of meeting anyone on the road.

'What did you say, Barney? You need to go?' she asked, reaching to the back seat for his lead.

She needed to get a feel for the place beyond what she could see.

She clipped Barney's lead on, and he jumped out of the car. The first thing that hit her was the silence. Rarely was she anywhere with such a deep, dark silence. Even in the early hours of the morning at her home there was a hum of something in the distance. She'd walked Barney many times in the middle of the night, and never had she felt such a thick, overpowering sense of nothingness.

She took her torch from the boot of the car. Every sound she made was magnified.

'Okay, boy, let's go this way,' she whispered, stepping out of the light cast by two ornamental lamp-post tops fitted to the stone pillars either side of the wooden gate. She was not going to see anything beyond those gates or the stone wall.

There had to be a break in the perimeter somewhere. She continued walking slowly to where the tarmac ended and wild bushes rose up out of shrubbery. She felt along the wall as Barney explored all the new smells that assaulted his powerful nose.

'Aha,' she said as her fingers curled around the stone where it ended. She moved a few more feet in until the bushes became too dense to push through.

The wall had given way to metal fencing that was waist high, which prevented her from stepping forward or even trying to push through the dense tree border on the other side of the fence.

Damn it, there was no way to see anything.

'Nice night for a dog walk, eh, Inspector?' she heard from the other side of the hedge.

Her heart jumped into her mouth, but she recovered quickly and spoke over her hammering heart.

'Yeah, you should invite us in for a little meander around your gardens.'

'I'd love to but my own dogs, Rocky and Tyson, are the gentlest Dobermans alive, unless they think someone is trying to encroach on their domain. Then they get a little testy.'

'You do know that we're going to nail you if you've hurt one hair on—'

'Inspector, I would expect nothing less, but I came to see if there was anything I can get you before I go to bed. Coffee? A snack?'

'I'm good, thanks,' she said to the hedge as she moved back towards the gate.

'Then I'll bid you good night.'

Kim offered no response as she forced down her rage. More than anything she wanted to scale this wall and see what was on the other side. He was watching them just as closely as they were watching him.

Was Grace in there? Was she alive? Was she scared?

'We're here, Grace and we're going to get you back,' she whispered into the hedge and then stood back.

The fact that she couldn't see a thing made her want to get over there all the more. But she couldn't. She had to consider that the man was goading her into making a mistake. Taunting her into doing something that would destroy any case in court.

Much as she hated to admit it, right now this man had her over a barrel and there was nothing she could do about it.

'Fuck you, Steven Harte,' she said, getting back into the car.

FIFTEEN

Alex savoured the anticipation until Emma was sound asleep.

After so long sharing a cell, she had come to know the woman's sleeping habits quite well.

The book she'd been reading had fallen from her hands and thudded to the floor. Next had come the light snoring which then changed to mumbling, signalling that she was in deep sleep.

She took out the phone and keyed in the number she knew by heart.

The woman answered on the second ring. 'Stone.'

Alex felt her lips turn up at the sound of her voice. She could hear the anxiety and trepidation behind that one word. She was receiving a call from an unknown number at midnight. Unlikely to be good news but impossible to ignore.

'Who is this?'

'It's your good friend, Alex.'

Silence.

Alex enjoyed the moment of confusion she knew the woman would be feeling after avoiding her calls.

'I don't have friends, and if I did you wouldn't be one of them.'

Alex laughed out loud. Oh it was good to hear her voice again after all this time.

'I've missed you, Kim.'

'What do you want, Alex?'

Alex closed her eyes and tried to visualise what she was doing. Was she sitting on the sofa beside that ugly mutt she'd adopted? Was she in her garage tinkering with old bike parts? Whatever she was doing, Alex knew that her thoughts would be focused on whatever case she was working.

'Well, it's been great catching up but I'm gonna hang—'

'I wouldn't do that if I were you, Kim. Not least for the fact that it'll continue to drive you mad wondering why I want to speak to you.'

Alex was already enjoying herself immensely. There was no person in the world she enjoyed interacting with more.

'I'll get over it, as I'm pretty sure you have nothing to say that will enrich my life.'

'Oh, I wouldn't be too sure about that.'

'Déjà vu. We've been here before. Don't you have any new schemes in your playbook? I expected more creativity from someone as diabolically evil as you.'

And there it was. So quickly they reverted to the pattern of their relationship. An ongoing battle with minor triumphs along the way. The battles hadn't always been psychological. Kim could still easily recall the time they had fought physically at the side of the canal for the life of a very special autistic young man named Dougie who had known what Alex was before anyone else. Kim had won and Dougie had lived. But as with their other battles, it had been close.

'What if I told you I had the power to change your life forever?'

'I'd say there you go bigging yourself up again. Isn't grandiosity a staple of your average sociopath? And let's be honest, as far as sociopaths go, you are very average.'

Oh, the inspector was in good form tonight but she knew her subject well.

'Someone backed you into a corner, Inspector? Your worse than usual mood indicates that someone is not toeing the line.'

'Fuck off, Alex,' she spat, awarding that point to her.

'I'm happy to listen. That's what friends are for.'

'You are neither my friend nor my therapist, thank God, and there's nothing I'd wish to share with you.'

'How about just a moment of your time in exchange for valuable information?'

'Okay, time starts now.'

'Oh, no, Kim. If only it was that easy,' Alex said. 'I mean in the flesh. I'd like you to visit so we can talk face to—'

'Not happening. You've had two attempts at me and both times you've failed. What could possibly make you think I'd go again?'

'Because you know I don't lie.'

Kim's genuine laughter met her ears. It was a sound she enjoyed regardless of the reason.

'Alex, you're a sociopath. You have to be a pathological liar to keep your membership.'

Good point, Alex conceded to herself. 'But I never actually lie to you.'

Silence.

'You know that the information I hold is truly significant and really does have the power to change your life. Knowing that will be a brick in your shoe until you know what it is.'

'I'm not playing—'

'Come any day. I'll clear my schedule, and I look forward to our mutually beneficial chat.'

Alex ended the call before Kim had chance to respond.

She felt confident that she had laid the bait.

Her old adversary would come.

SIXTEEN

'You didn't leave, did you?' Kim asked when she entered the squad room at 7 a.m.

Stacey shook her head. 'I'm fine, boss, honest. Got my head down in the canteen, took a quick shower and I'm ready to roll.'

Kim understood the detective constable's guilt at not being able to take part in the informal surveillance of Steven Harte, but Kim hadn't given it a thought. There were many things Stacey could do that none of them could. And it wasn't as if she hadn't made use of the canteen as a bedroom herself once or twice.

Kim was willing to bet Stacey had still caught more shut-eye than she had after the annoying call from Alexandra bloody Thorne. Despite her efforts to ignore the calls, the damned woman had managed to get her, and Kim didn't even want to know how she'd obtained a mobile phone.

It was only after the third time of wondering about the information Alex had that Kim realised the insufferable woman was right. She did want to know.

She pushed the thoughts away and glanced at the whiteboards.

'You've been busy,' she said as Penn entered the room.

She'd told him to take an extra hour, but he'd ignored her

instruction, and she couldn't blame him. Whatever they did, wherever they went, Grace's face would be in their minds until they returned her safely to her mother.

'Okay, the family liaison officer assigned to the Lennards is Bernadette.'

'Good one,' Stacey said, nodding her approval.

'Stace, keep in touch with her and be sure to let her know that if she needs us for anything at all, we'll be there.'

'Will do, boss,' Stacey answered.

'The ground search will resume in about fifteen minutes. The grid has been extended by a square mile, and we're waiting on information about wind speeds before we get confirmation of the helicopter deployment. Inspector Plant is the man on the ground coordinating the efforts so...'

'I'll check in with him, boss,' Penn offered.

She nodded her thanks.

Kim turned her full attention to some of Stacey's efforts during the night. One of the wipe boards held a twenty-five-year-old photo of Melody Jones along with dates, times and names of family members.

The second board held a photo of Grace Lennard, taken just a few days ago. Again, Stacey had included all relevant information.

'Anything from Wrigley?' Stacey asked.

'Who?' Penn asked.

Kim forgot that Penn had already gone when they'd talked about the detective the night before.

Stacey took a moment to fill him in before she took over.

'Yes, he is as grouchy as the rumours purport, and yes, he felt there was something off with the family. He didn't care much for the older brother and felt the whole family were too eager to profit from the situation.'

She turned to Penn. 'I want you checking background on anything to do with Grace Lennard. We have to make sure there's no one in her family involved, and when you've got a minute, I want to know how much money the Joneses have made out of Melody's disappearance.'

'On it, boss.'

'Stace, I want you to get me all you can on Steven Harte. I know his adult history, but I want his life before. I want to know how he did at school, any trouble he got into, what his relationship was like with his parents, his type of friends. Anything.'

If nothing else she wanted his vulnerabilities – something, anything she might be able to use when questioning him.

'Already started, boss,' Stacey said, pressing a few keys.

Kim poured a coffee from the pot Stacey had made.

'Steven Harte was born in 1967 on Hollytree Estate.'

'What?'

'Yep, I was surprised too. Kinda comes across as someone who has always had money, doesn't he?'

Kim nodded her agreement although she should have known better than to judge. She too had spent the first six years of her life on Hollytree.

'His father is unknown, and his mother was mentally ill.'

Kim frowned at the similarities.

'Apparently, his mother, Nita Harte, developed severe agoraphobia after giving birth. She didn't leave the high-rise flat for just over eight years. And neither did he.'

'School?'

Stacey shook her head. 'She signed him out when the authorities came knocking. A neighbour shopped for them once a week and a cousin took care of paying the bills, but other than that it was just the two of them stuck in that small flat for years.'

'Until?'

'It don't get any rosier, boss. A week after Steven's eighth birthday she hung herself in the bathroom.'

'Jesus.'

'Obviously Steven was taken into care. At first, he was terrified of the outside world. He didn't understand a lot of it. He ran away from the group home twice and tried to get back in the flat. The new tenants weren't thrilled, and no family ever came forward to foster or adopt him.'

Kim felt sadness begin to steal over her. She pushed it away forcefully. If this man had harmed any little girl, she would not offer him one ounce of her sympathy.

'He'd never been to a park, a beach, a forest – which I'm guessing explains his philanthropy now. At school, he was a loner. He had no social skills, and he was late into the school system. His intelligence helped him catch up on the academic side, but he never learned how to get along with other people. And he didn't really need to. By the time he was fifteen he outshone every pupil in his class and had already set his sights on college.'

'You didn't go home last night, did you, Stace?' Penn asked, raising an eyebrow at all the information she'd gathered.

Kim took a moment to digest it all. Normally she had a grudging respect for anyone who was able to pull themselves up from humble beginnings. On top of that he'd faced a childhood with a mentally ill parent. He'd faced his own mother's death years before he should have and had been abandoned to the care system. On a normal day, she would have gone into that room and shook his hand.

But there was also the possibility that he abducted and killed little girls.

'Okay, Stace, let's not go pinning a hero badge on him quite yet. He alluded to the fact there may be others like Melody Jones. Start looking into it,' she said as an alarm sounded on her phone.

Woody had texted her with an instruction to brief him at 7.30 a.m. Without Bryant's fussing to get there on time, she'd set a reminder. Good job because she'd forgotten all about it, and what she really needed was time to prepare her strategy for 9 a.m. when Steven Harte would return, followed closely by Bryant.

'Okay, guys, get to it,' she said, heading out of the office.

As she made her way upstairs, she was betting that the two of them were discussing Steven Harte and the likelihood of him being involved in the crimes. And maybe they were right but, if so, why had he walked into the station in the first place?

It wasn't even eight o'clock and her head was hurting already.

Kim knocked her boss's door and entered.

'Sir, you wanted— Oh, am I early?'

A man who appeared to be in his late sixties sat at Woody's briefing table, holding a zip-up document folder. Two large bags lay at his feet.

'No, Stone, for once you're bang on time.' He turned his chair towards the man. 'I'd like you to meet Derek Foggarty. I thought that given the need to interview this witness effectively, you might benefit from some expert help.'

'Sir, I was thinking the same thing. Is there any way we can get Alison—'

'Derek here is an ex-MI5 trainer,' Woody said, ignoring her. 'He is an expert in the field of interview techniques, and I think he could give you some valuable pointers.'

Kim felt her mouth begin to open before she closed it again. Her last performance appraisal had highlighted her disrespect for visiting experts. She hadn't denied it but most of them were complete dicks. She liked to choose which dicks got to come in and advise her team, but maybe Woody had pulled a blinder. The mention of MI5 was a showstopper, and any help she could get in extracting the information from Harte was welcome. For the sake of Woody and her next performance appraisal, she would give Derek Foggarty the benefit of the doubt.

He stood and offered his hand. Kim ignored it as she leaned down and took one of his bags.

'Jesus, what you got in here, a couple of interviewees?'

His face showed no humour as he reached for the other bag.

Woody closed the door behind them. Great, all she needed was a visiting dick with no sense of humour.

She was still going to give him the benefit of the doubt.

'You want to see the interview tapes so far?' she asked as they headed down the stairs.

'Not necessary. The techniques I teach are universal.'

Mistake, her mind screamed, wondering how long the benefit of her doubt was going to last.

SEVENTEEN

'You're early. Did he give you the slip?' Kim asked Bryant, who was sitting at his desk.

Steven Harte had said he'd return at 9 a.m., and it wasn't yet eight.

'Nah, he's downstairs. He left early, went to the gym, offered me croissants, which I refused,' he said, pointedly, to Penn, who shrugged. 'And then he came here.' Bryant leaned to the side and looked around her. 'Want to introduce your new friend?'

'Guys, please meet Derek Foggarty. Ex-MI5 and here to tell us how to question our witness.'

Kim wheeled a chair to the top of the office, close to the coffee machine. On Stacey's screen, Kim could see she'd already made a start on searching for any previous incidents of missing girls.

Foggarty stood in front of the door commanding their full attention. 'Okay, the presentation is broken down into four sections. Should only take about six hours. It's a slimmed-down version of the whole model.'

Kim said nothing as Derek closed the door so that his computer could project the slides onto the wall. She already knew this was not going to take six hours. They didn't have that kind of time.

Kim knew that from his seat Penn could see Steven Harte on the monitor and that was where his attention would stay.

'Let's start with the first golden rule,' Derek Foggarty said. 'The investigator should be unbiased and open-minded and definitely non-confrontational.'

Bryant turned and wagged a finger in her direction.

She crossed her arms and sat back in her seat.

'There are three main categories to the interrogation process: indirect questioning, direct questioning and a mixture of both. To clarify indirect—'

'We understand the difference. Please move on.'

In her mind, she'd allowed Derek Foggarty an hour to teach them something new that they could use.

'The desk between you should be free of clutter and you should establish rapport as soon as possible. Use flattery if necessary, and deceptive tactics are acceptable as long as not outrageous or unlawful.'

'You're stuffed, guv,' Bryant said behind a cough.

'Change words. Use take instead of steal. Use empathy. Ask various questions in different sequences at different markers. Listen for inconsistencies. Someone who is lying continues lying to cover previous lies. The investigator should always remain cool and good gestures go a long way like buying lunch. One good turn etc.'

Kim considered the thought of presenting Steven Harte with 'tell me where Grace Lennard is and I'll buy you a meal deal' strategy. She wasn't sure that was gonna fly.

'The investigator must possess ideational fluency.'

'Who?' Penn asked.

'The ability to shift one's thinking instantaneously as the situation warrants. Keep the subject in short-term thinking mode; the relief of coming clean. Avoid long-term thinking, like going to prison. Don't be adversarial. Interview is a dialogue; interrogation is a monologue.'

Foggarty paused to drive that point home. Oh, how she loved a sound bite, she thought as she watched the minutes ticking away on Stacey's computer screen.

'Without realising it, deceptive people convey a message in the words they choose to articulate the lie. Interrogation is more about elicitation. It's a process that is designed to influence or persuade an individual to reveal information that he has reason to want to conceal. I'd like to offer some statements that transition to interrogation mode.

'You seem to be thinking about something. Something is clearly on your mind. There is—'

'Next,' Kim said. She got the picture. Foggarty moved forward through his presentation by a good five slides. Time saved.

'It's been said that a guilty person just wants to be understood. It allows him to feel he's been forgiven. This is what monologue is intended to accomplish, and when doing so you should slow your rate of speech, lower your voice and offer the illusion of sincerity.'

Kim could see that the rest of her team were multitasking. Bryant was managing to tidy his desk. Penn was keeping an eagle eye on Steven Harte, and Stacey was interrogating Google while still appearing to listen. Yes, it was her team, all right.

'Tailor your monologue to elicit a confession. Rationalise the action you think they're guilty of. Project the blame onto someone else, minimise the seriousness, reward for honesty. There are three primary forms of resistance to the monologue: convincing statements, emotions and denials. To counteract, use the person's first name, articulate a control phrase, hold up your hand.'

Kim did just that to indicate he should go faster.

'Use bait questions like: "Is there any reason we'd find your fingerprints on that door handle?"'

'Next,' Kim said.

'Ask simple straightforward questions.'

'Next.'

'Avoid compound leading, negative or confusing questions.'

'Next,' Kim said, wondering idly if presentation slides could get whiplash.

'Be alert for follow-up opportunities.'

'Next,' she said again. 'And please don't think I'm being rude. I just don't want to waste your time or ours.'

'I understand, and I'm trying to keep it relevant.'

Kim nodded for him to continue.

'Avoid a checklist mentality. Keep note taking to a minimum and don't rush the pace between questions. Make the subject feel good about disclosing information and use catch-all questions to uncover lies of omission like: "What haven't I asked you today that you think I should know about?"'

He took a deep breath as though surprised he'd reached the end of the section alive. Kim took a bottle of water from the fridge and placed it next to his projector.

'Okay, now I want to go through some terms that may or may not be familiar but that you should be aware of.

'Baselining is where you compare observed behaviour with an established norm. This helps identify when the subject is lying or is uncomfortable because you have a baseline to compare it against.'

Stacey seemed to have stilled beside her. She was reading something with interest. Kim glanced across and saw the name 'Suzie Keene'.

'The cliff moment is the point where a person feels he has disclosed everything he can without suffering negative consequences.'

'Got it,' Kim said.

'A cluster is any combination of two or more deceptive indicators.'

'Okey-dokey,' Kim said, stealing another glance at Stacey's screen.

'Mind virus is the psychological discomfort a person feels when he receives information that has potentially negative consequences, causing his mind to race with hypothetical ramifications of the information.'

'Yep, got that too,' she said, moving her chair slightly closer to Stacey's desk.

'Okay, now I want to move on to the elicitation approaches: either mild flattery or provocation.'

'You can skip straight to the second,' Bryant offered, showing that he was still listening. He knew she was unlikely to use the first.

Derek ignored him. This man was clearly a textbook tutor. Listen and don't interact.

Now she could read better, Kim could see why the case on Stacey's screen had caught her interest. Suzie Keene was abducted two years before Melody Jones.

'There are eighteen approach techniques, and I'd normally go through them all, but we'll focus on a couple. Incentive-based approaches work like offering a smoke—'

'Or a cup of tea,' Bryant interjected.

'Never promise something you can't give. There's the emotional approach. Read your subject and appeal to greed, hate, revenge, love of family – whichever emotion will work.

'Equally you can use emotional hate. If you can identify a fear, you can play it up or play it down to get a result.'

Suzie Keene had been taken in the middle of the school holidays just like Melody Jones.

'Can I get an example?' Penn asked.

Kim offered him a look. Questions took time.

'Say your subject is scared of spiders. You can hint that you're going to let in a truck load, or you can assure him that if one gets in, you're going to protect him.'

'Got it,' Penn said.

'And finally, I'll mention some techniques for detecting deceit. Repeat and control the questions. Look for internal inconsistencies like timeline. Are they giving you too little or too much information? Is the information self-serving?'

There were no witnesses to the abduction of Suzie Keene. Just like Melody, no one saw a thing.

'Is there a lack of extraneous detail? Are they repeating answers with the exact same wording and details? Is it too rehearsed? Does their appearance match the story? Does the language match the story?'

'Go back,' Kim called out.

'To which part in particular?' Foggarty asked obligingly.

'Not you,' she said, no longer making any effort to hide the fact she was doing more than listening to his presentation.

'Further, further,' Kim said as Stacey scrolled back up the screen.

'There – read that bit.'

Why had she never heard of Suzie Keene? Why weren't her parents on the television appealing for information? And then she caught the important paragraph as Stacey reached the bottom.

Suzie had been returned.

This victim was still alive.

EIGHTEEN

'Not sure our new friend Foggarty was impressed with being cut short and bundled out of the squad room,' Bryant said as he drove.

'I think he was a bit more understanding once we explained we had a lead in our investigation of a missing child,' Kim said, but the man had looked slightly offended.

'It's not strictly a lead though, is it, guv? I mean we're going to see a grown woman who may or may not have been abducted by the same person who took Melody, who may or may not be the same person who has abducted Grace, who may or may not be the man sitting—'

'Okay, details boy, I get your point, but did you really think we were going to get anything valuable from his presentation?'

'Learning how to sleep with my eyes open was on the horizon.'

She rolled her eyes.

By the time they'd managed to shepherd Derek Foggarty out of the office and back to his car, Stacey had found a current address for Suzie Keene and Penn had been back on Harte watch. Kim guessed he was getting to know the man's baseline behaviour quite well.

'So, let me get this straight,' Bryant said, unwilling to let the silence between them settle. 'There was another little girl abducted two years before Melody Jones, so that's twenty-seven years ago, but she was found exactly one year later safe and sound?'

Kim turned to her colleague as he negotiated an island.

'You do know you get no points for reciting my exact conversation with Woody.'

'I'm saying it out loud to prove it.' He frowned. 'I was a constable then – how do I not know about it?'

'Two reasons: it was a South Staffs case not West Mids and the coverage got lost somewhere between an earthquake in Algeria that killed 171 people and the opening of the Commonwealth Games in Canada.'

'How closely has she been questioned? Do you think she can identify Steven Harte?'

'Shit, I was in such a rush this morning after no sleep that I forgot to pack my crystal ball, tarot cards and other fortune-telling devices, so I suppose we'd best just talk to her and find out.'

'A simple "not sure" would have sufficed, and while you were searching for your crystal ball, I was following Harte while explaining on the phone to Laura the type of wiper blades she needs for her car, which I now have the pleasure of fitting when I get home.'

'Don't say it as though you mind it,' Kim said.

'What I mind is that it was only ten minutes ago I was fixing stabilisers to her first bike and now its wiper blades to her car.' He shook his head. 'Doesn't matter how much time passes, you still want to protect them.'

They remained locked in their own thoughts until Bryant pulled up outside a small semi-detached house in Lower Gornal.

'Hope she's not gonna mind us dredging it all up for her,' Bryant said as they approached the front door.

'With an eight-year-old girl still missing I can take a little discomfort.'

A woman answered the door wearing a pencil skirt, heels, collared shirt and carrying a laundry basket.

Her pleasant features instantly contorted into concern as most parents' faces did when strangers knocked on their door.

Kim took out her ID and introduced them both. 'And your daughter is fine,' she added, to put her mind at ease.

'How did you know I have a daughter?' she asked, panicking.

Kim nodded towards the linen basket that was drowning in small pink garments.

'Oh, of course. I'm sorry, how can I help?'

Kim took a breath. She didn't know how much pain she was about to cause.

'May we talk to you about what happened to you as a child?'

'Sorry?'

For a moment Kim thought there had been some kind of mistake.

'The abduction?'

'Oh, yes, of course,' she said dismissively. 'Come in, but we'll have to chat upstairs while I do this, or I'll be late for work.'

Kim followed her upstairs and into the first bedroom on the left. Bryant remained in the doorway.

'Nice room,' Kim said, taking a quick look around.

A white quilt cover with daisies matched the pillowcase. A couple of Barbie dolls sat on the bedside cabinet. A small desk sat beneath a wall-mounted TV. Perhaps a little dated but spacious despite the three-quarter-sized bed.

'Cammie likes it. She'd love a computer up here but that's not happening.'

Kim smiled as the woman took out folded clothes and started putting them away.

'So, how can I help?'

'You were abducted twenty-seven years ago when you were nine years old. If it's not too painful, can you tell us about it?'

Susie smiled. 'I was away for a year, Officer. You'll have to be more specific than that.'

Kim found the word 'away' a strange choice – captive, kidnapped, gone, taken – but she let it pass.

'Did you see the man that abducted you?'

'Never. Not for the whole time I was there.'

'So he never touched you or...?'

'God, no. It wasn't like that,' she said with an expression of distaste.

Kim was confused. Yes, it had been a long time ago, but the woman showed no emotional response at all. Right now, she didn't know which questions to ask.

Kim took a seat on the bed. 'Please, tell us what you remember as long as it's not too difficult.'

'It's not difficult at all,' she said, putting leggings in the second drawer. 'I'm sure you've got the dates and times etc, but all I remember is going to look for the ball. Some older girls were playing rounders and allowed me to join in. They put me right out in the field. Lizzy Brown was batting, and I knew she could slog 'em, so I went right back as far as I could go. Still it sailed over the top of my head and into the bushes. Went after it, bent down, felt something over my mouth and that was the last thing I remembered before I woke up.'

'Where?'

'In a room; a nice room. It had its own bathroom. It was quiet, peaceful. I could hear birds. I was scared. I stared at the door for hours, terrified it would open and someone would come in and hurt me. I cried a lot while I waited and waited for something bad to happen, but it never did. Food and drinks came when I was asleep, and then comics and the TV remote and then books and then tests that were marked and returned. Never did understand geometry until then and now I'm an architect, go figure.'

'But you were separated from your family. Weren't you terrified?' Kim asked, trying to understand.

'At first, yes. I missed them like mad and I was petrified that something bad was going to happen to me, but as each day passed I felt safer, sure that no one was going to hurt me.'

'How could you know that?'

Suzie shrugged. 'I don't know. Maybe I just convinced myself of that so I could let go of the fear. After about a week I began to feel the relief.'

'Of what?' Kim asked, trying not to show her astonishment. Never had she had this type of conversation with the victim of a kidnapping.

'I wasn't happy at home. My parents had just announced they were getting divorced. I cried myself to sleep every night and did what every nine-year-old does. I blamed myself. I questioned everything I'd done from arguing about going to bed to leaving my plate on the floor. All I could think of was how to make them stay together. Here's another irony for you. My time away brought them closer and they're still together now.'

'Please don't be offended but you sound almost grateful that you were kidnapped,' Kim observed and waited for the eruption of denial.

'Such an ugly word and one I don't use in relation to my own experience. I was removed from my life for a while. I had a nice room, food, books, TV, music, school lessons, a birthday cake and peace and quiet. I felt no pain, maybe a bit lonely sometimes, but I also felt safe. I'd been removed from everything that was hurting me. It's difficult to explain but I felt protected. I knew he wasn't going to let anything hurt me. It did me no long-term harm, and I returned to normal life. It's no different to when children are removed from toxic situations by social services. They're placed elsewhere temporarily and then returned when the time is right.' She smiled. 'When I came back everyone was so pleased to see me. I was spoiled rotten all over again.'

Kim agreed that on the face of it she hadn't suffered. She had a nice home, a family, a good job. But how could she have been ripped from her family, held captive for a year and suffer absolutely no ill effects?

'And how did you leave?' Kim asked curiously. So far, she hadn't mentioned seeing anyone.

'The door opened. No words. Just a small van with the back door open. I got in and closed the door.'

'You didn't see anyone?'

She shook her head.

'What about the building, the surroundings?'

Suzie shook her head again. 'I didn't register anything. I just got into the van.'

Kim tried not to show her surprise at the trust she'd placed in her captor. He could have been taking her anywhere.

The news report stated that she'd been dropped a hundred metres from Old Hill police station.

'How long were you in the van?' Kim asked.

'You know, I was asked this question back then and I couldn't answer it. It could have been fifteen minutes; it could have been an hour.'

Kim calculated the difference in radius to the drop point from approximately seven miles to a 30-mile radius working on a rough speed of 30 miles an hour.

Kim raised an eyebrow. 'You really can't narrow it down?'

Suzie shook her head.

'Anything you remember about the journey? Was it bumpy, smooth, noisy, bendy?'

'I'm sorry, Officer, it's been so long ago now that any detail is lost to me.'

Kim had a sneaking suspicion it was lost to her twenty-seven years ago as well.

'If there's nothing further, I really must get off to work.'

'Of course,' Kim said, rising from the bed.

There was little point in posing any more questions to Suzie Keene, who appeared to have no memory of the important stuff, and Kim had the distinct feeling that she wouldn't tell them if she did.

Never had she heard of a kidnapper abducting a child to feed them, clothe them, educate them and then free them untouched and unharmed.

So why was Suzie Keene lying about the whole thing?

NINETEEN

'You know, Penn, I'm struggling a bit with this one,' Stacey said honestly. 'I can't peg this guy as a murderer.'

It was a feeling that had been swirling around her stomach all night. It had sat with her at her desk, it had followed her to the canteen while she got her head down for an hour and accompanied her into the shower block before the others turned up for work.

She'd seen the disapproving look on the boss's face, but she hadn't wanted to go home and relax when the others were pulling extra hours. Not that there was anything to go home for anyway. Devon's job as an immigration officer was equally as demanding as her own, and she had left early Sunday morning for a four-day sting operation in Kent. Their flat had felt empty the second she'd walked out the door.

It wasn't until Sunday night that Stacey had headed for bed around eleven and found an almost life-size cuddly giraffe on Devon's side of the bed. He'd been sprayed with Devon's favourite perfume and held a note saying he needed lots of cuddles. Everywhere she'd looked since she'd found little Post-it notes with messages from her wife.

She smiled at the realisation that they were over halfway, and that Devon would be home tomorrow evening. In the meantime, she had to try and alter her thinking on Steven Harte.

'Stace, we've already—'

'I know that but tell me honestly what you think. Do you feel that he abducted and killed Melody Jones and has kidnapped Grace Lennard too?'

Penn raised his head and took a good look at the screen.

Steven Harte was sitting comfortably and scrolling through his mobile phone.

'Okay, I will admit that he doesn't strike me as a murderer, but it's dangerous to assume that, and we can't get past the fact he brought himself to the station.'

'But look at all the good works he's done. Do murderous psychopaths really commit hundreds of thousands of pounds to good causes?'

'Again, Stace, I don't think one is mutually exclusive of the other. I think we've only got to look at Jimmy Savile to prove that one wrong.'

'I take your point, but I still have my doubts,' she said, sighing heavily just so Penn knew how much that concession had cost her.

'Well, there's nothing dodgy about Grace's family that I can see. Claire Lennard has one sister who lives in New Zealand, an elderly grandmother she helps to care for, a father who retired to Spain with his second wife four years ago and a cousin who is a barrister in Manchester. Barely a parking ticket between the lot of them. Very clean.'

'Squeaky,' Penn agreed. 'Now the Jones family are a little more colourful. One of Melody's sisters is in prison for armed robbery, and another had two kids before she was seventeen. Robbie's not been in much trouble, but he is making a killing on eBay. He's been selling gifts and donated goods on there for around fifteen years.'

'Traded up from the car boot then?'

'Oh yeah, and there's a noticeable upsurge after an appearance by Lyla, of which there are many,' he said, waving a list in the air.

'Go on,' Stacey said, sitting forward.

'By my count, over the years she's done at least ten documentaries – four of those were specifically about Melody and the rest were various unsolved crimes. Some were UK and a couple were for cable channels in other countries. She's done breakfast television a dozen times and that seems to be the big earner.'

'How much?'

'By my calculations, in the last fifteen years the family has made at least fifty-three thousand pounds from selling the tokens they've been sent. There's no way of knowing what payment or expenses Lyla has made from forty-three articles in the local and national press and the dozens of magazine stories, or what the family received in cash and vouchers.'

'I can hear the disapproval in your voice,' Stacey said, and she didn't disagree.

'Somehow, they managed to move off Hollytree, which I don't blame anyone for doing, but they profited from the disappearance and probable murder of their daughter or sister or whatever. It just doesn't sit well that the family were able to—'

Penn stopped speaking as his phone rang, surprising them both.

He answered it and listened, his face freezing by the second.

He offered his thanks and ended the call.

'I'd hold off on that medal for Harte's good works for a minute, Stace,' he said, making another call.

TWENTY

'You reckon we can find a way to tie Steven Harte to Suzie Keene?' Bryant asked as they headed back to the station.

'And charge him with what, taking her on holiday? You heard Suzie. He fed her, clothed her, gave her a big bed and a bathroom, educated her and then sent her home. If Harte was responsible, what could she say in court that would help us put him away?'

'He still kidnapped her. That's a charge,' he argued.

'And Suzie Keene, the victim, would be a fabulous witness... for the defence.'

'I can't get my head around it,' Bryant said. 'She was gone for a whole year. That's like ten years to a kid. She wasn't lonely. She didn't feel isolated. He never hurt her. He never even touched her, so what the hell did he take her for?'

'Bryant, on this occasion you are not alone in your confusion.'

'See, that doesn't give me any reassurance. I feel safer when I don't get it but you do. It's like when I was a kid and my mum—'

He shut up as her phone rang.

'Probably lucky you didn't get to finish that thought,' she said, taking out her phone and hitting loudspeaker.

'Penn,' she answered. 'Brilliant timing, as I think Bryant was about to compare me to his mother, which wouldn't have done him...'

'Boss, we've had a report. Bones have been found.'

Kim felt a cool shiver crawl down her spine.

'Okay. Where are we going?'

Bryant was now listening intently.

'That's the thing, boss. They've been found at Hawne Park.'

'In Halesowen? Didn't Stacey mention that as one of—'

'Yeah, boss. Steven Harte has been funding small projects there for years.'

Bryant had already done a full circle of the traffic island and was heading towards the location.

She thanked Penn, ended the call and scrolled down her contacts. Her boss answered almost immediately.

'You've heard, sir, about the bones at Hawne Park?'

'Of course. Are you on your way?'

'Yep, just a mile out. Harte has links to this location, so if the bones are human, we're gonna need some help in reading and understanding this man.'

One wrong move and they could lose him. He was clever. He was playing a game, and she had to make sure he didn't win.

'Okay, I'll see if Derek can return and—'

'Thanks, but no thanks, sir. He's a train the trainee guy who has absolutely no practical experience in questioning suspects.' She took a breath. 'There's only one person to help us with this one and if you can't get her, we'll go it alone.'

Woody said he'd see what he could do before ending the call.

Kim tried to use the remaining half a mile to prepare herself for what lay ahead.

Were they finally going to bring Melody Jones home?

TWENTY-ONE

Alex finished her poor excuse for a breakfast and headed back to her cell. The tasteless, mundane offering of porridge, cereal or toast did nothing to set her up physically or psychologically for the day ahead.

Oh, how she had once loved warm, freshly baked croissants with home-made preserves from the café a short walk from her home. It had been her favourite time of the day and the reason she'd never booked an appointment before 10 a.m. Nothing beat eating a leisurely breakfast made of the best ingredients while observing the trials and tribulations of people far more ordinary than she was.

It was both the breakfast and the feeling of superiority that helped her get through the day in her old life, but here only the sense of superiority was the same. There wasn't one person in the whole prison able to match her in intelligence. Another reason she was looking forward to a visit from Kim Stone.

She rubbed her hands with anticipation, unsure when the eagerly awaited event would occur.

In the meantime, she had plenty to keep her going to help secure the result she craved.

And this morning she was going fishing.

'Hey, Olivia,' Alex said, standing in the doorway of the cell next to her own.

'Hey, Alex. How was breakfast?' she asked. It was a meal Olivia never appeared for.

'Same old.'

Olivia Spencer was an educated, wealthy woman in her late thirties, doing a two-year stretch for the embezzlement of a children's charity that raised tens of thousands of pounds for underprivileged kids. Her own lifestyle with her husband, a local TV news anchor, hadn't been too shabby, but she'd been tempted by the large amounts of money she'd handled on behalf of the charity.

Olivia had made some mistakes in her few months at Drake Hall. Firstly, she'd thought that Warden Siviter would go easy on her because they had been friends through high school and college. She had found out quickly that the warden didn't play favourites.

Olivia's second mistake had been in thinking she could befriend her, that because they were both educated, professional women they would bond. Another mistake. Alex hadn't yet found a glue strong enough to bond her to anyone.

Upon meeting people, Alex worked through a checklist in her mind. Are they useful to me now? Will they be useful to me later? This woman's name was shit to the other prisoners, and her name would be worth nothing on the outside. As a woman who had actively taken money from deprived kids, she would struggle professionally and personally to rebuild any kind of reputation, and no one in here would say a word to her.

In truth, Alex didn't care one way or the other what the woman had done. She'd seen an opportunity to make some extra cash and she'd taken it. Her true crime had been in getting greedy and getting caught.

Alex had initially dismissed the woman until her personal little bone carrier, Emma, had furnished her with the information of

Olivia's and Warden Siviter's history. That had changed things substantially.

She had started slowly: the occasional smile, a wave as she passed by the door, sometimes sitting closer to her in the food hall, standing in her doorway to ask her how she was.

Today she moved into the room and took a seat on the bed.

'I swear these women are killing me. I never thought my biggest issue in here was going to be my need for a decent conversation.'

Olivia smiled as though she understood when she really didn't. Barely anyone in the whole place spoke to her. Her crimes against kids weren't enough to secure her a beating or a push down the stairs, but they had earned her the silent treatment. By now she must be desperate to just talk to someone.

'Talk to me, Olivia,' she said with mock drama. 'About anything other than your kids, your husband or what happened last night on *Corrie*.'

Olivia allowed the suspicion to fade and a half-smile appeared. 'What would you like to know?'

Oh, this really was too easy, Alex thought.

'Where did you go to school? I'm guessing you were privately educated?'

'I attended King Edwards Academy in Oldswinford,' she said proudly.

'Nice,' Alex said appreciatively. Clearly, Olivia's family hadn't been on the breadline even before she'd found herself a high-earning husband. 'I'm guessing that place was expensive enough to produce some notable alumni.'

'Oh yes. My year alone produced a poet laureate, a physicist and a ground-breaking heart surgeon.'

'Impressive,' Alex said.

'And a prison warden.'

Alex faked momentary confusion, as though it was taking a

little while for the penny to drop. 'Oh, this one? You were at school with Warden Siviter?'

'School and college.'

'You're joking?'

Olivia shook her head.

Alex frowned. 'That surprises me. I'd never have guessed. I mean it's not like— Never mind.'

'Not like what?' Olivia asked.

'Well, it's not like anyone would know, is it? She doesn't exactly do you any favours, does she, to say you once vaguely knew each other.'

Throw out the line.

'Oh, it wasn't vague. We were definitely friends. Right through to the end of college.'

Reel her in.

'Oh my goodness. That's a bit shocking, to be honest. I mean, I'm not sure what exactly she could do to make life more comfortable but surely there's something. Although, she is a bit of a "by the book" person, isn't she?'

'She wasn't always that way,' Olivia said.

'Really?' Alex asked with wide eyes.

'Pregnant at fifteen, baby adopted out, pregnant again at seventeen and miscarried.'

'Blimey, she was busy. She must really love the kids she's got now.'

Olivia shook her head. 'She hasn't got any. Can't have them apparently.'

'Oh no, what a shame,' Alex said.

The reminder of that realisation seemed to put a muzzle on Olivia's mouth. Her expression said that she felt like she'd revealed too much. Whether Warden Siviter gave her special treatment or not, this was personal information she was sharing. Very personal.

'Well, whatever her past, she's a good warden and I think we're lucky to have her,' Alex said, pushing herself up off the bed.

'Agreed,' Olivia said as Alex headed for the door. 'And obviously, Alex, what I've said must stay with you.'

'Of course, Olivia,' Alex said, feeling the smile rest on her face. 'I swear to you that I will never breathe a word.'

TWENTY-TWO

Hawne Park was located just 1 mile out of Halesowen. At 285 yards long by 165 yards wide it was hardly a sprawling site, but the area had been adopted by the locals and improved over the last twenty years. One of those improvements was a set of brand-new black gates on Short Street, which was currently full of vehicles. Residents were gathered around the tape that had been pulled across the entrance.

Kim pushed her way through, ignoring the questions from the more vocal members of the group.

'What've we got?' Kim asked the first uniform she saw.

He pointed to a group of people made up of construction workers and suits, none of whom she recognised. She stepped into the middle of them and saw what they were all looking at. The digger being used was small with a forked bucket. At the very edge was a collection of what appeared to be small bones.

'Are they human?' asked one of the suits she didn't recognise.

'And you are?'

'Jenson Butler, owner of Butler Building Limited. Micky called me as soon as he brought up the scoop.'

'He called you first?' she asked, appraising him. He had salt-

and-pepper hair and she guessed him to be mid-fifties. He appeared to be in good shape, although he didn't look like that was from getting his hands dirty.

'Of course he called me. I'm his boss and he didn't know what to do.'

'They all with you?' she asked, nodding to the other three suits.

'Yes, that's my health and—'

'I don't care. Take yourself and them to the cordon and wait to be spoken to.'

Even as she spoke, Bryant was shepherding people away. By the time it was just the two of them and a couple of uniforms, Keats was heading towards them.

'Finish your lunch first, did you?' she asked the pathologist.

'I shall not dignify that with a response, Inspector,' he said, walking straight past her and stopping at the bucket.

In this scenario, his job was not to immediately recover the body, it was to assess the likelihood of them being human remains, which was a whole different process. Nothing would be touched until he had made that call.

She and Bryant exchanged glances as he peered closely at the bones in the bucket.

'Any chance of a time of death?' Kim asked to lighten the mood around them. Finding bones was never a joyous occasion, but finding smaller bones was heartbreaking.

He ignored her. 'Yes, Inspector, my opinion is that these bones are human. We appear to have most of a small hand, and I suspect that is the thumb there,' he said, pointing to the left side of the hole.

Kim nodded towards Bryant, who stepped away and took out his phone.

'She's on her way,' Keats said with dread in his voice. 'I took the liberty of forewarning her of what I'd been called to, so she should be here any—'

'Is that you, Keatings?' came the familiar voice from behind them.

Despite the conditions, Kim couldn't help the smile that tugged at her lips.

Doctor A was a slight woman who measured no more than five foot two. Her hair was long and of the ombré style with the tips lighter than the rest. Her real Macedonian name was long and complicated, so everyone called her Doctor A. She was the most skilled and passionate forensic archaeologist Kim had ever worked with.

She offered her hand as the woman approached. There were few people she greeted with respect, and Doctor A was one of them.

Doctor A took it and shook it warmly.

'Good to see you again, Inspector, but not so good,' she said, glancing at the hole in the ground.

Kim nodded her agreement.

Doctor A approached the bucket. 'And how are you, my sweetheart?'

'I'm good, thanks,' Keats offered with a straight face.

'Of course, you are, Keatings, but I was talking to our charge,' she said, walking around the hole and looking in the bucket.

The wave of sadness that passed over her features confirmed what they already knew; that they were looking at the bones of a child.

Doctor A took out her phone. 'Bryan, please remove these people.'

Bryant didn't bother to correct her on his name. He'd already done it many times. It was never clear if her spoken mistakes were intentional, but she was forgiven anyway.

Bryant stepped over to the last remaining police officers and instructed them to leave, while Doctor A summoned her team.

'Okay, I will collect the bones from the ground and then work from your place, Keatings.'

'Lucky me,' he said, out of the woman's earshot. Even he wasn't brave enough to incite the fiery lady.

'Okay, shoot, shoot, all of you,' she said, taking an elastic band from her pocket. In just a couple of swift movements, her long hair was tied up and out of her way.

'Are we being dismissed?' Keats asked, standing beside Kim.

'Sounds that way.'

'Please feeling free to stay and watch me watch the bones until my teams arrives; however, I would have thought you had all got more pressing tasks. I will take care of the little soul.'

Kim didn't doubt it.

'And the accuracy of that statement may not change,' Keats said as they walked back towards the entrance.

'I know,' Kim answered. If they were looking at the bones of a child, they might never know if they had found a boy or a girl.

The walk to the gate was short, and privacy screens had already been erected.

Keats bid them farewell and headed to his van.

Another familiar face appeared before her.

'Like to give a comment to the community via the local press?' Frost asked.

'Yeah, I'd like to share that you are one annoying b—'

'Nothing right now, Frost,' Bryant interjected.

'Aw come on, Inspector, that's no way to speak to someone who's slept in your bed.'

'Spare,' Kim said to Bryant.

'I can assure you, guv, that needed no clarification.'

She shot Frost a look before moving away.

'You know, there's a very good reason why I am rarely nice to anyone. It only comes back and bites me in the ass.'

'Enough already about the night she stayed over,' Bryant quipped as they headed towards the high-vis jackets.

Kim approached the guy who had been operating the machine. 'You were on the digger?'

'Excavator,' he corrected with a chin-out attitude.

It was rather a grandiose name for a smaller-than-average piece of building machinery. Perhaps excavator was what the little machine aspired to be.

'And what were you doing?'

'Excavating,' he said, folding his arms.

'Oh, you're funny. You here all week?'

'Well, if you're gonna ask questions as dumb—'

'Not sure where your attitude is coming from, fella, but do us both a favour and drop it before we take this down the station. We like to get a detailed report from the person who discovered the bones.'

She held his gaze for a few seconds, appraising him. She'd met this type before. Middle-aged with a decent job but with a shady past and brushes with the law. The resentment for the police would accompany him to his grave. Not her problem.

'You need me to repeat the question?'

'Digging out footings for a wall, nothing major.'

'On whose instruction?'

'My boss,' he answered.

'And who instructed your boss?' Kim asked, trying to hold on to her patience. Petty arguments and power struggles were not going to help her. She'd learned from Bryant when to hold her tongue in check.

'And where is your boss?' Kim asked, looking around.

'Had to go. Urgent meeting.'

Kim stifled her irritation. She was pretty sure she'd told him to stay put. She had to admit that it took some neck to deliberately defy an instruction from a police officer. But she'd catch up with him later.

'Bryant, will you please find me someone I can speak to about—'

'Er... excuse me. I'm Roy Barber, chairman of the residents' association.'

Bryant offered her a satisfied look, as though he'd just made the man appear upon her instruction.

'Ah, Mr Barber, can you confirm what works were going on here?'

'Yes, we're building a small seating area for the residents to gather.'

'You couldn't use benches?' Bryant asked.

'Keep getting nicked, Officer. We put up a temporary camera. Well it was Sandra's old babycam; caught the buggers but your lot didn't pursue it. No justice and no bench.'

It wasn't a case that the CPS would entertain taking to court.

'We don't have a lot of money and we wanted something permanent. These guys gave us a good quote, dead cheap really. They did some work here about twenty years ago, so we were happy to use them again.'

'And does the name Steven Harte mean anything to you?'

His smile was wide on hearing the name.

'Of course. Most of the improvements we've made are because of him. He started helping us out some time in the nineties. If it wasn't for him our modest park would still be a forgotten piece of land covered in dog shit and used condoms.' The man frowned. 'Is he in some kind of trouble?'

Kim chose to leave the question unanswered. 'And recently?'

'We've not heard from him for a while, but he still makes a small donation annually to our committee funds.'

'When was he last involved in any major project works, Mr Barber?'

'Well, it would have been back in '95.'

Damn, that was a whole year before Melody Jones had been abducted.

'No, no, hang on. That's not right, it would have been '99 when he paid for some dead trees to be removed and some new mature trees planted.'

'And you're sure that was '99?' Kim asked. Three years after Melody had disappeared.

'Absolutely positive. He and his team were determined to get the job done before we hit the millennium.'

'His team?'

'Yeah, the guys who were here earlier.'

Kim felt the anxiety roll around her stomach. 'Butler Building Limited?'

He nodded. 'That's why we've used them again now of our own accord, as they did such a good job before.'

'So, twenty-two years ago Steven Harte brought in this same company to do some work?'

Roy nodded. 'As I understand it, Jenson Butler works on all of Steven Harte's projects.'

TWENTY-THREE

'Okay, guys, I think we finally have our answer to the "why now" question,' Kim said, sitting at the spare desk. A quick catch-up with the team and then in to talk to Steven Harte.

'You think he knew this was coming?' Penn asked, glancing at the screen.

'Makes sense.'

'Guv, do you think Steven Harte abducted Melody Jones and also has Grace Lennard?' Bryant asked.

'I do.'

'But why not just wait until we came knocking?' Stacey asked. 'He's got to have known we'd get to him eventually. Still doesn't make sense to me.'

'Stace, I know you're struggling to see him as the bad guy,' Penn said, 'but you gotta come on board with—'

'No, she doesn't,' Kim said. 'Stick with your gut, Stace. He hasn't admitted anything yet so we can't get carried away. We need a dissenting voice to keep our viewpoint open and other options available. We can't afford to focus on one lead only.'

Bryant put his hand in the air. 'Er, so, Stace is getting paid to sit here and argue with you?'

'Pretty much.'

'Where was the advert for that one? I'd have had a go.'

Kim saw his point, but she needed Stacey's objectivity to remain intact in case they were chasing the wrong tail. Her gut told her that Steven Harte was in this up to his eyebrows, but without solid evidence or a full confession, there was little she could do at this point.

'Boss, I think we may have another one,' Stacey said, looking away from her screen.

'Another what?' Kim asked as her heart leaped into her mouth. Another abduction? Another bone site?

'Another Suzie,' Stacey said, clicking furiously.

'What?' Kim said, placing her coffee back on the desk.

'I went back a couple more years. An eight-year-old girl named Libby Turner disappeared in '92. Two years before Suzie and four years before Melody Jones. Taken from an estate in Chester. No one saw a thing and guess what?'

'She came back?' Kim asked hopefully.

Stacey nodded. 'Yep, one year later she's found a quarter mile away from a police station, unharmed.' Stacey frowned as she continued reading. 'Libby went straight into the social care system.'

'Did they think her family was involved in the abduction?'

'Don't think so but she never lived with them again. I'll keep digging.'

'What the hell is going on?' Kim asked to no one in particular.

'Got an address here, boss. Currently lives just outside Wrexham,' Stacey said.

Kim looked to Penn. 'Reckon your old banger will get you that far?'

Penn laughed. 'I've told you. She's reliable.'

If not tidy, Kim thought, remembering the debris she'd had to move from the passenger seat one time Bryant had been otherwise engaged.

He stood. 'Stace...'

'Already texted to your phone.'

Penn grabbed his jacket and headed out.

Kim finished her coffee.

'Stace, I want to know every project that Steven Harte has worked on with Butler Building Limited and take a look at the employees and business finances as well. These two have a history and I want to know how far back it goes.'

Bryant knitted his hands together and placed them behind his head. 'I'll just kick back and...'

'You wish, Bryant. You're coming in there with me.'

After the morning they'd had so far, there were more than a few questions that Kim wanted to put to Steven Harte.

TWENTY-FOUR

'Hello, Mr Harte, thank you for coming in to speak to us again,' Kim said, sitting down.

'My aim is only to help, Inspector,' he said, sitting up in his seat.

'Of course,' she said, reaching into her back pocket. She slid a £20 note across the table towards him. 'That should cover Penn's supper for last night. He gets expenses.'

He held up his hand in refusal.

She pushed it further. 'Mr Harte, I must insist.'

She was not prepared to face bribery slurs in any potential trial. His defence could make a meal out of that one. Literally.

'Understood, Inspector, but I don't like the feeling of going backwards. I'm sure we agreed yesterday that you would call me Steven.'

'Okay, Steven, why are you here and what do you want?'

'I want nothing more than to assist you with your enquiries.'

'Okay, where is Grace Lennard?'

He smiled and sat back in his chair. 'I'm sure Grace Lennard is fine, wherever she is. We have many other things to talk about.'

Kim felt Bryant bristle beside her. Like her, he didn't appreciate Harte's attempts to control the direction of the narrative but they had agreed outside that she would lead the questioning.

'Where is Melody Jones?'

'Did you speak to her family?'

'We did and I'm intrigued to know why you sent us in that direction. Did you want to cause even more hurt? Don't you think they've suffered enough?'

'I'm not sure they've suffered at all, but I thought you'd be interested in her background.'

'Yes, we were very interested, but how did you know so much about her background? How closely did you follow her family?'

'Please ask me one question at a time,' he said, tapping the side of his head. 'I struggle to keep up.'

Bryant shifted in his seat. She was sure it was taking all his effort not to reach across the table and try to shake the information from him. Luckily for her, Bryant had excellent self-control because brute force was not going to work.

'I'm sorry, Steven, but I don't believe that for a minute. You are simply trying to control the conversation.'

He was no idiot, and neither was she.

He smiled. 'In answer to your first question, I knew so much about her background because like any concerned citizen at that time I watched the news, I read the articles, I saw the interviews. I watched as Lyla Jones frowned less and smiled more. I watched as the make-up she wore became thicker and better applied. I watched as her hair darkened and became styled. I watched her confidence grow along with her bank balance.'

'You know her finances?'

'I can imagine she was paid for many of her appearances. I watched as Melody's disappearance became less about Melody and more about her.'

Kim disputed none of it. 'But what were you hoping we'd find?'

He shrugged.

Kim couldn't help wondering if he was trying in some way to

ease his own guilt for taking Melody's life by trying to convince them her life hadn't been all that great.

'So, what else have you dug up while you've been gone?' he asked, meeting her gaze.

Kim was sure she heard a low growl from Bryant's throat at Harte's play on words but she'd decided before entering the room that she was going to share nothing of the discovery at Hawne Park.

If she was correct, that he was here because he had known Melody's body was going to be uncovered, he would be expecting her questions to centre around that. She wasn't going there until she had more information and could ask the questions she really wanted to ask. It was also important that he understood that he was not in control.

'We met with a woman named Suzie Keene. You might remember her.'

Amusement danced in his eyes, but he offered no response.

'Suzie Keene was nine years old when she was abducted in 1994. Kept from her family for a year.'

'Oh yes, I remember Suzie. I read a lot of articles about her and her family too.'

Kim saw what game they were playing and realised she had no choice but to play along.

'And what do you remember from those articles, Steven?'

'I remember thinking she was a shy and sensitive girl. Withdrawn. I felt she was having problems with her family when she disappeared. Her parents didn't appear very close when they did their television appeal. I heard they became close again while Suzie was gone, and then she miraculously reappeared sometime later and rejoined a happy family.'

'A year later,' she emphasised.

'It's a long time.'

'She claimed she was untouched.'

His face creased in disgust. 'Only a sicko would do that.'

'Then one wonders what kind of sicko had her at all.'

He fought down any emotion that was trying to show on his face. She noted that particular trigger for use if she needed it.

He recovered quickly. 'And how has she fared in life after her terrible experience?'

Kim would not give him the satisfaction of answering that one.

He tipped his head. 'I'm sure I read somewhere that she was now an architect. Is that correct?'

Again, Kim said nothing.

'Unbelievable, isn't it? That someone can experience an event in their life so unsettling and for it to have no impact on them in later life. In fact, one could even wonder if the experience was a positive one that—'

'She was ripped from her family and held captive for a year,' Kim said, unable to listen to his twisted perspective.

'I wonder if that's how she remembers it?' he said, tipping his head.

Kim took a moment to reflect over the things he'd said. There was nothing that he couldn't have got from the media outlets at the time. There was nothing specific to tie him to the crime. He was an intelligent man, and his answers were well rehearsed.

'I would imagine it was a staycation for Libby Turner two years later too, wasn't it? I've got a feeling you read a lot about her too?'

Kim was coming to realise that he couldn't hide the small bursts of triumph that came into his eyes. She made another mental note as he answered.

'Funny you should say that, Officer, because I remember her very well indeed.'

TWENTY-FIVE

'One minute I was playing hide and seek in the woods and the next I woke up in a room I didn't recognise.'

Penn nodded and encouraged her to continue.

Libby Turner had graciously agreed to speak to him and had guided him through to a sun room at the back of her detached new-build home on the outskirts of Wrexham.

It had the best light in the house to aid her business as a jewellery maker. The sun shone in and reflected off the stones, clasps and tools that littered an antique workbench.

'I was scared but I wasn't hurt. No one spoke to me. Food arrived in the night while I slept, but I couldn't eat because I thought the food was poisoned. On the second or third day there was a note. It simply said: "No one is going to hurt you".'

'And you believed the note?' Penn asked as she tucked a lock of curly blonde hair behind her ear.

'Actually, I did because underneath the words was a smiley face. Evil people don't draw smiley faces, do they? That was my eight-year-old logic, so I believed him.'

'Him?' Penn asked, jumping ahead. Had she seen her captor?

'I've just assumed all these years that it was a man. I never smelled any perfume or even heard footsteps, but I've always assumed it was a man.'

His hopes were dashed. They were not going to get a positive identification from this one either, but he was intrigued enough to keep listening.

'I started to eat the food and enjoy the space. The room was lovely. I had a big bed, my own bathroom. A television on the wall, a desk and a wardrobe full of new clothes and shoes. There was a window, but it was covered with some kind of mural. I tried to peel it off, but it was glued from the outside.'

'Didn't you miss your family?' Penn asked. He couldn't imagine being taken away from his parents and Jasper at that age.

A shadow passed over her face. 'I missed my friends more. They had been my lifeline.'

Why did an eight-year-old need a lifeline? Penn wondered but didn't interrupt.

'After a couple of weeks, the schoolwork started to appear on alternate days. If I finished my lessons, the next day I got comics and batteries for Fido.'

'Fido?'

Libby smiled. 'You know those electronic pet games. You had to feed it, walk it, train it and show it love by patting it.'

'So he brought you presents?'

She nodded. 'Games and puzzles. Normally it was something that kept the brain ticking over, something challenging that had to be accomplished. I remember one time when my bracelet broke. Oh I was so upset; my grandma had bought it for me before she died. It was the loop for the fastener that I couldn't find. Next day there was a pair of tweezers and a little clamp. I managed to work one of the circles of the chain so I could repair it. A few days later there was a box full of beads, string and fasteners, enough stuff to make a hundred bracelets.'

Penn glanced to the workbench.

'Who knew it would become my passion and my job?'

'Was there anything else he brought you?' Penn asked, seeking clues in his actions.

'Cough mixture,' she said. 'I got a cough, and medicine and throat sweets came during the night. He brought me a book that I hadn't asked for, but I read it and asked for another.'

'You asked?'

'I held the book up to the camera in the corner and nodded.'

So he'd had a camera on them the whole time. He'd been watching them for God only knew what reason.

'The camera didn't make you feel uncomfortable? Knowing you were being watched?'

She shook her head. 'It made me feel safe. I absolutely knew that no one could hurt me.'

Penn heard the emotion that crept into her voice. 'And had someone hurt you?' he asked gently.

Libby took a box of cigarettes from her desk drawer and opened the door to the back garden. She lit a cigarette and leaned against the door frame.

It didn't go unnoticed by Penn that all the talk about her captivity had prompted nothing but fondly recalled memories. Touching on her life in the real world had brought on the need for a nerve-steadying cigarette and the appearance of tension in her shoulders and face.

'It's not something I like to talk about.'

He remained silent.

Another draw on the cigarette, a long breath out and she was ready to speak.

'Those books that he brought me. They were true accounts of girls who had been abused. Their stories, their struggles, their triumphs.'

Penn didn't know what to say. He let the silence last until she was ready to fill it.

'My uncle had been touching me for a few months. He did the

usual, said that people would get hurt if I told anyone. I would cry myself to sleep trying to swallow the shame and disgust. I did what he told me to. I stopped eating and completely withdrew into myself. It was the fear you see. I became constantly frightened of his visits, of my mum finding out and getting hurt. I felt trapped and alone.'

She shook her head as though shaking away the experience.

'The books I read told me I wasn't alone. I came to understand that with one threat my uncle had taken away all my power. The stories I read gave me strength and encouragement. When that door finally opened and I saw the van waiting, I knew it was time to return to my life and put it right. I was only a year older, but it felt like a lifetime. I was bursting with my truth.'

'Did you see anyone in the van?' Penn asked. He wanted to hear her story, but he also couldn't miss any opportunity to learn something that might help their investigation and bring Grace Lennard home safely.

She shook her head. 'No one. I just knew it was time to leave. There was a mattress in the back to soften the ride. Sometime later, the van stopped and the door opened. Believe it or not, I hesitated. I felt as though I was leaving safety to plunge into uncertainty, but I got out and started walking. There was a police station, so I went in and told them who I was.'

'I read that you went straight into the care system.'

'On that very day, I told the police about my uncle. Lots of people came to talk to me but I really wanted my mum. And when she came, she broke my heart. She didn't believe me, and after hugging me, she asked me to take it back and tell everyone I was confused. I could see the pain it was causing her, but I couldn't put the words back in. I didn't want to. I was placed in temporary care until they sorted it all out. I missed my mum but I was happy. I was around other kids in a foster home, with a great family, and I felt no fear. I didn't want to go back to that, and my mother refused to believe it of her brother so I stayed in care. About ten years later he was caught abusing the child of one of his neighbours. He was prosecuted. My mum reappeared full of apologies and shame, but it was too late.'

'You lost a lot of time with—'

'Do you know one of the worst things to paralyse the life of an abuse survivor later in life, the thing that keeps them awake and fills them with rage?'

Penn shook his head.

'Staying quiet. Not telling anyone. Allowing the abuser to silence them. I'm not going to say those years after I came back were easy. They were difficult for many reasons but not because I was terrified and not because I hated myself. I've suffered much less than others because I found the courage to speak out. It was something that happened to me, but it hasn't shaped me.'

Although Penn had heard from the boss about Suzie's recollection of her time in captivity, it was strange hearing the gratitude behind Libby's words for the strength she felt she'd been given during that time.

'Was there anything about the journey back that you can recall?' Penn asked, dragging himself away from the emotional and back to the practical. And the reason for his visit.

She shook her head. 'It might have been fifteen minutes or fifty, I don't recall.'

'Any particular sounds or…?'

'Officer, it was twenty-nine years ago.'

Penn knew that nothing else was coming. She had no need to remember. She had no wish to help them catch the person who had taken her. She bore no ill will towards him.

Unless…

'Ms Turner, would it help your memory if I told you we think he's taken another little girl?'

He was shocked to see what he thought was annoyance cross her face.

'It wouldn't help my memory at all. I can't recall what I can't recall. And even if he has, I don't think you should be unduly concerned. If he has her, he won't hurt her.'

Penn almost said that the bones found at Hawne Park were likely to say otherwise.

TWENTY-SIX

'Yeah, I didn't get a lot else from him in there,' Kim said, once Penn had finished recounting the details of his meeting with Libby Turner. 'Although I think Bryant was close to flooring him once or twice.'

'I'm not a violent man but he really does test my patience,' Bryant admitted.

Kim could see his point. Frustratingly, Steven Harte was only giving her details that he could have read or learned during the time or since. And yet there was an intimacy to his recollection, a smile here or a frown there that hinted of involvement in the events as more than just an observer.

'Now we have two victims that want to shake his hand,' Kim said as a welcome figure appeared in the doorway. 'Well, you took your time,' Kim offered as a greeting as Alison Lowe, consulting behaviourist, stepped into the room.

'The urgency was communicated to me in no uncertain terms by your boss.'

'Sorry if we disturbed yet another day of you doing nothing useful except—'

'I got home at 2 a.m. this morning after consulting on a rape profile in Glasgow.'

'Good to see you're back to doing what you do best. Now take a seat,' Kim said, pointing to the spare desk.

Kim was pleased the woman was back out again consulting, after her absence from the field following a near-death experience with her team.

'Ooh, who's that?' she asked, peering at the screen that showed Steven Harte drinking his sixth cup of sweet tea.

'Guys, fill her in,' Kim said, checking her phone.

An email from Keats informed her that Doctor A and her team were now set up on site at Hawne Park.

'So, what do you think?' Kim asked, once the team had brought her up to date.

Alison fixed her with the customary emotionless stare. 'I've been here five minutes. I haven't asked one question or reviewed one minute of tape and you're asking me what I think. Jeez, I bet you're a cheap date.'

Kim raised a questioning eyebrow.

'Forget the glass of wine, bypass the starter and let's get to the main course.'

'You do know we've got a little girl missing?' Kim reiterated.

'Only seven minutes in and you're giving me attitude,' Alison said, shaking her head. 'That may even be a record.'

'Much as I'd love a chat and a catch-up over a leisurely coffee and Danish, we need to press on.'

'You're saying there was no contact of any kind?' Alison asked.

'Neither victim even saw him,' Kim offered.

'Is there any chance he was doing it just for them?' Stacey asked. 'Both victims benefitted some way from his intervention.'

Alison thought for a moment before shaking her head.

'Unlikely. Just because it wasn't sexual doesn't mean he wasn't getting something out of it.'

'Before we start on Harte, explain to me why both victims feel their abductor was some kind of god,' Kim said, pouring herself coffee. 'He took them from everything they knew and isolated them for twelve months. How can both victims forgive that fact so easily?'

'Stockholm syndrome.'

Kim groaned. 'Too easy.'

Alison rolled her eyes. 'Oh, how I love having to prove myself to you every time you request or rather demand my involvement in a case. I enjoy this part of the process so much.'

Bryant placed a coffee on Alison's desk. She nodded her thanks.

'Yep, I think I'm gonna need it.' She took a gulp. 'Right, just because you don't believe in something doesn't make it any less real.'

'My issue is that it's become a term bandied about all over—'

'As I said. It's a real thing and comes from an emotional attachment to a captor formed by a hostage as a result of continuous stress, dependence and a need to cooperate for survival.' She took another swig of coffee. 'Every hostage that was held captive in the Kreditbanken building in Stockholm in 1973 refused to testify in court, and some even attempted to raise money for their captor's defence lawyers.'

Kim folded her arms. 'Were they all vulnerable in some way?'

Alison shook her head. 'Strong bonds can be formed through negative experiences, just like soldiers on the front line. There are four major factors in order for Stockholm syndrome to develop. Number one, was there any previous relationship between captor and captive?'

'Not that we know of.'

'Two, is there a refusal by hostages to cooperate with police forces or other authorities?'

'Neither of them has offered us anything remotely helpful.'

'Three, did the hostages believe in the humanity of their captor?'

'Oh yeah,' Kim and Penn said together.

'And four, were they aware either consciously or unconsciously that their captor had their own skewed reasons for keeping them alive?'

'They both seem to think it was for their own good.'

Alison thought for a moment and then nodded. 'Yes, that makes sense.'

'In what universe?' Kim asked.

'Our natural instinct for survival rushes to the forefront of our subconscious. This becomes the driving force for our actions, beliefs and emotions. The victim's need to survive is stronger than the impulse to hate the person that has created the dilemma.'

'Oh, bloody hell, can someone get Foggarty back?' Kim asked.

'Not sure who Foggarty is, but in any situation where two opposing parties are reduced to the status of victim and offender, such as victims of domestic violence who stay with their abusers or sex workers regularly punished by their pimps, deep affection develops, as the captor is responsible for survival.'

'I get that but there must have been opportunities to try to escape. He brought food every night,' Kim argued.

'First of all, they were kids,' Alison said. 'Secondly, the hostages in Stockholm were there for only five days and formed deep emotional attachments to their captor. But imagine this. You're being held captive, and you anticipate that when the door opens, you're going to die. If your captor then brings you food and drink, it elicits a primitive gratitude for the gift of life.

'An American girl named Jaycee Lee Dugard was held for eighteen years. She had many opportunities to escape. She'd been given a false identity by her captor which she maintained until Garrido confessed. She explained it succinctly when she said that she had adapted to survive. How often do you think Bear Grylls goes home and drinks a glass of his own urine? But would he do it to stay alive? Of course he would. Our need to survive trumps almost everything else and that's emotionally as well as physically.'

'Not only do they not hate or blame him, they actually seem to have great affection for him,' Kim said, shaking her head.

'Natascha Kampusch demanded to see her captor's body after he took his own life. She broke down in tears and hugged his body. She later bought the house in which she'd been held captive and keeps a photo in her handbag.'

Kim had heard something like that but hadn't believed it.

Alison continued, 'Stockholm syndrome often dissipates after the trauma of the event, although it is possible to never fully recover.'

'Is that why they still have such deep feelings for him?' Penn asked.

'Very few victims acknowledge they suffered Stockholm syndrome. The steps to recovery require intense therapy, and recovery is different for everyone depending on the severity of abuse, length of time held and the psychological mindset before the event occurred.'

Alison paused for a moment as she appeared to digest everything she'd been told.

'A year in captivity is a long time. It's understandable that they developed these feelings of affection and loyalty. They're not going to tell you anything useful.'

Kim had already worked that one out.

'Believe it or not you're gonna have better luck getting it from him.'

'And you can help us with that?' Kim asked.

'Hold my beer, Inspector. Hold my beer.'

TWENTY-SEVEN

'What exactly do you want the boss to do?' Stacey asked her friend as they watched on the monitor.

'I'm going to watch everything back, but now I just want to see some live interaction to get a feel for his behaviour and traits.'

Alison had asked the boss to go in and let him know about the Hawne Park discovery. The boss had gone to brief Woody first.

'What are you doing, Penn?' Stacey asked as he drew a line down the middle of the whiteboard.

'Dates and names,' he answered without turning. 'All getting a bit confusing and I like to see stuff in black and white.'

She watched as he worked quickly forming tabulated columns.

Libby Turner taken 1992 returned 1993
Suzie Keene taken 1994 returned 1995
Melody Jones taken 1996

'So what went wrong?' Stacey asked as Alison busied herself with notebooks, pens and a couple of textbooks.

'With what?' Alison asked.

'Melody. If these three cases are the work of one person—'

'I think they are,' Alison interrupted, looking at the board.

'Why do you think so?'

'Look at the regimentation of the timings. The abductions occur every two years. The girls are kept for one year and then released, unharmed.'

'So I ask again: what went wrong with Melody? Why wasn't she returned unharmed after a year?'

'Maybe she saw him,' Penn offered.

'Or perhaps she didn't get into the van as easily as the others and there was a struggle,' Alison said.

'Could he have escalated?' Stacey asked.

'From what?' Alison asked. 'He wasn't being violent to them in the first place. We don't actually know why he kidnapped them. We know it wasn't sexual so my guess at this stage is some kind of twisted voyeurism.'

'No camera in the bathroom and a lockable door,' Penn offered. 'He wasn't watching them bathe or undress.'

Alison shrugged. 'I got nothing yet. I mean is there anyone else you can talk to, any victims prior to Suzie and Libby? If there was a change in his behaviour with Melody it might—'

'There are no similar incidents prior to '92,' Stacey offered.

'We really need to know why he killed Melody and not the others, and we need to know why it stopped.'

'Shit,' Stacey said as a cold shiver passed over her.

'What?' Penn asked.

'What if Melody was the first one he killed? What if that became his new MO? What if Melody wasn't his last.'

'Oh shit,' Penn said, returning to his desk.

TWENTY-EIGHT

'Hope your lunch was okay,' Kim said, stepping back into the interview room with Bryant right behind her.

Alison had instructed her not to bait him, and her boss had warned her to go gently. Do whatever it takes to find Grace Lennard had been his instruction.

It was clear that she was expected to play nicely with a man who, in her mind, had kidnapped two girls, killed Melody Jones and knew the whereabouts of Grace Lennard. She'd certainly give it her best.

'It was fine,' he answered. 'Not enough salt in the potatoes but it filled a gap.'

It was on the tip of her tongue to assure him she'd pass his comments to the chef. But knowing Betty Miles in the canteen, she could imagine the response and it would contain a couple of fingers.

'Good to hear,' she said, linking her fingers together on the table before her. 'Let's talk about your involvement with Hawne Park.'

'Of course, but it was so long ago that my memory might not be as accurate as you'd like.'

She wondered if his memory loss would include the bones that had been buried there.

'How did you become involved with Hawne Park?' she asked.

'I'm hardly involved with them, Inspector. I made a small donation to their cause many years ago, after reading about their plight in the newspaper.'

'You read a lot of papers, don't you, Steven?'

Kim felt Bryant knock her foot gently beneath the table.

No goading.

'I think it's good to keep abreast of events in your local area,' he answered.

'And what did you learn about the project?'

'That it was a small community initiative trying to make their surroundings a little more attractive.'

'And that kind of project appeals to you?' Kim asked.

'Inspector, I have been fortunate in my business dealings over the years. I have made much more than I ever need to spend. I've always known when to retreat from a situation so that I don't get caught... out.'

Kim felt the muscles in her jaw tense. He was playing with her. She knew that, and she had been shackled in how to respond.

'You donated a few thousand pounds to their nature programme and that's it?'

'Yes, that was the extent of my—'

'How about your connection to Butler—'

'Oh, wait a minute. How could I have forgotten? I also instructed the builders in some excavation work.'

Damn it. She'd been about to call him on a lie, but his sketchy memory had saved him at the last minute.

'That's Butler's builders?'

'Oh yes. There's no one better locally for digging... stuff up.'

Again, she felt the pressure of Bryant's foot against her own. Even he knew that Harte was trying to bait her.

'Well, he certainly dug up something interesting today.'

'Really, what?' he asked, leaning forward.

Oh, how she wanted to lean forward, grab him by the throat and squeeze until he told her where Grace Lennard was.

'Bones, Steven, and they appear to be human. Is there anything you'd like to share with us?'

'There are human remains in Hawne Park?' he asked, bringing his hand to his chin in horror.

His evasiveness and surprise were an act that he wasn't even trying to conceal.

'Do you know anything about them?' she asked.

Repetition, repetition, repetition, Derek Foggarty had said.

'It doesn't matter how many times you ask me the same question, Inspector, the answer is going to remain the same.'

'I don't recall you actually giving me an answer, Steven.'

'I'd mind that tone if I was you, Inspector, or else your colleague there might kick you beneath the table for the third time.'

'Okay, I'm not doing this,' Kim said, pushing back her chair. 'I am not going to treat you like a helpful witness when I know full well that you've been responsible for the abduction and murder of young girls. Consider this my exit from the game you're trying to make me play.'

She placed her hands on the table and leaned into him. 'Leave, don't leave but know that the next time we meet we'll be playing by my rules.'

He pushed back his chair. 'Inspector, you're going to regret—'

'Probably,' she said from the door. 'But I'll live with it because right now you're just wasting my time.'

As she stormed out of the door, Kim could picture Alison shaking her head with despair, but she could bear the man's silent triumph no longer. Every time he spoke he confirmed his involvement but not in any way she could use.

'I know, I know,' she said to Bryant as she leaned against the corridor wall.

'Surprised you kept your temper that long to be honest.'

'Yeah but now I've completely fucked our chances of—'

Kim stopped speaking as her phone rang.

She watched miserably as Steven Harte exited the building and headed for his car. If Woody had been watching, she knew he would be her next caller.

'Give me something good, Doctor A.'

'I give you all that I have, Inspector. The bones have all been recovered and they are of a small person.'

'Gender?'

'Unknown at this point, but I'm prepared to say we are looking at a little girl or boy no older than twelve years of age. I will keep you informed of our—'

'Thanks, Doc,' she said, ending the call.

Steven Harte's car was reversing out of a parking space.

Right now, he had the means, motive and opportunity to flee the country and never be seen again.

She sprinted outside and ran past his car as it headed towards the exit.

She stood in its path as it travelled towards her.

His gaze met hers. He didn't slow down.

She planted her feet and folded her arms.

The car continued to advance towards her.

Bryant headed towards her from the automatic doors.

Her heart was beating wildly in her chest, but she wasn't moving. She was not going to let him leave.

The car came to a stop an inch from her legs.

She'd never lost a game of chicken in her life.

'Guv, what the hell are you playing at?' Bryant growled.

She walked around the side of the car and opened the driver's door.

'Mr Harte, please get out of the vehicle.'

He did so with a smile on his face.

'I thought we weren't playing anymore. Have you changed your—?'

'Different game, different rules.'

He tipped his head. 'No, I don't think so. I liked the existing rules.'

'Mr Harte, in about thirty seconds, Bryant here is going to say something that you're really not going to like. So, before he does, I ask you one more time: what do you know about the abduction of Melody Jones and the whereabouts of Grace Lennard?'

He leaned back against his car. 'I've already told you I have nothing else to say.'

Kim turned to her colleague. 'Arrest him,' she said, before turning and walking away.

TWENTY-NINE

'For what?' Woody barked, pushing his chair forcefully away from the desk.

'The abduction and murder of Melody Jones.'

He rubbed his hand over his smooth head. 'Under what criteria? You have no—'

'To allow the prompt and effective investigation of the offence. And I was unlikely to get anything if we'd have allowed him to continue calling the shots.'

'You had one opportunity to try and prise the information out of—'

'Sir, forgive my interruption, but Steven Harte has been in control of everything since the minute he walked into the station. He is well aware of our scope while assisting us with our enquiries. I've cracked a hundred eggshells while tiptoeing around him in case I make a mistake with which he can beat us later, and I can still, hand on heart, state that he will not share anything he doesn't want to. I need him here by force not choice. I need the freedom to question him properly.'

During her speech, she could see that some of the tension had left his face.

'Not one mistake here, Stone. I'm warning you.'

'He's with Jack right now.'

After arresting him, Bryant had led Harte to the custody offi-cer, who was advising Harte of his rights. Jack would ensure that someone would be informed of his arrest and that he'd be offered free legal advice. He'd be given the opportunity to view the Police Codes of Practice, offered medical attention if he was feeling ill and be shown a written notice informing him of his rights about regular breaks for food and use of the toilet.

Kim guessed Steven Harte needed no such guidance, but there was a sense of relief that when Jack was done with him he'd be in a cell not the interview room.

'You do realise that you've destroyed any chance of him leading us to Grace Lennard?'

'He wasn't going to,' she replied. 'We've kept him on watch from the minute he left the station yesterday until he returned this morning. If she isn't in his house, he has her somewhere that she has access to food and water or she's already—'

'Let's not give too much thought to the already possibility,' he said, rubbing his head again.

He sighed. 'Leave the search warrant with me. It's going to take some creative wording to get a signature and I think you've got more than enough to do.'

Kim knew the restrictions that lay before her. If she didn't find something concrete soon, they would need to seek the permission of a superintendent to extend the detainment for a further twelve hours or a magistrate to keep him up to a maximum of ninety-six hours. If he wasn't charged in that time, they had to let him go. She already knew that getting any kind of extension based on what they had now was going to be like pissing in the wind.

'You've got twenty-four hours, Stone, to come up with some-thing good, so you'd better get out of my sight and make them count.'

THIRTY

'So by three tomorrow we need to charge him or release him?' Penn asked, frowning.

Kim knew he perfectly understood police procedure, so he was repeating her words in a 'need to get this to sink in kind of way'.

'We gotta get something, guys. We can't get this close and then release him. There's a little girl out there somewhere and we can't rely on Steven Harte to tell us where she is.'

They all nodded their agreement except for Alison.

'Thanks for following my guidance in there. Good job,' she said, holding up her two thumbs.

Kim raised an eyebrow.

'But to be fair you weren't going to get anything out of him.'

Kim already knew that. 'And the next time you give me advice, make sure it's something I can actually do. How much of that you expected me to take, I'll never know.'

'I got enough to make a start.'

'Good, now what you got for me?' Kim asked.

'Boss, me and Penn are already looking to see if Melody was his last victim,' Stacey said as Penn walked over to the board.

'So far every abduction seems to occur in two-yearly intervals.

He took Libby in '92 and released her in '93. He took Suzie in '94 and released her in '95. He took Melody in '96.'

'So you're thinking the murder of Melody marked some kind of change in his behaviour towards the girls but that he might have taken another one in '98?'

'Looking at it, boss,' Stacey confirmed.

'Okay, stay on it, Stace. Penn, I want a list of every inch of property he owns.'

'Okay, boss,' Penn answered.

Kim turned to the behaviourist. 'Alison, study every minute of footage we have and find me something I can use. We have to be able to control this.'

'On it,' she said, returning to the screen.

Bryant glanced her way, and she nodded towards the door. They had a lot to do and not much time to do it.

THIRTY-ONE

There was something instantly sobering about seeing the bones of a child laid out on a gurney.

Both she and Bryant took a moment to process the sight. They had visited this morgue hundreds of times over the years. They had witnessed bodies in every state of decomposition. They had observed tortured bodies and self-inflicted injuries. Most times they'd formed a vague storyline in their heads of the person's family, their life, their likes and dislikes from just the tiniest of clues.

Here, there was nothing, which made the situation all the more poignant because there was no meat on the bones – literally.

In some ways, Kim wished the skeleton hadn't been arranged quite so accurately. It showed just how small and defenceless this child had been.

'Bryant,' Kim said, regaining the attention of her colleague, who hadn't yet looked away from the table.

'We have the majority of the bones,' Doctor A offered sombrely. 'My team is still shifting for more tiny bones.'

Kim guessed the woman meant sifting but made no move to correct her.

'Any development on gender?' Kim asked.

Doctor A sighed heavily. 'There are a number of macroscopic methods for determining the sex of infant and juvenile skeletal remains which have been developed, but current standards generally recommend that we don't attempt them because the methods have a low level of reliability. Differences between male and female skeletons arrive from the interplay between genetics, hormonal variations, culture and environment. For individuals who have completed skeletal maturity, sex determination is considered to be reliable; however, skeletons can't always be placed into two neat categories. The traits relevant for sex determination exist on a spectrum from very feminine to intermediate to very masculine.

'Five categories are used in anthropological analysis: female, probable female, intermediate, probable male and male.'

'Can we not tell from the skull?' Kim asked, looking down at the tiny head.

Doctor A shook her head. 'The bones are not yet fully formed; boys typically show a more prominent chin, an anteriorly wider dental arcade, a narrower and deeper sciatic notch than girls. The assessment of these traits is accurate in approximately seventy per cent of cases.

'The most effective sex indicators do not begin to develop until adolescence, and some are not fully expressed until adulthood. Sex estimation in children remains problematic.'

Keats stepped forward. 'There is DNA analysis which requires good DNA survival and is very time-consuming.'

'What about peptide analysis?' Bryant asked.

'Who?' Kim asked as all eyes in the room turned towards him.

'I am impressed, Bryan,' Doctor A said. Even Keats was smiling.

'What? I like to keep up to date on stuff,' he offered with a shrug.

'I shall put our young victim back to bed while Doctor A explains,' Keats said, covering over the bones.

Bryant opened the door for Keats to wheel the trolley back to storage before they both focused on her response.

'Peptide analysis is a minimally destructive surface acid etching of tooth enamel and subsequent identification of sex chromosome. Tooth enamel is the hardest tissue in the human body and survives burial exceptionally well, even when the rest of the skeleton or DNA in the organic fraction has decayed.'

'Sounds expensive,' Kim noted.

'Sounds like there's a big but coming,' Bryant observed.

'It is prohibitively expensive and not yet in widespread use.'

Would Woody be prepared to commit thousands of pounds of their budget for one single state-of-the-art forensic test? She suspected not.

'Okay, given what you do know at this stage, what would be your classification of the five you listed?' Kim asked.

'I would state probable female aged between seven and thirteen,' she said as Keats re-entered the room.

'Thanks, Doctor A,' Kim said, turning to the pathologist.

'No pressure for something good from you after that, eh Keats?'

'I'm not a seal that performs on demand, Inspector. Although I should mention that the cause of death...'

'Yes?' Kim asked hopefully.

'Is likely to remain a mystery indefinitely.'

'Keats,' Kim moaned.

He shrugged. 'In the absence of any soft tissue, it is impossible to deduce. I can say that there is no obvious trauma to the remains that we have.'

'Damn.'

Keats moved away and recorded something on his clipboard. Kim got Keats's problem. If the victim had been stabbed but no bone had been nicked in the process, there would be no evidence as the flesh and organs were long gone.

'How long ago are we talking, folks?' Kim asked, unsure who was best to ask. If their answers differed, she would choose the one she liked the best.

'Twenty to twenty-five years,' they said together.

Keats held up his hand, uncharacteristically, to receive a high five. Doctor A looked at him as though he'd lost his mind and moved away.

Keats lowered his hand.

'That may be the first time I've see you two agree on anything but, really, can you not narrow it down any more than that?'

'Oh, Keatings, we forgot to mention the newspaper,' Doctor A said, holding up her hand to Keats.

'No, Doctor A, you do it after something.'

She shook her head. 'I will never understand you crazy Brits.'

'What newspaper?' Kim asked, ignoring this weird new dynamic between the two of them.

'The one that was lying on the body giving the exact date and time.'

'Oh funny.'

Doctor A turned to Keats. 'Now?'

'Yes now,' he said, finally getting the high five he'd been waiting for.

'I think I prefer you guys hating each other.'

'Yeah, it's a bit weird,' Bryant agreed.

'So there's nothing more?' Kim asked of them both.

It was negative responses all round.

Kim headed out of the morgue at speed.

'Slow down, guv – I ain't no Usain Bolt here. What's up?'

'We have nothing definitive, Bryant. We've arrested Harte for the murder of Melody Jones. Right now, we can't prove it was murder or that it was Melody Jones.'

'We can narrow it down ourselves,' Bryant said, now matching her stride.

'How so?'

'Builder's got to have records. It can't have happened after the guy had filled in the hole. He planted trees on top of it.'

'Bryant, there are days when you are worth your weight in gold. Let's go see what Jenson Butler has got to say.'

THIRTY-TWO

'Got anything else to eat, Stace?' Alison shouted across the office.

'Since you've already had my last packet of prawn cocktail crisps, my apple and emergency energy bar, it's safe to say I'm all out. But, hey, you're great for my diet.'

If Alison wasn't one of her best friends, Stacey would hate her for her ability to eat more than a small village without putting on an ounce of weight.

'I'll nip to the canteen for a snack run in a bit,' Alison said, turning back to the computer.

'What do you make of him?' Stacey asked. Her initial doubts about Steven Harte's involvement were coming under fire with every new piece of information.

'Hard to tell until I've watched more footage.'

'Why have you turned off the sound?'

'It's distracting.'

'What, listening to what he has to say?' Stacey would have thought his words would have been of paramount importance.

'I want to watch his movements, his expressions, his posture. Don't you ever do that?'

'What, watch TV with the sound off? Er... no, hearing the script tends to be necessary in following the plot.'

'Believe it or not you can pick up a lot by just the expressions and body language.'

'Okay, next time I rent a movie I'll be sure to watch it with no—'

'Oh, Penn, I love you,' Alison said as her colleague walked in the door.

'Wondered where you'd got to,' Stacey said, eyeing up the booty in his arms.

'Thought I'd best get some fuel before Betty closes it down for the night.'

Stacey could see he'd bought the last few cold sandwiches, sausage rolls, crisps and a selection of brownies and cookies.

Alison looked as though Santa had just dropped down the chimney.

'Penn, I swear if you're not married in five years' time, you're mine.'

He smiled as a little colour entered his cheeks.

'Any luck on missing girls?' Penn asked, ripping open a Mars bar.

'Yeah, I've tapped into a list that gives me every outstanding missing child since '96. Tells me what they were wearing and even what they had for breakfast.'

'Cool, didn't know you could do that,' Penn said.

'You can't, dipstick, and I wish it were that easy.' She consulted her notebook. 'Did you know that in the UK alone over a hundred thousand children are reported missing every year? Of that number, roughly ninety-eight per cent are reunited pretty quickly, but last report by the missing persons unit stated that over fifteen hundred children are long-term missing, which means they've been missing for longer than twenty-eight days. Searching for up-to-date information is a nightmare because the data for each year differs.'

'How can it differ?' Penn asked.

'Take the stats for 2018/2019. Almost seventy-six thousand kids were recorded missing by UK police forces; however there were over two hundred thousand incidents of missing children.'

'Why?'

'Because some children go missing multiple times per year.'

'But your guy sometimes brings them back.'

'Eat your cake, Alison, or tell me something I don't know.'

'Generally, most missing-children incidents are resolved quickly without harm. The majority of resolved incidents end within eight hours, with eighty per cent being resolved in twenty-four hours.'

'Concentrate on the fifteen hundred,' Alison said, looking away.

'Why?'

'Because the kidnapping of Melody Jones changed something in him. If she was the first murder, you can venture to say that any girls taken afterwards met the same fate. Something happened with Melody. Maybe it was his fear of being identified, but he crossed some kind of line. It's unlikely he would have gone backwards and started returning them.'

Stacey didn't disagree. The most prominent thought as she returned to her computer was: what did that mean for the fate of Grace Lennard?

THIRTY-THREE

Alex reached beneath her mattress and checked for her most prized possession – valued highly because it was a tool that was going to help her get what she wanted, and because it had cost her three weeks of her cigarette allowance. Not that she smoked, never had, but in prison it was currency, so you took it anyway.

She put the item back. She would need it soon but not today. It had to be presented at the right moment to have the effect she wanted. It needed to be the catalyst for everything to fall into place. She had to be sure that the recipient would appreciate it and know exactly how to use it.

Prisoners were pretty inventive when it came to fashioning weapons on the inside. One of the most common was a toothbrush shaped into a shiv. A more creative one was an eye gouger made of two plastic forks fastened together with the middle tines taken out. During her time she'd seen a razor blade comb. She'd seen a spiked glove made from gardening gloves and upholstery tacks. She'd even seen a paper shiv. A prisoner had ripped pages out of a book, wetted them down, rolled them super tight then dried them with salt. The result: a knife made of paper.

But Alex didn't need any such weapon for the next part of her plan. She had her mouth and that was enough for now.

She had waited until visiting hours were over for the day to make her next move.

She knocked and entered the cell four along from her own.

'Hey, Lisa,' she said, fixing the fake smile to her face.

Appearing friendly and interested was exhausting for her. Because she was neither, it took great care and energy to fake it. It was like acting in a demanding role twenty-four hours a day. Oh, the relief when the lights went out and the mask came off and she could allow her facial expressions to match the ruminations of her mind.

'Oh, you know, same shit different day.'

Alex noted immediately that her eyes were red-rimmed and puffy.

Good.

'How'd the visit with Rod go?'

Jesus, casual small talk was an effort.

'He didn't come,' Lisa said, picking at the bobbles on the coarse grey blanket.

Of course he hadn't. The visits from her boyfriend were getting scarcer.

She'd identified Lisa as the perfect candidate for her plan about a month ago.

It wasn't the first time the twenty-four-year-old had graced the cells of Drake Hall. Two years ago, she'd been inside for fencing stolen goods. During her nine-month stretch she'd got herself together and had left as a poster child for the rehabilitation process.

All had been rosy until she'd bumped into one of her old cronies, who had persuaded her to store some stolen jewellery. She'd only agreed because she and her boyfriend were broke, and she'd just found out she was pregnant and knew she could do with the extra money.

Someone tipped off the police, her house was raided and she was back in the slammer for a five-year stretch. Because of previous convictions, the judge had disregarded the heavily pregnant woman's pleas and had handed her the maximum sentence.

Up until the birth, Lisa had tried everything to get transferred to one of the six prisons in the country with mother and baby units, but there had been no spaces available. The boy had been removed from her care within hours of being born.

Lisa had fallen into a deep depression which was sad for her but fortuitous for Alex. Prison was not the place to develop mental-health problems. The staff tried their best, but they weren't trained enough to spot the signs or how to handle it. Luckily, Alex was on hand to help them out.

'So you didn't get to see the little one again?' Alex asked.

For the life of her she couldn't remember the little boy's name.

Lisa's eyes filled instantly with tears as she shook her head.

Good.

Raw pain was the best kind of pain to work with. She didn't want it easing off. She wanted the woman to be experiencing the sharp end of loss and loneliness.

'It's weird cos I can still feel the imprint of his tiny body against my chest. I can see every detail of his scrunched-up face. I just don't know how I'm going to bear being away from him until I've served my time.'

Alex did her usual trick of staring hard without blinking. Her eyes began to water.

'You have kids?' Lisa asked.

Alex paused before shaking her head slowly. 'Not anymore.'

The closest she'd ever come to having kids was the photo she had of two boys on her desk years ago, taken from a catalogue for the sake of appearances.

'I had two boys,' Alex said, sniffing.

'Had?' Lisa asked.

'Yes, when we divorced, my husband sued for full custody. As he'd taken all our money, I couldn't even fight him. He won and then took them to live in New Zealand. Men move on so quickly.'

'Oh, I'm so sorry to—

'It's okay.'

'Tell me,' Lisa insisted.

'Oh, you don't want to hear all that,' Alex said, knowing full well that she did. In her fog of despair, Lisa wanted some kind of reassurance that things would get better. That there was hope.

'Please tell me and then maybe I won't feel so alone.'

'Oh, I tortured myself first of all with visions of my husband with other women.'

Lisa paled. 'Oh my God, you don't think Rod...?'

'No,' Alex said, holding up her hand. It was fine. The thought had been placed and she didn't need to labour it. 'It's different for you. I was working long hours and wasn't available for him. He had an affair which turned to love apparently. I never suspected a thing.'

Alex began to insert pauses into her mini speeches. Time for Lisa to digest what she was saying. And right now, she'd be wondering how she'd find out anything from in here.

'His meetings went on later, and there was always an excuse why he didn't come home before midnight. Obviously, that's different for you. Rod comes to see you every chance he gets.'

'H-His van broke down,' she said miserably.

'Of course it did,' Alex said. 'Anyway, we tried to work on it for the sake of the boys. He loves his kids so much.'

Lisa brightened. 'Rod loves Josh so much.'

'But neither of our hearts were in it. I told him that things would be better in a few years once I'd built my practice. If he could just be patient for a couple of years, we'd have the life he always wanted.'

Just like Rod has got to wait for you for a couple of years. This point was worth labouring.

'But he couldn't wait. A couple of months into our fresh start, the late nights started up again.'

Lisa's face fell just an inch as her fingers began picking again at the blanket. 'And the boys?'

'The more I fought to hang on, the harder it was on them. For their sake I had no choice but to let him go.'

Alex sighed heavily so that Lisa would appreciate her martyrdom and her sacrifice. She needed to leave lots of little seeds to germinate in her mind.

'Once they'd left, I tortured myself with visions of him finding someone else. I used to lie in bed picturing them together. I worried that my boys would forget me. The thoughts turned to him falling in love, him marrying someone else. Of my boys getting attached to someone else as their memories of me faded away. I was tortured by pictures of someone else putting them to bed, some other woman reading them a story. Of another woman's face being the last thing they saw before falling asleep.'

Alex paused as she could see the terror building in Lisa's eyes.

'But the worst thing I could imagine, and there being absolutely nothing I could do about it, was the thought of them calling someone else mummy.'

A strangled cry escaped from Lisa's lips even as she covered her mouth in horror.

'I'm sorry. I shouldn't have unloaded like that. Our situations are completely different. I'm sure, I mean, I wouldn't have thought any of that would happen to you, but the pain is still so raw, even after six years. It doesn't take much for it all to come spilling out.'

'It... it's okay,' Lisa said, trying to get her thoughts in order.

Alex shook her head. 'I wouldn't tell anyone else this,' she said conspiratorially, 'but when the pain was at its worse, I'm surprised that I found the strength to carry on.' She stood and headed for the door. 'Most days I just wanted to die. It's a pain that never goes away, and as a mother yourself, I know you understand.'

Alex offered one last half-smile before turning and leaving the cell.

The half-smile turned into a real one.

Yes, this part of her plan was definitely on track.

THIRTY-FOUR

Butler Building Limited was located on a small trading estate just outside Quinton. From the car park, Kim could see that the business had grown over the years and had taken the premises either side of it. To the right of the two-storey building was a double metal gate that appeared to be for equipment and materials storage.

The three reserved spaces outside the door were occupied with a new BMW, Jaguar and Mercedes.

'Company appears to be doing okay,' Bryant said as they passed the collection of vehicles.

'Top brass are always the last to suffer anyway,' Kim said, pushing open the heavy glass entrance door.

The reception area was pleasant and unfussy. The chairs appeared comfortable, but there were no flowers or magazines to soften the space. The walls were filled with framed montages of what she assumed were high-profile projects at varying stages of construction.

She frowned as a woman appeared at the desk.

Bryant stepped forward.

'May we speak with Jenson Butler please?' He held up his ID.

The woman picked up her glasses from the desk and peered at it closely.

'We spoke with him briefly at Hawne Park,' Bryant clarified.

'Oh dear, that's where the bones were found, isn't it? Are they human?'

'If we could speak with Mr Butler,' Bryant pushed, pleasantly but firmly displaying one of his many interpersonal skills. He could temper two emotions to the correct degree to get the desired result. It was a skill that had not been bestowed upon Kim. She would ask once and then shout. There was very little scope in between.

Bryant moved away from the desk to offer privacy as the woman picked up the phone. He took a moment to peruse the gallery, and the same frown that had made its way onto her face appeared to be mirrored on his.

It was definitely something they'd address when they spoke to the man.

'He'll be just a couple of minutes,' the woman said after ending the call.

Bryant gravitated back to the desk. 'Have you been here long?' he asked, leaning on the counter as though it was his local bar.

'Twenty-nine years,' she said with pride in her voice.

'Really? You must have left school exceptionally early.'

Kim was pleased to be facing the other way to hide the smile that tugged at her lips. The man was a charmer, and she could understand why. Those words out of the mouth of another man might have come off smarmy, but not Bryant. He delivered the words matter-of-factly without the schmooze, which added an authenticity to his words.

'Oh, thank you. Yes, I was quite young when I started here. It was nothing like it is today. Billy Butler, Jenson's dad, started the business with a digger, a loader and a couple of guys. He grew the business to a team of eight, but it was Mr Butler Junior who took the business forward to where it is now.'

'And where is that?' Kim asked, turning.

'We employ over three hundred staff and work in every county in the UK. We've built some high-profile buildings all around the country and—'

'Thanks for the PR speech, Barbara,' Jenson Butler said, appearing behind her. 'But I don't think the officers are interested in our portfolio.'

'Sorry, Mr Butler. I was just—'

'Would you like to follow me?' he asked, pointing to a door to the right of the desk.

Kim couldn't help noticing the use of the formal salutation from Barbara when addressing her boss. The woman had been with them for almost thirty years. Was she not almost part of the family?

'Yeah, I remember when you didn't have to feel guilty for printing off a piece of paper,' Barbara mumbled as Kim passed.

Kim knew that many companies were going paperless in their efforts to be green and environmental. Others were doing it just because it was being forced on them by accreditation bodies. No policy, no membership.

And this company clearly wanted membership at the cool table, Kim thought as she entered what she assumed was the meeting room. The table was the biggest single sheet of glass she'd ever seen. At the centre was a switchboard-type phone, and a pull-down projector hung from the ceiling. There was no piece of paper in sight. It looked good until she factored in the level of engineering needed to produce that table and the transport to get it here. Clearly some of the policies were for show and certification.

'You rushed off earlier, Mr Butler,' Kim noted as she took a seat. 'I trust the emergency is now resolved.'

'What emerg— Oh, yes, of course. My apologies.'

Kim was sure that no emergency had required him to leave site. He just hadn't wanted to hang around.

'Although, I'm glad of the opportunity to pay you a visit. Barbara was just giving us a little history of the business.'

A flash of annoyance flitted across his face.

'It was all complimentary,' Kim assured him. She didn't want to get the woman into trouble. 'She was only commenting on how you had grown the business from what your father built.'

'Aah, yes. Much of the time Barbara wishes for those old days back when she called my father by his first name, and they would have quick coffee chats together throughout the day. We require a different level of professionalism these days,' he said stiffly.

'I'm surprised she's still around,' Kim observed.

'She's a caveat,' he said regretfully.

'A what?'

'A caveat in the contract my father drew up before allowing me to take over the business.'

'Oh, so you inherited her?' Kim asked.

'For as long as she wants to work or her death, whichever comes soonest.'

Had there been any trace of humour in his words she might have found that funny, but his tone only demonstrated his annoyance in not having any control.

Good job, Butler Senior, Kim thought.

'So, those bones at—'

'Before we begin,' he said, holding up his hand, 'do I need my lawyer here?'

'For what?'

'Well, we did uncover the bones. I didn't know if—'

'Mr Butler, have you done something wrong?' she asked.

'Not that I'm aware of.'

'Then I think we're good. I'd like to know a bit more about the business if you don't mind.'

'I'm sure Barbara gave a suitable summary of our history but, in a nutshell, my father worked off the back of word-of-mouth recommendations: small house extensions, minor commercial repairs and refits. Worked consistently within a twenty-mile radius without placing one advert for thirty years.'

'And you joined the company...?'

'After university and a few years out in the real world putting my business degree to good use. I came on board when my father decided he wanted to slow down. That had always been the plan.'

'You took the company in a different direction?'

'Absolutely. We stick to my father's principles but upscale it and apply it to bigger projects.'

'And you worked at the Hawne Park site many years ago?'

He nodded. 'I can get you the exact date but it was August '99.'

Exactly what the residents' committee chairman had said.

'Are you sure?' Kim asked.

'Of course I'm sure.'

If that was true, Harte had either kept Melody for three years instead of the one year he'd kept the others or he'd had the body located somewhere else.

Butler took out his phone and began texting. His fingers were quick and nimble.

'I'll have the exact dates shortly,' he said, placing his phone on the table.

'And is that how you met Steven Harte?' Kim asked. 'On the Hawne Park project?'

'No, we met in our first year of university. Not many guys from the Black Country at Oxford that year. Our accents set us apart.'

Kim tipped her head and frowned.

'I've worked hard to soften it over the years, Inspector. Got sick of being called a Brummie.'

Kim smiled. 'So you've been friends for...?'

'Hang on. I wouldn't exactly say we were friends. We got along and we passed the time of day, but other than our accent, we didn't have a great deal in common. I started to make friends and asked him to come to a couple of parties or a sports event, even just for a pint, but he was always busy.'

'Doing what?' Kim asked.

He shrugged. 'He liked taking photos.'

'Of girls?'

Butler laughed. 'No. At least that I could have understood but it was birds, trees and flowers and shit... sorry, stuff like that.'

'And you kept in touch all these years?' Kim asked. Strange to say they hadn't even been friends.

'Not really. We lost touch while he was out there making his millions. I was working in London, as I said. First I heard was when he called the company and asked me to quote for a job. We were still doing the smaller stuff, so we met up and had a chat.'

'And that was Hawne Park?'

'Yes, which was the seventeenth to the twenty-first of August '99,' he said, consulting the message that had flashed on his phone.

'And had he changed in the years since you'd seen him?'

'Not a bit. He was still quiet and studious, pleasant enough but a bit detached.'

'Wife or girlfriend?'

Butler paused and looked up, searching his memory.

'You know, not in all the years I've known him has he ever mentioned the name of one female – or a male for that matter.'

It was as though he'd only just realised that himself.

'And you've worked regularly for him ever since?'

'He's a good customer, and he's not a bad name to throw around to attract other business.'

'And did Steven Harte ever visit the building sites once he'd instructed the work?'

'Oh yes, it was a job and a half to keep him away. He annoyed a couple of the older guys sometimes with his attention to detail, but hey, he's the customer. He can be as anal as he likes.'

'And was he? Anal, I mean.'

'Absolutely, but the result was always worth it. He knew what he wanted and wouldn't settle for anything less.'

'Would he visit the site after hours?'

Butler laughed. 'It wouldn't surprise me. He liked to be sure his instructions were being— Hang on, you're not trying to say he put those...?'

'I'm saying nothing, Mr Butler. I'm just getting background on the working relationship between the two of you.'

'Are you sure I don't need my lawyer?' he asked suspiciously.

'Not unless you've committed a crime since the last time you asked.'

'Okay, please continue.'

'Did you or your guys report any strange activity around the area at the time?'

'Bloody hell, Inspector. It's been over twenty years.'

And that was always going to be her problem. Except Grace Lennard wasn't twenty years ago and neither was she dead, Kim prayed, but to find her Kim had to know everything possible about Steven Harte and his associates.

Butler shook his head. 'If we had I'm sure we would have reported it at the time.'

Bryant took out his notebook and Kim watched him scribble a reminder to check suspicious activity around a community park in '99.

'Just one last thing, Mr Butler,' Kim said, recalling her and Bryant's puzzlement in the reception. 'I can see from your pictures out in the reception area that you've worked on many high-profile buildings around the country, projects worth hundreds of thousands if not millions of pounds.'

'That's true,' Butler answered as his chest puffed out.

'Then why on earth would you be interested in taking on such a tiny project worth a couple of hundred quid for a small community job?'

'Because we were asked, and we like to keep our best customers happy.'

'Roy Barber from the residents' association is a good customer?'

He laughed. 'No, we refused him.'

'So who?'

'Steven Harte asked us to reconsider the request. It was him that asked us to dig up Hawne Park.'

THIRTY-FIVE

'Bloody hell, your boss needs a refresher on rapport posture,' Alison said, sitting back in her chair.

Stacey groaned. 'Alison, we've already had one guy come and lecture us. We don't need—'

'We're talking basics here, Stace. The idea is to get answers from this guy.'

'So what's she done wrong?' Penn asked, rolling his chair closer.

'She started well. She was businesslike, not hostile or over friendly. But she never controlled her temper or masked her distaste or disgust. She's supposed to stay emotionally detached and relaxed, but you can see the tension in every part of her body.'

'He is trying to play her like a violin,' Penn defended.

'And who are you analysing, the suspect or the boss?' Stacey asked.

'Both at the minute because I can't work out if he's feeling genuinely tense or if he's mirroring.'

'Whatting?' Penn asked.

'It's when someone imitates the movements or gestures of

another person to enhance familiarity and liking. I don't know if he's feeling his own tension or picking it up from the boss.'

'Well, you've been doing plenty of scribbling so you must have spotted something.'

'Grooming,' she answered. 'He touches his ring…'

'Touches his what?' Stacey called out.

'The ring of his cup. It's non-verbal deceptive behaviour, where anxiety is dissipated through physical activity in the form of grooming either oneself or the immediate surroundings.'

'He asks for a lot of tea,' Penn offered.

'Often, he touches his face or head before messing with the cup; it's another form of non-verbal deceptive behaviour, this time prompted by discomfort associated with circulatory changes triggered by the fight-or-flight response.'

'What if he just has an itch or a mild skin condition?' Penn asked.

'That's why we look for clusters,' Alison explained.

'Not every skin condition produces clusters, you know,' Penn offered with a cheeky smile.

Alison chuckled before continuing. 'Clusters of behaviour. Non-verbal clusters include grooming gestures, hand-wringing, inward curled feet, pursed or biting of lips, slumped posture, finger tapping, a shift in blink rate, shrugs, clenched fists, winks, closed eyes and fake smiles.' Alison smiled and took a breath. 'There are more if you want me to—'

'But how can you tell if the smile is fake?' Stacey asked, intrigued. 'Everyone is different.'

'The muscles around the eye sockets are the most difficult to control. Only one in ten people can do it. Forcing a smile to reach the eyes is difficult to do. Only genuine happiness can control the orbicularis oculi, the eye orbiting muscle.'

'How about verbal clusters?' Penn asked.

'Qualifying statements like "to tell you the truth". Repeating the question verbatim, non-spontaneous response time, weak tone of voice, dodging questions, inappropriate detail, objections to irrelevant specifics, dismissive attitude. More emphasis on persuasion than facts.'

'But what if a person naturally speaks or acts that way?' Stacey asked.

Everyone was different. Some people had idiosyncrasies that could be interpreted inaccurately.

'That's why we need a baseline behaviour against which to compare it. Just like a polygraph interviewer will ask baseline questions before starting a lie detector test. He needs to establish normal physical responses against which he can compare the set questions. I need baseline behaviour before the boss began questioning him.'

'But we don't have that,' Penn said. 'The boss put him in the room and the camera started rolling.'

Alison smiled. 'Luckily for me your boss decided to keep him waiting for a while in the foyer. It's not much; I can only gauge some non-verbal behaviours, but it's enough to detect marked change in his interview demeanour.'

'So did he do it?' Stacey asked, leaning forward.

Alison laughed. 'I've been here a couple of hours, watched his interviews once and you want me to answer a question like that?'

'Okay, is there any question you can answer?'

'Ask me if there are any particular indicators of deceit.'

'Are there?'

'Yep, about ten of them.'

'And?'

'So far, our man in there has shown just about every one of them.'

THIRTY-SIX

'Who do you reckon Woody had to sleep with to get this through so quickly?' Bryant asked as they headed to the home of Steven Harte.

'I think it falls under the don't-ask-don't-tell policy.'

'Do we have one of those?'

'We're not the bloody army,' she said, rolling her eyes.

But she'd thought pretty much the same thing after Woody's call as they left the premises of Butler Building Limited.

Quite frankly, she didn't care what body part he'd sold to get the search warrant. He'd assured her it would be at the premises by the time they got there, and right now they were no more than a few minutes away from his address in Wombourne. She used the time to offer up a silent prayer that they were about to find Grace Lennard alive and well and completely unharmed.

'Bit too easy, guv,' Bryant said, voicing the nagging thoughts in her head.

'Shut up, Bryant,' she snapped.

He did as she'd asked until he passed three police vehicles and Mitch's van. The gate to the property was already open and their lead forensic tech was already here.

'How did they get the gates…? Oh, I see,' Bryant said, taking a better look.

Metal plates had been removed to reveal the mechanism that could be wound manually.

They passed through the gates and stopped as Inspector Weaver waved them down.

'You'll be wanting this, I expect,' he said, passing her the search warrant through the window. 'We're cracking on with the external search, but the front door has been accessed ready for you. No one has entered.'

'Are the dogs contained?' she asked of Rocky and Tyson, his two Dobermans.

'No dogs, marm,' he said, shaking his head.

'Thanks,' she said, closing the window. Another lie he'd told her.

Bryant moved forward slowly as Kim thought how strange it was to now be on this side of the wall after trying her hardest to just get a looky through the hedge barrier during the night.

She already knew that it was by far the grandest, most expensive property they'd ever visited.

'How much?' she asked her colleague.

'Four to five,' he answered as they approached the property along a sweeping gravel road to a circular raised lawn placed perfectly central to the front of the house.

'Make that closer to five,' Bryant said as a stable block and coach house came into view.

'It's a good-looking house,' she observed. 'And it's going to take a while to search thoroughly.'

'Master of the understatement there, guv,' he said, pulling up in front of the white-painted Regency property.

A double green door had been removed, and Mitch stood suited and booted, ready to enter.

She got out of the car and took a moment to appreciate the

beauty of the house and its surroundings. A total of twelve arched windows graced the front of the property.

'Grade II Regency Gothic,' Mitch said, walking towards her with his phone. 'Last sold twenty-five years ago for half a million but probably now worth closer to five.'

Bryant smiled smugly.

'What else does Rightmove tell you?' Kim asked, approaching the front door.

'That it has ten bedrooms, five bathrooms, a good few reception rooms and a cellar.'

'You got the floor plan of when it was sold back then?'

Mitch nodded.

'Text the link to me and to Bryant as well,' she said, stepping inside the property. 'And get to the cellar as quickly as you can.'

The hallway was a stunning space, lovingly restored, with a geometrically tiled floor and high ceilings.

'Bloody hell,' Bryant said from behind.

Kim pulled her gaze away from the ornate cornicing and delicate ceiling roses. They weren't here to appreciate the property's beauty.

'Okay, you take upstairs,' she instructed Bryant as both their phones tinged receipt of a message from Mitch, who was briefing members of his team who had just arrived.

'If I'm not back in an hour, it's because I've moved in.'

Kim laughed as she took the pair of gloves being offered but she completely understood his sentiment.

Despite it being a grand sprawling property, there was something comfortable and welcoming. It had been restored to its former glory without being overdone. There was no unnecessary grandeur. Surprisingly, it was still a home.

For one person, she reminded herself. This was all for one man who lived alone and wasn't known to have formed any romantic attachments in the last thirty years.

'Don't forget to look for CCTV equipment,' she called as Bryant headed for the stairs.

A wave over his shoulder showed he'd heard.

She loaded the floor plan to her phone and got her bearings.

Surely, Grace was here somewhere. She prayed they were going to come across a locked room and behind it would be a little girl, perhaps frightened, disoriented but alive and unharmed.

She took the first left into the dining room. The easy, gentle theme of the hallway flowed perfectly into the next space.

She walked the room, opening and closing drawers and cupboards, her analytical eye looking for anything out of place. This was an initial cursory search but she didn't want to miss anything. The hardwood floors guided her back to the hallway.

She worked her way through the sitting room, a cloakroom, drawing room, music room and snug, looking for anything obvious but she couldn't help noticing the floor-length curtains, the intricate pelmets, the ornate cornicing and delicate chandeliers. Every room had a spectacular view of the surrounding land.

By the time she reached the kitchen, her hopes of finding Grace were dwindling. She opened the door of the double fridge and freezer. Both of his earlier victims had been taken care of with one hot meal, sandwiches, drinks and occasional sweets. It was the greenest, leafiest fridge she'd ever seen. It looked nothing like her own, which held a half tub of Lurpak butter, a few cheeses and her one nod to good health, which was a few small bottles of Actimel.

She saw no evidence of feeding a child.

But wouldn't he be expecting this? she asked herself. He had come to the police station. He'd arranged for the digging to be done at Hawne Park. It wasn't much of a stretch to believe he'd cleared out his fridge.

He saw this coming before he'd even stepped into the station.

Kim continued her journey around the kitchen and back into the hallway with a sinking feeling. Grace Lennard was not here.

There was no way Steven Harte would have led them to her until he was good and ready.

She had the unsettling sensation of being an actor, that she was following a script that had been written a long time ago.

'Nothing obvious upstairs,' Bryant said, arriving in the kitchen. 'All ten bedrooms and three bathrooms checked as well as another two reception rooms.'

'Cellar is all clear,' Mitch said, following closely behind Bryant. 'Although if you did want to keep someone captive, you could easily do it down there. Six separate rooms all as creepy and dark as each other.'

'Not his style,' Kim said, considering the accounts of the girls he'd brought back. Both had spoken of a van parked right outside a front door. There had been no mention of dark, enclosed spaces.

'Still gonna start down there,' Mitch said, right before she suggested it. Melody Jones had never come home. There was no body but there might be traces of DNA. Steven Harte had bought this house around the same time Melody had disappeared. There was a chance she could have spent time here.

'Floor plans?' she asked.

Mitch nodded. 'As they were when the property was sold.'

Bryant nodded his agreement.

No rooms had been added since he'd taken ownership of the house. There were no secret spaces added designed to keep someone prisoner.

'Nothing obvious outside in the coach house and outbuildings,' Inspector Weaver said, arriving in the kitchen.

Kim refreshed her phone and held up the details of the house to the inspector.

'How many acres?' he asked.

'Forty-seven. And every one of them needs to be checked and searched.'

He ran a hand through his brown hair. 'Well that's me sorted until retirement,' he said, reaching for his radio. 'Best get on to the boss and get some more bodies.' He paused. 'Actually, that wasn't the best choice of words I could have used but you know what I meant.'

Kim nodded. Thank God there was no blooper reel at the end of each case.

'Just one more room,' she said, stepping towards what she was sure was Steven Harte's study.

The push of the door met with no resistance, and the impact upon opening the door was immediate. This room was located at the back of the house. Double doors were right in front of her. As with every other room, the view was breathtaking. Every angle had something different to offer: mature trees, the lake. She'd even seen a couple of geese.

But none of that compared to the view of a wisteria tunnel framing a path that led to the gate of a walled garden.

'He's not short of stuff to look at, is he?' Bryant said, following her gaze.

It was getting more and more difficult to keep in her mind that this was the home of a man who liked to abduct and murder young girls.

She stood and took a moment to inhale what was probably the most personal space in the house for Steven Harte.

It was the space where he would keep the things most important to him.

Bryant was already opening and closing desk drawers. He was going to come up empty. She knew that now. Harte knew they'd be here sooner or later and had prepared his home accordingly.

Her gaze took in the walls and the glass display cabinets fixed to every available space. Many of them were encased butterflies.

She took a closer look. She'd never paid much attention to butterflies, but seeing them so close together she could see the different sizes and shapes and, above all, the colours. Each butterfly was labelled with a name like Macedonia Grayling, Sinai Baton Blue, Island Marble. With twenty to twenty-five in each frame, she was guessing there were hundreds. There were other frames, all housing some kind of colourful insect. One was labelled as Plant-hopper, some kind of hard-backed insect with unique camouflage design. There were Jewel Beetles, Flame Skimmer Dragonflies, Orchid Mantis, Nettle Grub Caterpillar.

Kim knew this was no ordinary insect collection. Every item was unique and vibrant and exotic. She was sure you could look at these displays every day and still find something you hadn't noticed before.

'Okay, Bryant, we're out,' she said as he completed his first circuit of the room. 'Mitch, special efforts for the hard drive that's running the CCTV.'

He nodded his understanding.

'Guv, don't you think a secondary search—?'

'She's not here, Bryant,' Kim said. 'There may be some kind of clue, which I'm confident Mitch will find, but right now I want another chat with Mr Harte. I think I've worked out one of his secrets.'

THIRTY-SEVEN

'Anything on his phone?' Kim asked once she'd taken her first sip of coffee. The day was moving fast, and every hour without evidence to charge Steven Harte was running down the clock.

'Sent to Ridgepoint, boss,' Stacey said. 'I can't get into it. I mean, he's a software developer,' she said as a defence.

'That's how he watches them,' Kim said. His home was open and available because he knew he'd left nothing to find. If his phone was locked then there was a reason for it.

'His phone must monitor the gate security system too,' Penn offered. He'd known their every movement when they'd had him under surveillance.

'Mitch has already prioritised trying to find the hard drive at the house, but gee up Ridgepoint, Stace, and make sure they understand the urgency of getting into that phone.'

'Well, he sure couldn't stay off it when you weren't around,' Alison said.

'Fuck,' Kim growled. He'd probably been watching Grace the whole time. The path to finding her was in that phone, and they just couldn't get into it.

'But if he's watching her she's still alive,' Bryant offered as the printer kicked into life. Kim had asked Stacey to print off photos of all of the little girls. Little blobs of Blu-Tack were rolled and ready for her to put them on the board.

'Okay, Penn, projects he's undertaken?' Kim asked.

'We're talking hundreds, boss. Some local, some national. He's funded small projects and others costing thousands. I still haven't got all of them.'

'Narrow them down. By tomorrow I want to know every project that has involved any kind of construction, and at the top of the list I want the ones where he used Butler Building Limited.'

'Got it, boss.'

'Property?'

Penn groaned. 'Another bloody maze of paperwork and red herrings. So far, I've found seven separate UK companies that trace back to Steven Harte, and three of them own substantial property ranging from disused warehouses to farmland and forestry. We've also got money being moved around the EU, so I suspect there are other companies abroad used for tax purposes. Any one of them could own land.'

'Keep at it,' Kim said, although the feeling in the pit of her stomach told her they weren't going to find Grace that way. All it took was one small property on one farm in the midst of such a sizeable portfolio.

'Once I've got all the properties listed I'll do a radius travel assessment.'

Kim nodded her agreement.

There was a timeline between him taking Grace from the day centre to him arriving at the station. He could only have travelled so many miles and back in that time. Penn loved a puzzle, and he was bloody good at them.

'Stace?' Kim asked once the photos had been lined up on the wall.

Stacey had arranged them in chronological order starting with Libby Turner, the jewellery maker who was being abused. Suzie

Keene, the architect who'd had a miserable home life. Melody Jones whose family appeared to love the money more than her. And Grace Lennard who had been taken from the day centre yesterday.

'I'm down to sixteen potential victims after Melody was taken. Just need to cross-reference a few more things to narrow the list down further.'

'Tomorrow morning?'

'Absolutely, boss.'

'Alison?' Kim asked. The behaviourist had had a couple of hours now.

'Well, he sure doesn't like being called a sicko, so I'd stay away from that,' Alison offered.

Yeah, she'd gauged that much from his reaction herself.

'He's very good at hiding his true emotions but not quite good enough. He's a bit of a leaker.'

'A what?'

'Real feelings leak out. We can't see our own faces. Micro-expressions are the ones you need to watch out for. They flash in 1/25th of a second. Our facial expressions are directly connected to our thoughts and emotions. They are almost impossible to squelch.'

'Squelch?' Kim asked, wondering if these were actual technical terms.

'Oh yeah, squelching is a thing when you try to hide the real emotion. See, we can't anticipate our feelings to what's about to be said, so the brain isn't quick enough to hide the initial response.'

'Jesus,' Bryant said. 'All this squelching and leaking reminds me of some dodgy films I watched at university.'

'TMI, Bryant,' Kim said, cringing. 'So, I know you can analyse our conversations after the fact, which is all well and good, but give me some pointers on what I should be looking for when I'm back in the room.'

'Okay, people will often subconsciously touch or try to cover their eyes when being deceptive. Men tend to rub their eyes. Notice his blink rates. Liars blink more. Look for asymmetrical expressions. Genuine emotions are balanced so when they're forced it sometimes looks lopsided. Look for gestures that match the emotion. True emotional indicators are usually expressed simultaneously. Feigned indicators occur in quick succession.'

'Example?' Kim asked.

'If I'm outraged I'll cross my arms as I scowl. If I'm forcing it the action will come after the emotion. Watch for the duration. Genuine expressions rarely last longer than five seconds. A fixed emotion will stay longer.

'Another obvious one is nodding that moves in the opposite direction. Liars rehearse their words but not their gestures. If a person who normally gesticulates freely stops moving their upper body, they're probably being deceptive. They're giving more away by trying to give nothing away if that makes sense. Also look out for emblems.'

'Is this a special language?' Bryant asked.

'Things like winks, shaking fists, the V-sign. If they're used outside the normal context, it's a red flag for deception. The use of illustrators decreases when someone is lying.'

'Oh, Lordy,' Bryant moaned.

Alison used her hand to make a cutting motion. 'That's an illustrator. It's directly linked to speech and is used to emphasise a spoken point. And one final point for now. Liars don't mirror. As explained earlier, the act of mirroring is a comfort move. Liars are more likely to pull back if you sit forward.'

Kim had come across mirroring many times before. It was a technique Alex Thorne had tried on her in the past. The thought of the woman brought a roll of anxiety to her stomach, but she pushed it away. Her focus right now was on Grace Lennard and those other little girls whose photos were now on the wall.

'Hope to be more specific once I've watched your interaction live and played back all the CCTV in slow motion,' Alison continued.

Kim nodded absently as her eyes darted from one photo to the next.

'Such pretty little girls,' Alison said, following her gaze.

'Exactly what I've been thinking,' Kim said as she headed for the door.

THIRTY-EIGHT

This time when Steven Harte was led into the interview room, Kim was waiting for him. She was sure that if the man was experienced in spotting micro-expressions he would have spotted her satisfaction in seeing him dressed in the paper jumpsuit and being instructed what to do and when. His days of wandering in and out of the station of his own volition were over.

'Good evening, Mr Harte. Would you like a drink?'

He nodded. 'Tea with…'

'One sugar. Yes, we know,' she said, nodding to the constable.

Bryant took a moment to repeat his rights. She was taking no chances on this one.

'And would you confirm that you have waived your right to legal representation at this time?'

He nodded.

Kim glanced towards the tape recorder. 'Please state your answer.'

'Not at this time.'

Kim regarded him for a few seconds, looking for any of the pointers Alison had offered, but right now he looked calm and relaxed.

'I trust that you're being taken care of,' Kim said.

Alison's last words had been to let him have his tea.

'The food is as I imagined it.'

'You expected to be taken into custody?' she asked, raising an eyebrow.

'Of course,' he answered.

Again, the feeling that she was playing a part, following a script.

'We spent some time at your home today.'

He smiled and from what she'd learned, the crow's feet told her the expression was genuine. There was no tension. She'd been right. Grace was not there.

'It's a very nice home. Sympathetically restored but a massive space for one.'

He said nothing.

She waited.

'Sorry, Officer, but that was an accurate statement, not a question. Is there something about my home you'd like to know?'

'Why don't you share it with anyone?'

He leaned back in his chair and met her gaze. She noted that he had not looked at Bryant once.

'Having a partner doesn't define me. I don't understand the opinion that everyone must be half of a pair, unless you're Mormon and it's a whole different set of rules. It may be beyond your comprehension that I am perfectly able to function and be content as a single being. It is the wish of others that everyone must be coupled up. I am perfectly happy being alone.'

Actually, she could comprehend it. Perfectly.

'Are you married with children?' he asked, tipping his head to the side. He clearly already knew the answer.

'Jenson Butler seems to think you've had no intimate relationships at all,' she said, ignoring his question.

Harte threw his head back and laughed uproariously.

'Oh my goodness, you're taking the word of my builder on the history of my love life?'

'He appears to have known you for some years.'

'We met at university. We talked now and again. We had little in common, but he was a familiar face. We didn't speak for years until I contacted him for a quote, so I fail to see how he can be an authority on my personal life when we've worked together no more than a dozen times over the last twenty-five years.'

Kim hoped Penn was listening. Now he'd know roughly how many joint projects he was looking for.

'You're not married now?'

'This isn't important.'

He was right but she wanted to test his reaction on whether it was a sore point. She'd detected no regret in his response. It wasn't something she could use.

'The house is very different to where you grew up, isn't it?'

The first sign of tension entered his jaw. 'It's not important.'

'Oh, I think it is,' Kim pushed. 'I know the Hollytree Estate very well. I also know where the exact property is that you grew up in. I know the main thing you can see from the window is the bins. It's the rubbish – it's the spot for drug deals and human defecation.'

'And how would you know all that, Inspector? Unless, of course, you've experienced life there first-hand.'

'Mr Harte, we're not talking about—'

'But maybe we should. Maybe we should take a minute to explore the depth of decay that breeds like vermin within Hollytree.'

Kim felt her cheeks warm at the glint of amusement in his eyes, leaving her in no doubt that he knew exactly where she'd spent the first six years of her life.

He continued. 'Maybe we should discuss in detail how much harder it is to succeed at anything if that's where you started. I think you have a better understanding than most that anyone who leaves that estate alive does well to avoid drugs, alcohol or a mental institution?'

Kim struggled to hang on to her composure. She would not let him take her back there, and she would continue her line of questioning.

She cleared her throat. 'I agree that it is where much of life's ugliness comes to visit at different times of the day. It's a cesspit. How long was it again that you never left the home?'

'You know the answer to that, Inspector, and now I have a question for you.'

'You don't get to ask the—'

'What did you promise yourself?'

'I'm sorry. I'm not sure what you mean.'

'During those long hours of fear, hunger, despair. All those days of being powerless, of not knowing if you were going to eat that day. Would your mentally unstable mother drag herself out of bed to make a sandwich? If today you would taste something hot or if the grumbling pain in your stomach would worsen? When you were eating two-day-old crusts from the bin to keep your body functioning. When your only window out to the world was a view to the filthiest, seediest things life had to offer. What was your "when I'm big" promise to yourself?'

Kim said nothing but she knew exactly what he meant. She had promised herself many things. When I'm big I'll have a fridge full of food. When I'm big I'll drink all the orange juice in the world. When I'm big I won't let myself feel frightened. When I'm big I'll be able to protect Mikey from the world.

Kim felt Bryant's foot against her own. A simple gesture but one that brought her out of the past.

'Mr Harte, I will not be drawn away from the matter at hand,' she said forcefully. 'But if we're talking about your "when I'm big" promises, I now know what you promised yourself.'

Realising the moment had passed and she was firmly back in

the present, he shrugged as though he had no interest in her opinion.

'It's your pursuit of beauty. You promised to surround yourself with beautiful things: furnishings, wildlife, paintings, nature, colourful insects, anything beautiful – including innocent little girls.'

The realisation had started to dawn on her while walking around his house. Everything was breathtaking, tasteful. Everywhere he looked, something pretty was waiting for him. When she'd seen the line-up of photos of the girls she'd been struck by the beauty of their innocence.

'The room that you kept them in is no different to the display cases that house your butterflies and bugs. All that was missing were the pins in their wings. It's all so you can watch them, enjoy them.'

'Appreciate them,' he added.

'The girls?'

'The butterflies.'

'Except little girls aren't like butterflies. They weren't made to be encased and observed for the viewer's pleasure. They are not part of someone's exotic collection. They are human beings ripped away from their families, their homes, to be—'

'I think we've already established that not every child has an idyllic childhood, Inspector.'

'Is that how you justify it to yourself? Is that your criteria – pretty and unhappy? If so that makes it somehow acceptable to you?'

'I'm saying that some of the names you've mentioned to me don't appear to have suffered as a result of their experience.'

'But you couldn't have known that,' Kim said, trying to keep her composure. She was talking about him, and he was talking about someone else. One slip, just one slip was all she needed.

'Sometimes a little period away from your problems—'

'One year is not a short period of time, Mr Harte, and of course your first two victims adjusted; they had no choice but to adjust to their environment while you observed and ogled them.'

She saw a faint look of distaste at her intentional use of the word ogle.

'One year to a child is half a lifetime. Why did you keep them so long?' she asked.

He weighed his words for a moment.

'The average butterfly has an adult lifespan of two weeks or less. There's a point during this time that the butterfly is at its best, at its most beautiful stage of being. It reaches its optimum unspoiled beauty before time and other insects get the opportunity to age and maim it.'

'So when you talk of other insects you mean humans, you mean life and age in relation to little girls. You take them at what you feel is their optimum beauty, observe them and watch them and then set them free?'

'I'm talking of butterflies.'

'And I'm talking about real-life little girls.'

He said nothing.

'What went wrong with Melody?'

His face hardened.

'Why wasn't she set free like the rest?'

He folded his arms and regarded her silently. His face was emotionless.

Now she'd brought it up, she had no choice but to commit to that line of questioning.

'Why didn't you set Melody free once she'd aged past your optimum expectation?'

No response.

'Why is Melody not out there living her life like the first two?'

No response.

'Did you decide that looking was no longer enough?'

No response but another tightening of the jaw.

'Did she fight back when you tried to touch her?'

No response but she could see he was struggling to keep the emotion from his face.

'Or did you feel so guilty afterwards that you'd succumbed to your true desires?'

She saw the almost imperceptible movements of his head to the side.

'Was there something about Melody that woke those urges in you?'

His gaze fixed on her.

'Did you kill Melody and bury her at Hawne Park?'

His eyes blazed.

'Did Melody die because she knew you were a paedo—'

'Stop,' he said, slamming his fist down on the table.

'Is there something you'd like to say, Mr Harte.'

'Yes, Inspector, there is something I'd like to say. I think it's time to call my lawyer.'

THIRTY-NINE

'Hope you all got something from that,' Kim said as she and Bryant entered the squad room. 'Cos it looks like that's the last intimate chat we'll be having.'

Steven Harte had been handed back to Jack, the custody sergeant, to make the necessary calls.

She wondered briefly if he was trying to run down the clock. It was almost seven and his legal representative wouldn't be attending until the morning, which meant he was now off limits for at least twelve to fourteen hours of the initial twenty-four she had to hold him.

No matter how much control she thought she had, he was still calling the shots.

'Glad to see you followed my advice,' Alison said, nodding at the screen.

'You stay calm and rational while interviewing the sicko,' Kim snapped.

'I meant about the tea,' Alison said easily. 'I'd have kicked him in the bollocks about two minutes in but hey ho, that's why I do the job I do.'

Kim laughed loudly and wondered if Alison was one of those

people that was impossible to offend, but she guessed the behaviourist knew her well enough by now to accept there was no malice behind her tone. Just frustration.

Kim kept her attention on Alison. 'You got anything for me?'

'Oh, I think I've got some stuff, but I'd like to go over the recording a few times before I report.'

Kim nodded her acceptance. She wasn't getting another run at him until tomorrow anyway.

'Stace?'

'I've ruled out more girls, boss, but I'm still in double figures.'

'Penn?'

'Started whittling down the projects, boss.'

She glanced around her team. 'Has anyone got anything that's gonna help us find Grace Lennard this side of some much-needed sleep?'

Her team looked exhausted. They had pulled out all the stops to provide surveillance on Harte last night, and Stacey hadn't even been home at all. She knew Stacey's wife, Devon, would understand, having a high-pressure job herself.

A collection of despondent 'nos' was the reply. If there *had* been the chance, not one of them would choose to leave, however rough they were feeling.

To prove her point, their efforts in collecting their belongings were sluggish, as though she might change her mind.

'Seriously, guys, go get some rest. Briefing at seven.'

'Okay, whoever wants me most gets to give me a lift home,' Stacey said to Penn and Alison. 'I have a hot date with a chicken curry and a furry giraffe.'

Alison raised an eyebrow before answering. 'Not me tonight, matey – I'm hanging on here for a bit.' She was cleared to view the footage but not remove it from site.

'Gotta go the other way, Stace, to pick up Jasper from Billy's house. It's brother-bonding night, which consists of picking up a

McDonald's and then me watching him fight his mates on the Xbox.'

Kim glanced at Bryant.

'Well, even though I wasn't even in your top two I'm happy to drop you off.'

'Oh, Bryant, you are my knight in a shining Astra,' she said, heading for the door.

He stood. 'Stace.'

She turned just in time to catch his car keys.

'I'll be down in a minute.'

He waited for a few seconds and then looked pointedly at Alison.

'What?'

'I reckon Betty's all but giving away any leftover muffins right now.'

'Ooh, back in a minute,' she said, launching herself from the room.

'What now?' Kim asked, folding her arms.

'Hey, I caught that micro-organism on your face just then, and I'm not gonna have a go about anything.'

'Micro-expression,' she corrected him unnecessarily.

'Watch him, guv. He's trying to get under your skin. He's drawing too many parallels with you. I don't know his game, but it's not me he's playing it with. It's your attention he wants. Just something to bear in mind.'

Bryant had been afforded the luxury of sitting and watching the whole exchange.

'Thanks, Bryant, now get lost and give Jenny my love.'

He offered her a mock salute and headed for the door.

A small part of her regretted not telling him about Alexandra Thorne. He was a wise man, and she trusted his judgement.

But with what she was about to do, she wasn't equally sure she could trust her own.

FORTY

Alex knew something special was happening, and she didn't need to ask the guard what it was. She didn't get marched over to the visitors' centre at eight o'clock for any old caller. It had to be someone with power, someone with authority and someone who didn't like to be told no.

She was heartened to see the detective inspector sitting at a table in the centre of the room looking straight at her. As usual she was dressed from head to toe in black, her long legs stretched out and crossed at the ankles.

Her face was unreadable, but Alex had an idea of what she was feeling. Her curiosity had outweighed her determination to stay away, and right now she was feeling pretty mad at herself for giving in to her own emotions. Oh, she did enjoy those little revelations of humanity in the woman.

'How lovely to see you, Kim,' Alex said, taking a seat. 'Thank you for coming.'

'Cut the bullshit, Alex. What do you want?'

'I'm just offering appreciation for your efforts at this time of—'

'Normally when you ask to see me it's because people are going to get hurt, so who is on your hit list this time?'

'We'll get to that in a minute. Firstly, tell me how you are. It's been a while. You look tired.'

'Because I'm dealing with a psychopath.'

'Well, I'm pretty sure we established that years ago. I've never pretended—'

'Not you, Alex. You're not the only psychopath in town, and you're certainly not the most challenging.'

But I'm the one you've driven 40 miles at night to see, Alex thought with satisfaction.

'Tell me about it – get it off your chest. I might be able to help.'

'Oh, Alex, don't act out of character. The only person you've ever been able to help is yourself.'

'Try me,' she said. She hadn't enjoyed anyone's company this much since the last time Kim had visited. 'If you're so sure you're dealing with a psychopath, it takes one to know one.'

And he or she has your current attention, Alex thought, reading the distraction in her eyes. She was here but not all of her. Alex swallowed down her irritation. She wanted, expected and demanded all of the woman's focus to be on her.

'I really would like to help,' she said as earnestly as she could manage.

Kim sighed. 'I've got a guy who abducts young girls, keeps 'em for a year and then brings them back, safe and sound.'

'Sexual?'

Kim shook her head. 'Don't think so.'

'Strange answer but okay. Physical harm, psychological harm?'

'No, and no.'

'What does he do, take them to Disneyland?'

'He watches them.'

'That's it?'

'Yep. Feeds them, clothes them, educates them and watches them.'

'He's not a psychopath.'

'His third victim didn't come back.'

'He's not a psychopath.'

'How can you say that? You're the one who explained to me that not all psychopaths are violent. You told me they want what they want. Well, he wants to lock up little girls and feed off their beauty. You don't think that's psychopathic?'

'Not at all and you should be pleased.'

'Hang on, how can you be so sure he's not a psycho? I've given you about four sentences.'

'If all he does is watch the girls, he's not what you think he is. Sociopaths, as I like to call us, don't sit and watch anything. We have to be involved, we have to be playing a game, competing, doing something. Our brains aren't wired to sit and appreciate beauty. The emotion is too high. We want to own, possess, battle, win. Watching something mundane is just not interesting.'

'He voluntarily came to the station to assist with our enquiries but has as yet admitted nothing.'

'Now that is interesting. He's clearly playing some kind of control game, which might mean he's narcissistic or a control freak. You say his third victim never came back?'

Kim shook her head. 'And we've found the body of a young girl at a site with a strong connection to him.'

'Have there been any since number three?'

'We're looking, but if there were, they didn't come back either.'

'Hmm, interesting' Alex said. She would have liked to discuss this more, but she'd already seen the guard glance at her watch.

Being a respected police officer got the woman an out-of-hours visit but it didn't give her the right to stay all night.

'Okay, I'm glad—'

'Why should I be pleased he's not a psychopath?' Kim asked, frowning and showing that she really did listen to every word.

'Because it means he has a weakness. He has a vulnerability. However evil you think he is, there will be a string you can latch on to and pull until it unravels him. You just have to look closely enough to find it.'

Kim appeared to be considering her words, but she now needed to move this along. Much as she'd enjoyed their conversation, this meeting was about her and now she wanted the inspector's full attention.

'I asked you to visit because I've got a parole hearing at the end of the week.'

Kim's head lolled back as genuine laughter rolled out of her mouth.

'Thanks, Alex. I really needed that. It's been quite the day, but the drive was worth it.'

'I'm serious.'

'I know. You're never anything else but – that's what's funny. Who the hell is going to let you out of here? You haven't been rehabilitated. You haven't changed. You can't change and you don't even want to. After getting the additional years slapped on you for trying to murder everyone that stood in the way of your appeal, I wouldn't get your hopes up too high.'

Alex pushed down her irritation. It was the response she'd expected. Pleasantries were over and it was now down to business.

'Oh, I do have high hopes, Kim. I am going to get out and, what's more, you're going to help me do it.'

Kim's gaze was now alert and cold. 'And why the hell would I want to do that?'

FORTY-ONE

Kim felt the air cool between them, as though someone had flicked a switch on the aircon.

She was still kicking her own ass silently for turning up at all. Damn that curiosity when it came to Alexandra Thorne.

What she really wanted to do was haul Steven Harte back into interview room one and ask him if he'd chosen her specifically because she had started her life on Hollytree. Was he under some kind of illusion that gave him a pass or that she would feel an affinity with him that would prevent her doing her job?

'Because I have two pieces of information that you want,' Alex replied. 'The first I'll give you for free as a good-faith gesture, but the second has a price.'

'What's the first?' Kim asked, willing to play along. For a while. The tension eased by the genuine laugh was creeping back into her neck.

'Your mother is dying.'

'Oh, Alex, for fuck's sake.'

'I thought you'd want to know.'

'She's my mother. I can ring up any time I want to find out about her health.'

'But you don't.'

'Because I couldn't give less of a shit if she dies or not.'

The staff at Grantley Care Facility, home for the criminally insane, were under strict instructions to contact her only when the woman died.

'You really want to leave things like this between the two of you?'

'What the fuck has it got to do with you?'

'I care about your well-being, Kim.'

'No, you don't. You care about trying to get inside my head, and the fact I won't let you anywhere near me with a lock-pick and a battering ram frustrates the life out of you. You said it yourself a moment ago: psychopaths like to play games and they like to win.'

'This isn't about me.'

'Oh, Alex, everything in your world is about you. Your motive right now is for that information to have some kind of negative effect on me, for it to bring back the memories, but you fail to understand that my mother died the day she walked out of that flat and left me and my brother chained to the radiator.'

Kim paused and reined in her emotions. She would not be baited into talking about Mikey.

'How the hell do you know this anyway?' she asked, hiding her rage at this woman's attempts to control her with information.

'We're still in touch.'

Kim was stunned and then wondered why she should be surprised. She'd thought this woman could surprise her no more, and yet she still managed to pull something unexpected out of the bag.

Alex had made contact with her mother a few years ago, pretending to be her. She had offered the woman forgiveness in Kim's name, and then tried to use Kim's hatred towards her mother as a manipulation tool. Kim had assumed that once the deception had been uncovered, the letters had stopped.

She should have known that Alex wouldn't stop before she'd

wrung every single ounce of twisted potential out of her mother.

'I apologised for my deceit, and she now knows me as your friend.'

'Bloody hell, that's almost as much of a stretch as you pretending to be me. And, much as I'd love to stop and chat, if that's the best you've got...'

'Oh, it's not even close, so please sit back down as we don't have much time.'

Kim remained standing. She was getting a bit fed up being told what to do. This woman was either going to spill her poison or not but, judging from the guard's repeated glances at the clock, she didn't have long to do it.

'We've become close, your mother and I. We've corresponded about many different things. She's opened up to me; she trusts me. She's told me things that she's never told another living soul.'

Kim felt the nausea rising within her. The two people she hated most in the world forming some kind of sick attachment behind her back was beyond twisted.

'Okay, enough build up. I can hear the suspenseful music playing. Spit it out.'

'You may want to sit back down for—'

'Okay, I've had enough,' Kim said, moving away from the table.

'It's big, Kim. It's something you've always wondered about, and I'll tell you on Thursday when you bring your letter of recommendation for my release.'

Kim turned. 'There's no information you could have that would induce me to—'

'Oh, but you're wrong there, Kimmy,' Alex said, using the name her mother had called her.

Alex walked towards Kim until they were inches apart. Her voice was low and menacing. 'Bring that letter and I'll tell you something that will change your life forever.'

'You don't have that power,' Kim spat.

'I don't, but your father does, and I know who he is.'

FORTY-TWO

Kim didn't let the air out of her lungs until she reached the safety of the car. Only then did she take some deep breaths to clear the swimming sensation in her head. Swimming or drowning she wasn't sure which.

'Well, that was a blast, eh, boy?' she said, pulling Barney towards her. Right now, she needed the grounding reassurance of her best friend. He was happy to oblige and jumped onto her lap, forcing himself between her and the steering wheel.

She wrapped her arms around him as she tried to make sense of what she'd just been told.

Her father. The words sounded strange in her head. Mixed in with the emotions rolling around her head was the realisation that she had one.

She had given it great thought as a child. In every children's home and every foster home, she'd prayed he was going to come and rescue her. That somehow, despite Mikey's death, he would find a way to make it all okay. It had never happened, and the only father she'd ever known was Keith, the man who had fostered her from the age of ten to thirteen.

From him she had gained her love of motorcycles and restoration. She had learned to start and finish a project and to do it right. She had learned from both Keith and her foster mother, Erica, how to open your heart, just a fraction, to people who cared about you.

Over the years she had thought less and less about the man who had fathered her and her twin. She and Mikey had become the result of a one-person process.

The fact that she had a blood relative out there somewhere was blowing her mind. It was a link to Mikey.

All kinds of questions were running through her head. Had he known about them? Did she have brothers and sisters, cousins? Were any of them like Mikey? Did they have his characteristics – that sparkle in his eye when he laughed, the habit of using his hands when he told her a story?

'Fuck you, Alex,' she growled as the emotion started to build in her throat.

And what response had she been expecting in relation to the news about her mother? Kim already knew that was an appetiser, a snippet, a power play to show Alex had the scoop on her mother. It was a minor triumph. She was welcome to it. She had known the day would come that she'd receive this news, and it wasn't that she didn't know how to feel. It was the fact that she didn't feel anything at all.

What narked her was Alex's continued insistence in trying to force some kind of reaction, an epiphany that she had to act or lose her chance forever. She had no intention of visiting her mother and the barrier of indifference would remain in place. But damn Alex for keeping on pushing.

She pushed the other feelings aside and held on to the anger. That bloody woman always managed to stir something up inside her. She had known any mention of her father would lead right back to thoughts of Mikey, her one vulnerability, her one weakness that Alex was fully aware of. And that was what made her dangerous.

'I swear, Barney, that woman—'

She stopped speaking as her phone rang.

Barney jumped back onto the passenger seat as she fished in her back pocket to retrieve it.

She frowned as she answered it.

'Hey, Keats, you forget where you live or something?'

'Just clearing up after the Macedonian tornado swept through.'

She smiled at the apt description. Both brilliant minds but completely different ways of working. There were times that she needed both, and much as she liked to bait Keats, he'd spent the day surrounded by the bones of a child.

'I was just checking my emails before I left. I've received the dental records for Melody Jones. I haven't had a good look yet, but I thought I'd let you know they were in.'

'Keats, have you lost your mind?'

He'd called her to tell her he'd received an email.

'I can't forward it to you right now, as I've closed down my computer and have an early meeting tomorrow morning, which means I probably won't get around to sending it until, say, ten o'clock.'

'Keats, what the hell are you trying to tell...?'

Her words trailed away as she realised exactly what he was trying to say, without actually saying it and getting them both into trouble.

She thanked him and ended the call.

What she'd just learned was not going to help them one little bit.

FORTY-THREE

'Okay, guys, look lively, no time to waste,' Kim said at exactly 7.01 a.m. Her team appeared rested and alert. Good – they needed to be. This morning they were going to have to hit the ground running.

'We have to prepare for the fact that it might not be Melody Jones we've found at Hawne Park.'

Four expressions of surprise rested on her.

'Why would we do that, boss?' Penn asked. 'The timeline of her disappearance fits with the date of the construction works.'

'Only if he kept her longer than the others or stored her body elsewhere before burying her there. Melody was taken in 1996 and the works were carried out in 1999. That's a three-year gap. Plenty of time to stick to his one-year schedule of abduct and release or kill. We need to be sure it's her, and we need to do it by ten o'clock.'

'Why's that, boss?' Stacey asked, raising an eyebrow. 'We have Harte until 3 p.m. before we need the extension.'

Not if he's been arrested for the wrong girl, she thought, which she was sure was the reason for Keats's late-night call. Without stating the words, he had been telling her the dental records were

not a match for Melody Jones and had given her time to do something about it. She wasn't the girl in the grave, but it was the crime
for which Steven Harte was being held.

Right now, she could claim deniability. She hadn't actually
been told. Because once she knew for sure she would have to
action it. It was a grey area and she wouldn't pass that on to her
team. Keats had given her until ten o'clock to make something
happen.

'Just work with me, Stace,' she said to the detective constable.
She took a breath and then a sip of coffee.

Stacey nodded.

'Harte's lawyer will be in some time this morning and they'll
want a good chat, so we've got a few hours. Stace, I need you to
identify any other victims that might be our girl in the ground.
Once you've done that, I want dental records for every one of
them.'

Stacey made a note and began tapping.

'Penn, I want you coming at it from the other angle. If Melody
isn't the victim at Hawne Park, where is she buried?'

Kim didn't add that she needed one or the other by ten o'clock
or Steven Harte would be leaving this station a free man at exactly
five minutes past ten.

He nodded his understanding.

'Any progress on the property searches?'

Penn groaned. 'It's like a maze, boss. I've found two corporate
umbrellas: one in Jersey and one in Portugal. Each header
company splits into six divisional operations, and each needs to be
searched separately with Land Registry. I've done two so far and
ruled out anything that's more than thirty miles away.'

'Keep at it, Penn.' She turned to her right. 'Bryant, see what
you can find out about Butler Building Limited as a company.
There's something about that guy that's not ringing true.'

'On it, guv,' he said, turning to his computer.

Bryant wasn't a natural data miner but right now it was all hands to the wheel.

Finally, she turned to Alison, who was mushing three Weetabix into a muddy, milky pool. Today, she had come prepared.

'You got anything for me?'

Alison put the bowl aside. 'Oh yes, I definitely have some observations if you'd like to pull up a chair.'

Kim did so, hoping Alison had something she could use. Right now she needed every one of her team to be at the very top of their game.

FORTY-FOUR

'Shoot,' Kim said, wheeling her chair next to Alison.

'Inappropriate choice of word for a police officer, no?' Alison asked, opening up her notebook.

'You've been busy,' she observed, seeing all the hastily written notes.

'I've watched the interview ten times now – normal speed, slow speed, with sound, without sound – and every time I discover something new.'

'I was in there ten minutes.'

'Yes, but they were quality minutes for deducing real and faked emotions. I'm going to point out some things, but if I try and show you everything we're still going to be sitting here way past your 10 a.m. deadline. So here we go, and although you'll find it hard, try not to interrupt.'

Kim snorted.

'Firstly, Harte is brought into the room by a constable and before he fixes the blank expression on his face, there's a brief flash of warmth. It's the first of many micro-expressions I'm going to mention but he is genuinely pleased to see you.'

'He didn't look at Bryant once,' Kim noted, watching the video.

'Bryant's not even there. He's totally inconsequential.'

'Er... guys, right here,' Bryant said, waving across the desk.

'There's no one else in this game but you and him. Even when Bryant is reading him his rights, Harte never takes his eyes off you. He's relaxed at this point and is showing no sign of tension.'

'Did he really expect to be arrested?'

'Okay, clearly the "no interruption statement" fell on deaf ears. The answer is yes. He was definitely expecting this. His palms are open, and his mannerisms are in line with his speech. As we move on and you talk about his home, we see genuine happiness. The involuntary movements cause crow's feet and narrowed eyelids. At the same time, the corners of the mouth curve up. As brief as it was, it was the only time I've seen it on his face, and that's what I mean when I say some genuine emotions will seep out without his knowledge. When you talk about his home and he rebuts you for not asking a question, we see a flash of contempt.'

For this Alison went to the marker she'd noted on the video.

'See here. Unlike the other basic expressions, contempt is asymmetrical. One lip corner is pulled in and back. He feels that that line of questioning is beneath you.'

Kim would never have spotted that had she not been shown.

'His responses to you about partners and his need for one all appear to be genuine, but look at this little leaker.'

She scrolled to the next marker.

'His eyebrows are up, his eyelids widen and the mouth drops ever so slightly. He is definitely surprised at Jenson Butler's comments on his love life.

'When he tells you that the questioning isn't important, there's a flash of impatience. He actually wants you to get to what matters. He wants to talk about the girls.'

Alison paused as though expecting interruption. Kim said nothing.

'The first signs of real tension only come when you mention his childhood. Watch what he does.'

Alison played the footage.

'He traces the ring on his cup,' Kim observed.

'That's why I asked you to let him have tea. I wanted to see what prompted him to touch it. It's his comforter. It's his version of grooming. Make sure he always has tea. It'll tell you a lot.'

'Got it.'

'Next we have a good example of deceit. When you tell him that you know why he takes the girls, he shrugs as though he couldn't care less. The movement is one-sided and his eyes narrow. He cares very much what you have to say and shows no surprise when you say it, but watch what happens next.'

Alison played about twenty seconds of footage and then stopped it.

'That was his butterfly speech, and it's clearly about the girls, but did you notice anything?'

'Nothing,' Kim replied honestly.

'Exactly. There is not one movement or expression change when talking about the butterflies. That tells us that he does have great control of his actions and you really are looking for just the odd clue. Get him talking about the girls without the butterflies and take away his tea and I'd be interested to see how much control he can maintain.'

'Got it,' Kim said.

'When you move on to his justification for taking the girls, he maintains his composure. I can tell you now that he absolutely doesn't believe he's done anything wrong. He truly believes he's been a saviour to the girls he's taken.

'Your use of any word that hints of impropriety is offensive to him. He is annoyed but not yet angry. I think he's annoyed that you don't get it.'

'Oh, I get it, and I still think he's a sicko.'

'Now here's where it gets even more interesting. Your first mention of Melody is the only time I've seen genuine sadness on his face. Look – the corners of the lips pull down, his cheeks rise in a near squint and his upper eyelids droop. Also, true sadness is revealed through reliable muscles in the chin. As you get more aggressive and direct in your questioning about Melody, he scrunches up his nose and raises his cheeks and upper lip. He is disgusted that you think he did anything sexual to her. As you bait him further, the disgust turns slowly to anger.' She jumped again to the next marker. 'Look at his pulled-down eyebrows and narrowed, pulled-in lips. You are really winding him up at this point.'

'Yes, that was my intention. I wanted to push him, but do you have any clues as to why he asked for his lawyer?' Kim asked, sitting back. 'He waived the right to representation when he walked into the room. He knew what he'd been arrested for, so he knew what he was going to be questioned about. He knew we were going to be talking about Melody, so why wait to say he wants a lawyer?'

'I can give you more than a clue for his reasoning, and it has nothing to do with Melody. It has everything to do with you.'

'Explain,' Kim instructed.

'Your disapproval has prompted him to call a lawyer. It may be that he's punishing you by adding a barrier to your communication. He sees the similarities between the two of you; where you spent your early years, a mother with mental illness.'

Kim bristled. Previously, Alison had worked the case with them where someone from her near past had recreated crime scenes based on her distant past. Much of her childhood had been laid bare for the consumption of her team. Alison had almost lost her life. It bothered Kim less that the team knew of her beginnings than the fact that it was part of her work. Again.

'Do you think he chose this nick because of that?' Kim asked, realising Bryant had noted this before anyone and had already warned her.

'Without a doubt,' Alison offered.

'So he's expecting some kind of concession perhaps. He thinks I'll go easy on him because I understand where he came from?'

Alison shook her head. 'I don't think he's expecting anything specific in return. He doesn't think you won't do your job, but he's disappointed, and I think it's because you don't get him. It's important to him that you do.'

'Why?'

'Steven Harte appears to have formed emotional attachments with the girls he's taken, and whether you like it or not, he appears to be forming one with you.'

FORTY-FIVE

It was exactly 8 a.m. when Kim received the call that Harte's lawyer had arrived. It was no later than 8.01 a.m. that Kim groaned upon learning who it was.

'It's Kate Swift, people,' Kim said, putting down the phone.

A collective groan travelled around the room until it reached Alison.

'Who's Kate Swift?'

'An ambitious, ruthless but brilliant solicitor who normally encourages her clients to go along the no-comment route. She's a cool fish. We've had her here a couple of times, but not many of our normal clients can afford her prices.'

'You think he'll close up now?' Bryant asked.

Kim shrugged. After what Alison had said, it depended on how badly he wanted to punish her.

'Stace?' she asked, feeling the noose begin to tighten around her neck.

'Going as quick as I can, boss,' she said, without looking up.

'Be back in a minute,' Kim said, heading out the door.

Maybe a quick word with his solicitor would help move things along, she thought to herself as she descended the stairs.

· · ·

'Ms Swift, good to see you again,' Kim said, standing in the doorway to the foyer.

If Alison could see her now, she'd be screaming, 'Liar.'

'We'll bring your client through shortly, but if I could just take a minute of your time.'

'Just a minute,' she said, looking at her watch pointedly.

The woman had not changed since the last time they'd met. She still wore a smart navy trouser suit with heels that lifted her a good three inches. Her white shirt was crisp and clean. Her long black hair was tied in a ponytail that stretched halfway down her back. Her face was attractive and not needing much cosmetic enhancement.

'Obviously I'm eager to speak with my client.'

'Your client has abducted an eight-year-old girl. We need to know where she is.'

'That's your job, Inspector, not mine.'

Any hope Kim had of appealing to the woman's humanity was disappearing fast.

'Ms Swift, we're pretty sure he's responsible for the abduction and murder of Melody Jones, twenty-five years ago. Your client is dangerous.'

'Has he confessed to any crime?'

'Not yet.'

'And he's been arrested and not charged?'

'That's correct.'

'Then you have suspicion but no evidence?'

'Oh, we will have,' Kim said, realising she was getting nothing from this woman.

'Then I suggest you get it by three o'clock this afternoon or my client will be walking out of here and back to his life.'

Kim had the urge to reach out and slap the polite formality out of her.

She had the feeling Kate Swift's client could have been witnessed setting fire to her own grandmother and she'd still want a DNA test done on the matches.

'We will get him, Ms Swift,' Kim warned, opening the door to let her through.

'We'll see, Inspector. We'll see.'

FORTY-SIX

Less than five minutes after letting Kate Swift onto the premises, Kim saw Mitch pull into the car park with the trailer.

Although the request had been put in yesterday, the team's priority had been in searching the house. He'd assured her he'd be here bright and early to impound the car.

She would swear she heard her whole team sigh with relief when she headed out to meet him. She was like a ticking clock pacing around the squad room. They had just over an hour and a half before she had to go and release Harte without charge. Once that email landed in her inbox, her hands were tied.

She grabbed the evidence bag holding the keys to the Mercedes Estate as she passed by the front desk and met Mitch as he was positioning the tow truck.

'Wanna go over it together before I hitch her up?'

Kim nodded and offered him the evidence bag.

'Anything at the house?' she asked while he completed the chain-of-evidence forms.

He shook his head. 'We're looking for something two feet square in a property the size of a small village. Nothing found to link him to Grace Lennard yet.'

Kim wasn't expecting it. The timeline suggested he wouldn't have had the time to take her to his home and then to wherever he'd stashed her.

If she was right about Steven Harte being the kidnapper, Grace Lennard had been in this car.

'It's very clean,' Mitch observed, opening the rear door.

'Too clean,' Kim said. There was nothing in the rear of the car.

She considered her own car boot. There was de-icer and a scraper that never got removed during the summer months, a pair of muddy boots for when she took Barney for a walk in the rain, a foot pump just in case, a bottle of water for the occasional radiator overheat, amongst other stuff.

'Mine's got more crumbs than the floor of Greggs bakery, as well as tools, carrier bags and all kinds of shit that doesn't need to be there. I treat my car like another room,' Mitch said.

Most people did, Kim thought, looking around for the source of the sickly sweet smell that was now escaping from the confined space.

She found it in the front passenger footwell.

'Summer rose air freshener,' she said, looking around the front of the car. It was spotless – nothing in the door pockets, nothing on the console, nothing on the floor.

'Excuse me,' Mitch said from behind.

He reached in and opened the glovebox. Empty.

'He prepared it beforehand,' Kim said. There was no way he could have fitted in this level of cleaning between depositing Grace wherever he'd left her and arriving at the station.

Mitch moved to the back of the car, removed his glove and began to touch certain points above the wheel arches and behind the back seats.

'Sticky. Four corners of the space. He taped some kind of covering and then threw it away somewhere. Reduces our chances of finding anything significant.'

Of course it did, Kim thought, but her mind was focused on the only thing that had been left in the car.

'Check for urine,' Kim instructed, patting the carpet in the back of the car. There had to be a reason for the air freshener. He'd been trying to mask the smell of something, and he'd had a terrified eight-year-old girl in the back.

'Anything else?' Mitch asked, closing the front passenger door.

Kim stood away from the vehicle, wondering exactly what else it could tell them. She'd already seen there was no satnav that she could interrogate.

'The tyres,' she said. 'Take samples from each tyre before you move it.'

The results from any kind of analysis on the car were not going to be immediate.

She took an anxious look at her watch and headed back upstairs.

The clock was ticking.

FORTY-SEVEN

Alex wondered if she'd ever get bored of replaying last night's conversation over and over in her head.

Just seeing Kim again after so long was almost enough, but being able to witness the beginnings of the rollercoaster she'd set in motion had been just perfect.

Those hours, the months, the years of keeping in touch with Patty had been worth it. She had known if she persevered for long enough, she'd get something she could use.

When she'd started laying the groundwork to ask the question, she'd never realistically expected an answer. The technique had been quite simple. In every letter she would ask Patty questions about her teens, then her early twenties. Any response would then be magnified. If Patty had said she loved to go to the seaside, Alex would reply back with a dozen questions about the seaside. Who did she go with? How did she get there? Eventually she'd mentioned a 'him' and the 'him' had turned into a first name and then a surname. If she'd had a wish list of information she'd hoped to gain, the identity of Kim's father would have been right there at the top. She was surprised Patty could remember, but according to Patty, he had been the only one.

Alex tried to imagine the thoughts that might have been going through the inspector's mind. She would think that Kim would be filled with rage that she, of all people, had been trusted with the information.

If she knew Kim at all, she'd guess that her thoughts would have turned to curiosity. That same need to know that had brought her here. She could imagine all the possibilities that were running around her head. Was he alive? Was he a good person? Had he known about them? Did he have a family? Did she have relatives?

Kim had spent more than thirty years thinking the only blood relative she had left was the woman she hated with every cell of her being. How would she be reacting to the possibility of family, and how best would Alex be able to manipulate those feelings if she chose to?

Knowing Kim, she wanted another little Mikey to replace the one she'd lost, and if that was her motivation to return with a letter recommending her release, all the better.

She pushed the pleasurable thoughts away for now. The conversation would keep her company for hours to come, but right now she had to focus on plan B. And this particular plan she was hatching was going to result in death.

It was just a case of how much.

FORTY-EIGHT

'Stacey, I'm not kidding. If you can do anything to fray my nerves just a little bit more, I'd appreciate it.'

Stacey said nothing.

'Stace, it's three minutes to ten and—'

'A whole two minutes has gone by since the last time you told me. Of the five potentials, I've managed to get four sets of dental records. I'm waiting for the fifth. What more do you want me to do?'

'There's an email gonna land in the next few minutes which will force me to go down there...'

Stacey's email tinged at the exact same second as hers. She put her phone face down on the desk. She knew what hers was going to say.

'Stace?'

'Shh...'

'Stace?'

'Just give me—'

'Stace, we don't have—'

'It's a match,' she cried, throwing pieces of paper in the air.

'Thank God for that,' Kim said as a cheer travelled around the room.

Stacey let out a huge sigh of relief and then sobered. 'Boss, sorry I shushed you.'

'It's okay. Print me the details of our victim.'

She picked up her phone and opened the email from Keats which stated exactly what she'd expected. The body at Hawne Park wasn't Melody Jones.

She typed an email response to Keats.

Thank you for this report. We have identified the victim and will send along details shortly.

We appreciate your assistance.

She waited for just a moment as Stacey collated the details. Keats's response was short.

Good to know.

She sent a silent thank you to the cranky pathologist who only ever took the side of the victim. Without that call last night, she would now be on her way to let Steven Harte go.

She took the piece of paper from the printer. 'Bryant, you ready to...?'

'Take someone else, guv,' he said, without taking his eyes from the keyboard. 'There's something here I want to check out.'

'Okay,' she said, nodding towards Stacey, 'Come on, hero of the hour – you're with me.'

FORTY-NINE

Kim and Stacey headed down to the interview suite in silence. Never far from Kim's mind was the image of Grace Lennard. They were approaching forty-eight hours and Kim had to wonder about the girl's access to food, water and fresh air. She ignored the voice that said there was a chance these needs were no longer a problem for the little girl.

She pushed the thoughts away as she entered interview room one.

Harte and his lawyer appeared to be sitting in silence.

Stacey closed the door behind them.

Kim took a seat, switched on the tape and introduced herself.

'And with me is Detective Constable Stacey Wood.'

She paused.

'Mr Harte, we have received notification that the remains found at Hawne Park do not belong to Melody Jones. On that note, you are no longer being held in connection with the abduction and murder of Melody Jones.'

A faint look of triumph passed over the face of Kate Swift, but Harte's expression showed no surprise.

'We have identified the body as six-year-old Lexi Walters, who was abducted from Leasowes Park on the seventeenth of August 1998. I am therefore now arresting you for the kidnap and murder of Lexi Walters. You do not have to say anything. But it may harm your defence if you do not mention when questioned something which you later rely on in court. Anything you do say may be given in evidence.'

She paused and took a second of pleasure in the surprise that he quickly tried to hide.

There was no doubt that he'd expected them to find the body, but she suspected he hadn't thought they would identify her so soon.

Both of them waited for her to say more.

She pushed back her chair. 'I'm sure that gives you two more to talk about, so we'll give you some time.'

Now she had to go and inform Lexi's parents that they could finally bring their little girl home.

FIFTY

Kim left Woody's office and headed back to the squad room. She had taken the opportunity to update her boss after her conversation with Harte and his lawyer.

'And Keats just happened to ring you to tell you that there was a delay in sending you the email confirming that the remains didn't belong to Melody Jones?' Woody had asked.

'Absolutely.'

'But he didn't tell you what the report said?'

'Absolutely not.'

'So when did you start looking for alternative victims?'

'First thing this morning, sir. Just a gut thing but I can assure you that no rules were broken, and Steven Harte and his lawyer were informed of the findings within minutes of the email coming through.'

'By which time you happened to have correctly identified the remains?'

'Yes, sir.'

He raised an eyebrow.

'Police work happens in mysterious ways, sir.'

Assured that nothing improper had occurred, Woody had

commenced writing a report on the timeline of events which would be entered into evidence and would cover her back and other parts of her anatomy.

'Good work, guys,' Kim said, walking back into the room.

A pensive silence met her arrival.

'Who died?' she asked, looking around.

'No one, but Bryant has found something you're not going to like.'

How had Bryant uncovered anything? He'd been given the job of background checking the builder.

'It's Jenson Butler, guv,' he said, turning to his computer. 'The man was questioned back in '96 in connection with the disappearance of Melody Jones.'

Every positive feeling deserted her.

Was there really a chance they had just arrested the wrong man?

FIFTY-ONE

'You don't think we should have gone to see Gum first?' Bryant said as they headed towards Mucklow Hill.

The knowledge that Inspector Wrigley had spoken to the building company owner twenty-five years ago was still spinning around her head. She wanted to speak to both men as a matter of urgency, but one other visit came first.

'Nope, I think this family has waited long enough, don't you?'

'Fair point,' he said.

'So, you wanna do a bit more data mining instead of being out...?'

'Hell, no,' he said, shaking his head. 'I can barely find my way around a squirty keyboard with two fingers...'

'Qwerty,' she corrected.

'See, what the hell kind of word is that?'

'Oh, Bryant, shut up and drive.'

'Well, it's not like we had far to go,' he said, taking the first right after the B&Q Island.

The houses were a mixture of detached and semi-detached properties that were built in the mid-nineties. The new red brick used on every property showed some signs of weathering, but the buildings still looked like members of the same family.

Bryant parked in front of one of the detached properties with an immaculate garden.

As they stepped onto the path, an attractive woman in her mid-fifties stepped out of the box porch, holding a cup of coffee. She was clearly headed for a bench in the corner that was bathed in the morning sun.

'Mrs Walters?' Kim asked.

The woman nodded and waited.

Kim introduced them both as they showed their IDs.

She chose her next words carefully. She didn't want this woman to feel any false hope for even a minute, and any sentence that began with 'we've found Lexi' could give the wrong impression.

'Mrs Walters, would you like to take a seat?'

She shook her head and waited.

'Mrs Walters, the remains of a young girl have been found at Hawne Park.'

'Is it Lexi?' she whispered.

Kim nodded. 'Confirmed by dental records.'

The mug slipped from her grip and smashed on the ground.

Not one of them looked at it.

'Let's go inside,' Kim advised, touching the woman on the elbow.

She turned as though in a dream, and the two of them followed.

Kim was surprised when they walked directly into the kitchen on the front of the house.

'It's why we bought it,' Mrs Walters said, filling the kettle.

'No, thank you,' they both answered.

'Please, have tea,' she said, with her back turned.

'Okay, thank you,' Kim said, understanding that she needed a minute to allow the news to sink in. One of the hardest things to deal with was the hope. It had kept her company for twenty-three years and now she had to let it go.

'You're sure it's Lexi?' she asked.

'Yes.'

'H-How old was she when she died?' she asked, spooning coffee into the cups. She then added a tea bag, and Kim was thankful that there was no expectation to drink them.

'No older than seven,' Kim said gently.

Lexi had been taken in 1998 when she was six, and the building works had been completed towards the end of '99, before the millennium.

Many years this woman had waited with hope for the return of her daughter, and for twenty-two of those years, the hope had been futile. But Kim was surprised to see what looked like a sigh of relief shudder through her back.

'Is Mr Walters...?'

'Dead. Two years ago next month. He never got over it; neither of us did,' she said, placing the hot drinks on the table at which they'd sat.

Bryant glanced her way. He'd obviously noted the mistake too.

Mrs Walters sat. 'My husband eventually wanted us to try again for more children, but I couldn't. All I could think was that if Lexi came back, she'd think we'd tried to replace her. I couldn't bear the thought of trying to love another child, to play with it, to laugh with it while Lexi was going through God knows what.' Another shudder passed over her but of a different kind. 'Just another layer of guilt, and I didn't deserve the happiness of a second chance.'

She paused and looked from Kim to Bryant and back again.

'I'm sorry, you must think I'm awful. I haven't cried yet. I don't understand why not.'

'Please don't apologise, Mrs Walters. Your brain is dealing with many emotions. It'll process them one at a time. The tears will come and then you can begin to grieve.'

She nodded.

'Mrs Walters, can you tell us what happened that day, at the park?' Kim asked.

'Not sure how much it matters now but of course. It was a weekday and I'd had to take the day off work at short notice. It was the school holidays and my childcare arrangements for that day had fallen through. There were quite a few other kids there, but I didn't really know anyone. I only looked away for a minute. I was an accountant, and Paul was an account executive for a petrol company. We were both ambitious. I wanted it all and I ended up with nothing.'

Kim waited.

'I never went back to work,' she said, regretfully. 'I couldn't face it. Felt too guilty and too angry.'

'About what?'

'My boss hadn't been thrilled with my last-minute request for time off. I took a work call and got caught up with trying to resolve whatever problem it was. I was distracted and took my eye off my child. It seemed like just a minute, but when I finished the call and looked around, she was gone.'

'One parent thought she'd seen Lexi heading off towards the ducks. I searched every inch of that park, but I knew she was gone and that it was my fault.'

Sadness filled her eyes as she stared off into the distance, reliving the whole event.

'Mrs Walters…'

'Please don't waste your breath, Inspector; when I say I looked away for a minute, I'm trying to excuse myself in your eyes. It was probably closer to ten or fifteen. I resented being at the park. I wanted to be at work. Of course, it wasn't until we lost her that we both realised we hadn't made enough time for our child.'

Kim appreciated the woman's candour but still felt she was being too hard on herself.

Bryant leaned forward. 'You can't blame yourself, Mrs Walters. You didn't ask anyone to take your child. Lexi should have been safe at the park. The person who took her is to blame, not you.'

The woman offered him a look that said she was grateful for the sentiment, but she would stick with the feelings that had kept her company for decades.

She continued. 'A massive search was arranged. Less people turned up each day. Contact with the police got less and less. They assured us that the case would remain open and that any fresh leads would be followed up. Then everyone went on with their lives except for us. We waited and hoped and waited.'

She sighed. 'The news you bring me is in many ways a relief. There's no more waiting and no more imagining the pain she might be going through. In the years since, with trafficking becoming more common, my nightmares turned to visions of Lexi being abused and trapped and beaten and—'

Kim held up her hand as the woman's eyes began to redden. This conversation was no longer in the abstract. It was real and the emotion was coming.

'Mrs Walters, your daughter was alive for only one year after she was taken.'

The tears were rolling openly over her cheeks now.

'Oh my God, you have no idea how much it means to hear that my baby didn't suffer for years and—'

'Mrs Walters, there are no wounds to her body to indicate prolonged suffering, but the full circumstances of her abduction are not yet clear.'

'Oh, thank God,' she said as the tears now came thick and fast.

Kim took a moment to consider what it was about Lexi that had attracted him. Kim had seen the missing person's photo. Lexi had been a beautiful child, but there was something more at play here.

Suzie had been enduring a miserable home life as her parents had contemplated divorce. Libby had been abused by her uncle. Melody was an invisible child, wanted by no one. So why Lexi?

The word neglect shot into her mind.

In his own sick, distorted view, the man had thought he was doing them all a favour.

FIFTY-TWO

'So how'd the date go?' Alison asked, turning to face her.

'Huh?'

'Giraffe and curry.'

'Food was okay but the conversation was shit,' Stacey said.

'And yet you have this lurking smile on your face,' Alison observed.

Stacey tipped her head. 'How exactly does a smile lurk?'

'It's hovering around your mouth.' Alison slapped her forehead. 'Aah, Devon is back tonight and you're already anticipating the—'

'Alison, shut it,' she said, allowing the smile to break free. And indeed that was the reason for it. No matter what the day brought, Devon would be waiting for her when she got home. And she couldn't wait. Geoffrey had been a very poor substitute.

'You're clearly bored so do you want something to do?' she asked Alison, who was busy drumming her fingers on the desk while staring at an empty screen. She'd just had a conversation with the boss which had done nothing to lighten her workload.

'Oh, how I'd love to be listening in on their conversation,' Alison said.

'Yep, but there are laws against that,' Stacey said. The camera to interview room one had been switched off while Harte consulted with his lawyer for the second time.

'I don't want to listen to his words. I want to listen to his body.'

'And if you happened to just lip-read something he said, we could be looking at a mistrial.'

'Details. Details. Details.'

'I've got jobs you—'

'Not authorised, Stace,' Alison reminded her.

'Details. Details. Details,' Stacey threw back at her even though she knew it was true. Alison was assisting them on a consultancy basis about his behaviour, and it was tempting to try and use her as another pair of hands.

'Anything I can help with?' Penn offered.

'Took your time offering there, buddy. You okay?' she asked, looking closer. There was a line of tension running along his jawbone. Penn was the first person to offer to help anyone, and the fact that he hadn't meant something was distracting him.

'I'm good, thanks, Stace.'

'Jasper okay?' she asked.

The tension line tightened. 'Yeah, he's good.'

'Hey, if there's anything wrong with my cooking buddy, I'll—'

'He's fine. Just leave it.'

The second sentence cancelled out any truth in his assurance that all was well.

'Okay, but if you wanna talk about—'

'He snuck out of Billy's, and he likes a girl,' Penn blurted out.

Stacey waited.

Penn stared at her meaningfully as though she should get it.

'Sorry, Penn. You're gonna have to help me out here. What do you mean he snuck out? Did he go alone? Did Billy's mum not know?'

'I mean he didn't tell me he and Billy were going out. I thought he was just gonna play Xbox.'

'He's sixteen years old. He went out with his mate. Big deal.'

'Don't minimise what he—'

'Well, don't blow it out of proportion then. What part of being sixteen don't you remember? He's a good lad. Don't turn his Down's into your disability.'

'Bloody hell, Stace,' Penn said as some of the tension left his face. 'Don't beat around the bush.'

'Sorry, didn't mean to be harsh, but you gotta trust him. He's amazing and what's wrong with him liking a girl?'

'She doesn't have Down's,' he answered.

'So what?' Alison asked.

'Well, if he ever gets the courage to talk to her, she'll probably reject him and then...'

'Oh, Penn,' Stacey said with despair.

Alison turned towards Penn and took over. 'See these teeth – crooked as a mountain range when I was a kid. Asked a boy out and he said no because of my braces. I mean, his loss, obviously, but it broke my heart.'

Penn smiled tolerantly. 'Not exactly the same thing though. You could straighten your teeth.'

'The heartbreak was real at the time, Penn. The reason didn't matter.'

'Want to know how many times I got rejected because I'm black?' Stacey asked. 'And no amount of braces was gonna change that. What we're saying is that heartbreak when you're a teenager is inevitable, matey. It's going to happen and you can't protect him from everything.'

Penn held up his phone. 'He's texted. He wants to stay at Billy's again tonight.'

'Bloody hell, that kid gets out more than I do,' Alison said.

Stacey caught his gaze. 'You know, Penn, maybe if you had a bit more going on in your own social life, you wouldn't be obsessing so much over loosening the reins on Jasper.'

'Okay, I feel truly outnumbered now so let's get back to your work problem, Stace, cos I can't cope with both of you.'

'I'm just not sure how much the boss's new criteria is gonna help me narrow these girls down.'

'I thought you were down to a shortlist of five,' Alison said.

'That was for girls that went missing in '98. We've got a whole new batch to consider for the year 2000. I'll check any details against the dental records I've already got, but none of these others fit the specifics I've just had from the boss.'

'Which are?' Penn asked.

'Troubled, possibly abused, neglected or something?' she said, turning back to the screen.

'Why? Grace is none of the above,' Alison said.

'How do we know?' Penn asked.

'Boss said they're a proper little team,' Stacey said. 'I've checked out the whole family and there is absolutely no evidence of any kind of mistreatment.'

'Not always obvious to outsiders,' Alison said. 'And as she's the current victim, the one who we're hoping is still alive, I'd be focusing on—'

'Without actually ringing up Claire Lennard and asking if she beats, starves or neglects her child, I have absolutely no way— Oh, hang on,' Stacey said, pressing a few keys. The day-care centre had sent over all the footage they had of Grace for the day she disappeared. There were seven files, the last two being what the boss had already viewed at the scene on Monday. It had all been sent to Ridgepoint for the techies to interrogate forensically.

She loaded the footage of the events later in the day. Grace wasn't hard to spot given the photo on the board.

Stacey watched as the little girl appeared for the roll call as all the staff and children gathered outside the shed at the end of the garden. Grace stepped in and out of the sunlight as she moved around the groups. Stacey couldn't help but smile at the obvious excitement of something out of the ordinary happening on a bright, sunny August day. As the sun moved slowly around, the group was cut in half by the shadow being cast from the shed.

Stacey watched the girl for any signs of isolation, sadness, of Grace appearing withdrawn or uncomfortable. She saw nothing as the girl bobbed around amongst her peers.

Stacey continued to watch her until the moment they were allowed to resume normal activities. Grace stepped out of the shadow of the shed and into the sunlight as she headed back to the planting spot out of sight.

Stacey's smile turned to a frown as she rewound the footage by just ten seconds to where Grace stepped out of the shade and into the sun.

She watched it again and the frown stayed on her face.

'What's up?' Alison asked from across the room.

'Maybe nothing but give me a minute. There's something I need to check.'

Stacey went back to the first file of footage to see if her suspicion was correct.

FIFTY-THREE

'Wait here,' Kim said as Bryant parked the car in front of an end terrace less than a mile away from The Dog in Tipton. Gum's registered address was within staggering distance of his favourite watering hole.

The exterior of the property appeared to be a visual representation of the man himself: neglected, worn out, unkempt, derelict. No one else needed to see what his life had become.

Bryant took no offence as he undid his seat belt and sat back in his chair.

She got out of the car and waded through the weeds and moss-covered path to get to the house. Four bin liners of rubbish were attracting a colony of flies outside his front door. The stench was overpowering.

She knocked the door, already wondering if she really wanted to enter, but those thoughts were pushed aside by the knowledge that this man had once been a great detective and many families owed him for achieving justice on their behalf.

'What the fuck do you want?' he asked, opening the door.

'A minute of your time,' she said, keeping his arrest and conviction record in her mind.

'You can buy it at The Dog at seven o'clock,' he said, attempting to close the door, but her foot was already in the way.

'Just a minute, Gum – that's all I want.'

He swore and stepped aside. His foot brushed another bin liner that was waiting to be put outside.

'Some little shit has nicked my wheelie bin again, and the council won't collect black bags anymore.' He shook his head as Kim walked past the bag that was starting to smell as bad as its buddies just outside the front door.

He guided her into the kitchen and picked up a can of beer from a collection on the kitchen work surface. He'd brought her into a room where there was nowhere to sit, and she wasn't sure she would have wanted to anyway. The smell in the kitchen was a mixture of old frying fat and alcohol.

'I remember when we had real bin men, the ones that picked up your tin bin, chucked it over their shoulder and tossed the contents into the back of the truck before putting it back outside your front door.'

'Gum, why did you question Jenson Butler in connection with Melody's disappearance?'

'Because we knew him?' he answered quickly, with no pauses for recollection. Despite the abuse to his body, his brain was still sharp, and it appeared that every memory associated with Melody's disappearance was still fresh in his mind.

She leaned back against the countertop and folded her arms. 'How?'

He swigged the last of his budget beer and tossed the can towards the bin. It missed. He reached behind and opened another.

'One of my first jobs as a detective back in '89 was to take the statement of a girl and her parents claiming she'd been raped by Jenson Butler.'

'Are you kidding me?' she asked.

'Her name was Sylvie and she was thirteen years old.'

'Oh, shit,' she said, pushing her hands into her pockets.

'Obviously, he claimed it was consensual, and they'd met after a pub crawl to celebrate something or other to do with his education.'

'He was at university?' she asked.

'Final year.'

'So how did he get out of it?' Kim asked, trying to fathom the complexities this added to her case.

'He didn't. He was convicted of the crime and served twenty-four months.'

Kim shook her head. 'Gum, that stuff has finally got to your brain. There's no conviction record on the PNC, and nothing on the Sex Offenders Register.' Both of these would have been checked by her colleague and flagged up to her.

'Sex Offenders Register didn't start until '97 and wouldn't have been indefinite anyway, as he was sentenced to less than thirty months.'

Okay, she got that, but his conviction should still be on his record.

'Butler pleaded no contest.'

Kim rolled her eyes. Pleading no contest meant that while you weren't admitting guilt, you were allowing the court to determine your punishment.

'But his conviction would still have to remain on record until he's one hundred years old,' she said, citing the rules for data retention.

He took a swig of his drink and nodded. 'Those are the rules now and in place since 2006, but before that a process called "weeding" was carried out.'

She'd heard the term and understood that it meant the removal of convictions and all associated evidence like fingerprints and DNA.

'It wasn't an automated system and there was little rhyme or reason to the process, but some crimes that should have been kept weren't, and some that should have been destroyed were kept. Hence the need for an automated system that can count to one hundred.'

'Bloody hell, Gum, why didn't you say any of this the other day?'

'You never mentioned his name as a person of interest, and there was nothing to tie Butler to Melody's abduction. We expected him to lawyer up immediately but he didn't.'

'Why's that?'

'Because he had a pretty solid alibi of being on a construction site thirty miles away with more than a dozen members of his team, a site foreman and the main contractor.'

'Jesus Christ,' she said, rubbing at her forehead.

'Is he a person of interest now?' Gum asked, narrowing his gaze. His eyes were bright and alert, and he had barely touched his beer since they'd started talking.

'Right now, Gum, your guess is as good as mine,' she said, heading out of the kitchen. She needed air for more reasons than the overwhelming stench of filth.

She needed to process the fact that Steven Harte was doing business with a convicted sex offender.

FIFTY-FOUR

Kim hadn't expected to be back at Butler's premises quite so soon.

'Mr Butler is in a meeting,' Barbara said. 'I can't disturb him,' she added, looking flustered.

It was clear the woman had a very different working relationship with Butler Junior than she'd had with Butler Senior.

'I'm afraid we must insist, and if your boss would prefer us to sit in here wearing full high-vis uniform until his visitors leave, that can be arranged.'

There, the woman had something to threaten him with that had come directly from her.

'I'll be back in a minute,' she said, leaving the reception area.

'Isn't it strange how one piece of information about someone can change your entire opinion about that person?' Bryant asked once they were alone. 'I remember before becoming a police officer, I worked with a bunch of guys in a warehouse. One guy, salt of the earth, do anything for you. Most popular guy in the place until he let out in conversation he often drank and drove. Most folks cooled towards him after that.'

Kim understood what he meant in relation to Butler. Yesterday they'd viewed the pictures on the wall, impressed by the scope of his works, the growth of the company, the number of employees from the local area. All of those things were still true today and yet none of it counted for anything after what they'd learned.

'Inspector, what is the meaning of this interruption? Your demands will not—'

'Mr Butler, I suggest we take this somewhere private.'

'I don't need privacy to tell you that I am not available to speak right now. Please make an—'

'This is your last warning to make this private, Mr Butler; otherwise we will have this conversation now and we will have it here.'

He hesitated before huffing and motioning for them to follow him.

They passed the glass meeting room they'd used the day before and entered a much smaller room with a round wooden table and four chairs.

'Inspector, please give me the name of your superior officer, as I fully intend to make a formal complaint against you.'

'His name is DCI Woodward and he's used to it. As you're in a rush, I'll get right to it. Is there any reason you chose not to tell us you're a convicted sex offender?'

He opened his mouth to argue and then fell into a chair.

She waited for an answer to her question.

'I don't tell everyone I meet.'

'Not even the police officers who are investigating the abduction of young girls?'

He shook his head. 'It has nothing to do with me.'

'Your company carried out the construction work where our victim was buried. Do you want to tell us more about it or do you want to give your lawyer a call? Either way we're going to have the conversation.'

'It was a mistake,' he said, rubbing furiously at his forehead. Kim was sure Alison would tell her that he was trying to rub the memory away.

She offered her own non-verbal communication. She folded her arms and said nothing.

'I was celebrating the end of term. I was drunk, and she looked much older.'

'Which defence would you like to use, Mr Butler?'

'A bit of both, but I swear I didn't know her true age. She told me she was seventeen.'

'And she was?'

'It happened a week before her fourteenth birthday.'

'So she was thirteen?' Kim asked to be clear.

Bryant put his hands in his pockets as Butler winced at her words.

'She looked much older; she was wearing make-up, mature clothes. She looked old enough.'

'For sex?'

He nodded. 'I swear I didn't know. It was totally consensual. I was roaring drunk. I can't even remember.'

'Mr Butler, which defence would you like to stick to: that it was consensual, you were roaring drunk or you can't remember? Both the second and third would prevent an accurate recollection of the first.'

When his brain caught up with her words, the colour flooded his face.

'The accusation came from her parents, not the girl.'

'I would imagine that it was the girl that told her parents. So it's the same thing really. Ultimately, she was thirteen years old. Were you charged with statutory rape?'

'Yes.'

'And you pleaded no contest.'

He nodded. 'Maybe I should have tried to fight it, pleaded not guilty, but I was advised to offer no plea and accept the punishment.'

'Which was?'

'A three-year sentence and forty hours of community service. It wasn't fully explained to me that I'd likely spend more than a year in prison.'

'Sue your lawyer,' Kim said without sympathy. His right to understanding the rules had disappeared when he'd slept with a minor.

'And you were questioned in connection with the disappearance of Melody Jones in '96?'

'Briefly,' he said, as though it was a minor event that he'd forgotten. 'But I wasn't even in the area when that girl disappeared.'

That girl.

'And I had a cast-iron alibi that—'

'Was provided by people that work for you,' she clarified.

'I wasn't there, and I'm not a pervert,' he protested strongly.

Kim neither agreed nor disagreed. The facts were the facts.

'You were at university when you were convicted of rape?' Kim asked, having a sudden thought.

He nodded.

'And you say you sought advice from those around you?'

'Yes.'

'Was one of those people Steven Harte?'

'Most likely. He was an intelligent, trustworthy guy, so yes, there's a good chance I asked him for his advice.'

So Steven Harte had known the man was a sex offender and had chosen to do business with him anyway.

FIFTY-FIVE

Stacey had wanted to be completely sure before she said anything to her colleagues and, most importantly, the boss. After reviewing all of the footage of Grace Lennard from the day of the abduction, she was pretty sure she was right.

'Alison, Penn, come take a quick look at this,' she said.

Penn wheeled his chair around the desks, and Alison followed behind.

Stacey had taken all the clippings of Grace from that day and formed a slow-motion montage.

Once they were in position she played it.

Grace in the huddle with the others.

Grace moving back to the vegetable garden.

Grace entering the premises first thing wearing a yellow cardigan.

Grace in the kitchen having a biscuit and a glass of juice without the cardigan.

'Stace, what are we supposed to be looking—?'

'Just watch,' she said, noting that Alison was already starting to peer in more closely.

Grace in the hallway taking something from her unicorn backpack.

Grace heading outside just behind a couple of other girls.

'Play that bit again,' Alison said.

It was the bit where Stacey's finding was most obvious. She rewound and froze the frame.

'Ah,' Alison said.

Penn shook his head. 'I still don't— Oh, yeah. Is that what I think it is?'

Yes, that was exactly what he thought it was.

Grace Lennard had a whopping great bruise all down the left side of her arm.

FIFTY-SIX

'You know when you're just not convinced,' Bryant said, heading towards the home of Claire Lennard.

She had listened silently as Stacey had called through her findings once they'd finished speaking with Jenson Butler. Her immediate reaction had come from her stomach, which had reacted against the thought that Claire Lennard had in any way harmed her child.

'For once we agree on something,' she said as Bryant entered the area of Kate's Hill.

'Everything in that house screamed love and warmth. Did you see the little clay model figures?'

Kim nodded. She had noticed them too. It looked like a family of three modelled from craft clay that had clearly been done by a child, but it took pride of place between two family photos on the fireplace. It was always the small things.

'Got no choice but to have the conversation though,' she said, even though her stomach was rebelling against it.

The unease did not lessen as Bryant parked behind Bernadette's Ford Fiesta, which appeared to be in the same spot it had been on Monday.

The liaison officer answered the door with a smile.

'You not been home yet?' Kim asked, stepping inside.

'Nope. World War Three is raging back at home, and I am remaining Switzerland. I'm needed more here right now.'

'How is she?'

Bernadette sighed. 'As you'd expect, not great. She won't eat, she won't sleep, she won't wash, she paces all the time. The adrenaline is surging around her body and she doesn't know what to do with it. I think she feels she's letting Grace down if she allows any kind of normality to settle. The fact that she's got nothing to do to help find Grace is making things worse.'

Great. Kim was pretty sure that the questions they had for Claire were not going to brighten her day.

'Is that the inspector?' Claire asked, appearing in the doorway from the lounge.

Kim hid her surprise at the appearance of the woman. There was no judgement in the fact she hadn't changed clothes since Monday or that her hair was unwashed and uncombed. Her face was pale, emphasising the red-rimmed eyes that had developed hairline creases on the lower lids.

'We haven't found her yet,' Kim said, answering the only question in her eyes. 'But we are following up leads.'

Fatigue appeared to be slowing her reactions, but it still only took a few seconds for her expression to change to suspicion.

There was no point lying to her. Claire knew that if it was a simple update she was after, she could have called Bernadette. That was her job.

'Shall we sit down, Claire?' Kim asked, stepping towards the doorway to the lounge.

Claire allowed herself to be ushered into the room and took a seat on the two-seater sofa. Kim took the single chair, and Bryant stood just outside the doorway.

Kim turned towards Claire and leaned forward in the most open and non-judgemental stance she could think of.

'Claire, we need to ask you a couple of questions about your relationship with Grace.'

She looked genuinely perplexed, which gave Kim no comfort in having to press on.

'I know the two of you are close but is there any time you've lost your temper with her?'

'Absolutely. There are times when I snap. I'm a single parent, still grieving and I'm only human.'

Kim felt the unease grow in her stomach.

'Have you ever lashed out or pushed—?'

'Get out,' Claire said, standing up and pointing towards the door.

Kim ignored her and remained seated.

'How dare you try and twist my words? When I said snapped, I meant verbally. Sometimes I've shouted when it wasn't necessary. I may have overreacted occasionally.'

'But never physically?' Kim asked evenly.

'Never,' Claire said, sitting back down.

'I'm sorry we have to ask, but Grace has this bruise – it's a big one – on her left arm.'

Claire appeared confused for a second until the fog in her memory cleared.

Kim raised an eyebrow as Claire lifted her T-shirt as high as her lowest rib. 'Does it look a bit like this one?'

'Similar,' Kim said, and waited.

'Paintballing, last week – and before you ask if Grace is too young, they do special days for kids' events. It was a classmate's birthday. They take extra precautions but nothing can defend against a twelve-year-old little shit who wants to break the rules. Got us both.'

Kim was both relieved and curious in equal measure.

'You thought I'd done that to her?' Claire asked.

'We had to ask. We hope you understand.'

Claire looked as though she wanted to argue the point but didn't have the energy.

'Claire, has Grace ever had such bruising visible before?'

She shook her head. 'Not that I can think of. Why?'

Because that means Steven Harte had to have seen Grace some time since the paintballing event to feel that she was being mistreated.

'Claire, there's something I need you to do for me and it may be very important.'

Her earlier defensiveness was forgotten as her eyes lit up with the prospect of doing something to help.

'I need a list of every place the two of you have been since the day that Grace got the bruise. I need the day and the times as close as you can get them.'

'Okay, I can do that but...'

'Trust me, it'll help,' Kim said, standing.

Harte had to have seen her sometime between the paintballing day and Monday lunch time, when she'd been abducted from the day-care centre.

If there was any way they could catch Steven Harte on CCTV at any one of the locations, it could be enough to rattle him into revealing something.

Kim left the house with a feeling of relief at the explanation offered them by Grace Lennard.

You couldn't always tell the kind of person you were dealing with. She had spoken to people not knowing they were murderers, rapists, armed robbers so good was the disguise they adopted, but her gut had told her that Claire Lennard had done nothing wrong. Just as her gut told her that Steven Harte most definitely had.

FIFTY-SEVEN

'I've got one,' Stacey called out. Right after putting the phone down to the boss, she had resumed her search for more potential victims.

'So have I,' Penn cried out straight after.

'Well, aren't I just the party pooper then?' Alison added.

'Eight-year-old Paula Stiles,' Stacey continued. 'Abducted fourteenth of August in 2000 from a day trip to a wildlife park in the Cotswolds. She was on a trip with twenty-six other kids from a children's home in Evesham. Oh, Jeez, look at that face,' she added, turning her screen.

'Just as pretty as the others,' Alison agreed. 'It's in the parameters of his favourite dates, and she was in the care system.'

'Apparently, there was no family member to do the public appeal, and it was done by one of the care workers who actually got her age wrong.'

A sense of sadness stole over Stacey for that fact alone. Who had been waiting for this child to come back? Who had been praying for her safe return? Who had been crying into their pillow because of her absence? However fond the staff had been of Paula Stiles, they'd had another two dozen kids at least to take care of.

'Bloody hell,' Alison said. 'Who the devil did the kid have to come home to?'

'She didn't. That's the point,' Stacey said, feeling a rage begin to burn within her. All these little girls just being picked off as though they were nothing, as though someone felt they had the right to just pluck them from their lives.

'Okay,' Penn said, moving around pieces of paper. 'Should we continue along the same timeline of him keeping them a year?'

'I think we have to,' Stacey said. 'Lexi Walters was taken in '98 and buried in Hawne Park one year later. Same time frame as the ones he brought back.'

'Okay, Harte only worked on one project with Butler in the year following Paula Stiles's disappearance.'

'And?'

'Well, let's just say the boss is gonna love this one.'

FIFTY-EIGHT

'Really, guv?' Bryant asked, as they pulled into the car park of Wyley Court on the outskirts of Bewdley.

'Well, it would suit the history of the place, wouldn't it?'

'Oh yeah, the missus came here a couple of years back and it gave her the heebie-jeebies for days.'

'Bryant, what exactly is a heebie-jeebie?'

'Dunno, but I'm sure they had a hit with "Night Fever" or something.'

Kim rolled her eyes in response.

Wyley Court was an Italianate mansion built in the seventeenth century on the site of a former manor house.

It was sold in the eighteenth century to the Denleys of Northumberland. The family appeared to live relatively peacefully for a couple of years until John Denley began philandering around the local area. One night, in a fit of jealous rage, Eleanor Denley cut the throats of all four of her children before throwing herself from the roof of the building. Unable to bear the loss, John Denley had gifted the house to the village along with a sizeable donation. Trustees from the village were appointed to oversee the upkeep.

When the money had begun to dwindle, the clever Victorians had attracted paying visitors with tales of the macabre and ghostly sightings of the Denley children. The ground floor had been turned into a museum celebrating all things horrific, showcasing the most horrendous murders and attracting visitors from around the world. Over time the site had become known as a paranormal hotspot and now hosted all kinds of ghost-hunting teams that performed vigils and seances.

'How the hell do we find the right person?' Kim asked as they parked in a car park that was already three quarters full.

'Follow the crowds,' Bryant suggested as they fell into step behind a group of Chinese tourists all sporting hefty cameras around their necks.

They reached the end of the queue, which snaked around the building.

Kim walked alongside the waiting line to some loud tuts and filthy looks.

Two ladies dressed in matching black T-shirts were operating a ticket booth at the front of the queue.

'Excuse us,' Bryant said as Kim stepped into the next available gap.

She showed her ID. 'Who's in charge?'

'Er, our day manager is Rory Duncan.'

'Can you get him for us?'

'I'm sorry. He could be anywhere. We're very busy.'

'It's urgent. Please ask him to meet us at the fountain.'

The girl nodded, and Kim stepped out of the way.

Bryant followed her back outside as they passed directional boards pointing them towards 'Ghoulish Gift Shop', 'Horrific Hall-way' and 'Choking Chamber'. The sign for the plain old 'Tea Room' was letting the side down a bit.

'What's the fascination, Bryant?' she asked, standing in front of the 'You are here' board.

'Not sure, guv. I deal with enough horror every day.'

'Absolutely, the scenes we witness…'

'Oh yeah, that as well,' he said, smirking.

'This way,' she said. 'We've got to head through the rose garden, then the cottage garden and the fountain is right in front of the maze.'

'Your orienteering skills are amazing, guv.'

'You know, Bryant, you're always not funny, but there are times when you are even more not funny than usual.'

'Clearly your linguistic skills are—'

'Holy shit,' Kim said as they exited the cottage garden.

Before them was the jewel of the extensive manicured gardens. The lush lawns and planted areas all appeared to have been formed to accommodate the grandeur of the fountain.

'There's not a smaller one somewhere else is there?' Bryant asked with dread in his voice.

Kim found herself hoping the same thing.

The plaque told her it was called 'the Perseus and Andromeda fountain'. The bowl of the fountain was in the shape of an eye. The edge of the fountain was a shin-high stone wall going all the way around. An ornate statue in the middle spouted out twenty jets of water at varying heights, with one vertical spray reaching a good seventy feet into the air.

'I'm gonna guess that this is Rory Duncan coming at us right now,' Bryant said.

The suited man was small but speedy, as though he'd been shot out of the archway that led from the cottage garden.

The lanyard around his neck swung to and fro like a sped-up pendulum.

'Are you the police officers that demanded my immediate attention?'

Kim was quite impressed. It was a good walk from the house to the fountain, and to maintain this level of irritation the whole way showed determination and vigour.

'We are indeed, Mr Duncan. We'd like to know more about this fountain.'

'You summoned me for a history lesson?' he asked, reddening even further. Kim half expected his polka-dot bow tie to start spinning.

'Only recent history, for example the renovation works that were carried out about twenty years ago.'

'Why would you possibly need that information?'

'Just humour us, Mr Duncan. We understand that it was quite a big job.'

'It didn't start out that way. There was an issue with the water supply to the centre statue. Everything external was checked before digging out the actual fountain. We did question ourselves on that decision, but it's a big draw for the people not interested in the gory stuff, and it's an original part of the site, historically integral to the building.'

Kim wondered how historically important 'Choking Chamber' and 'Horrific Hallway' were to the historic integrity of the building.

'One of our benefactors came forward and volunteered to foot the bill to get the fountain working again. He agreed with us about its importance.'

'And did he know the extent of the work involved?'

'None of us did until the excavation work began to determine the cause of the water supply cessation.'

'But it's a fountain,' Kim said, thinking that the water was just recycled from the base over and over again.

'It doesn't replenish to the degree it needs to. Rainwater helps to keep it topped up, but water evaporates in sunlight and as you can see...' He pointed to the sun's position, which told her it was being baked every day.

'In all honesty, we weren't sure of the water source, as previous problems had always been with the fountain heads.'

'So how extensive was the work?' she asked.

'We thought it would be some damaged pipes or worn fittings, but it was nothing of the sort. The well had run dry.'

'Sorry?'

'The water source had been an underground well which had simply run out of water.'

'And your benefactor didn't mind the rising cost?'

'No, he was very generous. He even brought in his own construction company to ensure it was done properly.'

I bet he did, Kim thought.

'So what work was required?'

'The crew had to dig down a good ten feet to make the well safe and then install a brand-new water replenishment system that feeds right from a collection tank, and which is also hooked into the water mains if the system ever gets too low.'

'Sounds like a lot of thought and work went into the project.'

'It did, but Mr Harte was very hands-on. He was here at all hours checking the progress. They were both incredibly diligent.'

'By both you mean Mr Harte and Mr Butler.'

He appeared surprised that she knew both names.

'Absolutely, yes. Their hard work and commitment, not to mention money, has ensured that this little beauty need never be disturbed again.'

Kim took a moment to consider everything she'd learned in order to make a judgement call.

There was the history and integrity of the fountain. The upheaval to the property and their business; the inconvenience to them and their customers. On the other hand, there was the involvement in the project of both Steven Harte and Jenson Butler, as well as the possibility that a little girl rested beneath it.

She turned to the day manager. 'I'm sorry, Mr Duncan, but we're going to dig it up.'

FIFTY-NINE

Alex headed to her first meeting of the day. There were two pieces to put in place today and a third tomorrow, which would pretty much guarantee her release with or without the inspector's recommendation.

Stone was her failsafe. Her last resort if her carefully constructed plot went wrong. She was the cherry on top of the cake, and what a delicious cherry she was.

It took her only a moment to spot Stella in the dinner hall. She was at the far end sitting next to Titch, a blonde woman of generous proportions in both height and width.

Stella Mackinley was serving ten years for running a crystal meth lab out of a barn in rural Warwickshire. So volatile had been the equipment and chemicals that police had been unable to enter until deemed safe by the fire service.

There were few things that bothered the women collectively, but anything that involved harming children got their attention. And Stella had sold to teens.

The drug itself was known to be highly addictive due to the long-lasting euphoric effect, a high that went on for as long as twelve hours, much longer than cocaine.

Knowing that she was unlikely to last the stretch unharmed, Stella had wasted no time in enlisting the first muscle she had come across. Titch would do anything for a couple of extra quid to shovel down the gummy bears she was addicted to. And that was her payment for protecting one of the most hated women in the prison.

There was only one thing that Stella wanted more than protection and that was control. And Alex was going to offer it for a price.

She walked down the food line and headed over to the table, sitting two spaces away from her target.

Both Stella and Titch eyed her suspiciously but continued eating.

Alex reached to her side and positioned the phone at the edge of her pocket. She adjusted her position on the seat.

The phone made a noise as it met with the ground. Alex paused one second before reaching to pick it up. She made a show of looking around.

'That a fucking phone?' Stella asked, still looking at the spot on the floor where it had landed.

Alex said nothing and continued to eat.

Stella scooted across to the seat that had separated them.

'I said, is that a fucking phone?'

'Shh,' Alex said, looking around. She knew no one else had seen or heard.

'I need to use it.'

Of course she did. She had an empire to run, and it wasn't easy with recorded phone calls.

Having the ability to call Inspector Stone directly had been nice, but this had been her real plan all along.

'Can't do. I need it. I've got calls to make.'

'Give me that fucking phone or you'll be eating a mouthful of fist.'

'From who?'

She inclined her head towards Titch.

Alex smiled in response and leaned around her.

'Hey, Titch, that iPod still working okay for you?'

She nodded while scraping up the last of her cold custard.

'Sound, mate, sound.'

Who knew that a cheap device loaded with Barry Manilow songs would buy her protection for her entire stretch? She had known. She had made it her business to know and that's why she always got what she wanted.

Stella's face creased in irritation. Titch would never touch her.

'Threatening me is never going to get you what you want.'

'So what is? You want me to fix you up with some...?'

'Not a chance. I wouldn't touch your filthy product.'

'So you're just like all these other bitches in here. Wanna shank me the first chance you get.'

'If you want honesty, Stella, I don't give one fuck how many lives you've taken or ruined with your pharmaceutical enterprise. Neither would I care if you'd been wrongly convicted and are completely innocent. I don't care.'

She moved to bring her legs from under the table.

Stella put a hand on her arm.

'You want something else?' she asked, licking her lips.

Alex burst out laughing. 'Er... that would be no.'

She stood. 'Sorry, Stella, but there's nothing you have that I want.'

'Not right now,' she said cagily.

Alex almost laughed at the ease of the task.

'Go on.'

'Well, it never hurts to have a favour in the bag, does it? You never know when you might want help with something.'

Alex appeared to give it consideration, as though she hadn't been expecting the offer.

She sat back down. 'Okay, but it won't be today. I've got my own stuff to do.'

'When?'

Alex thought about it. 'Meet me tomorrow in the library. I'm in there working at two. I'll make sure it's private.'

Stella looked to her sidekick.

Alex shook her head. 'Not a word and don't bring her or you're not getting the phone. If she knows anything, she'll tell for two packets of sweets, and I'm not losing this phone for you.'

Stella considered her options. Risk being alone for a short time and get to use the phone or keep her protection and get nothing.

Alex pushed herself up from the table. 'Okay, choice made. See you—'

'No, no. I'll do it. I'll be there but you gotta make sure the place is empty.'

'Oh, you can bank on it,' Alex said, walking away.

As she neared the door, she noticed one particular prisoner watching her closely.

Good. That's what she'd wanted, and it looked as though her second meeting of the day was going to come to her.

SIXTY

'Nothing,' Penn said. 'I can't find one thing on the man.'

The boss had asked him to go deeper on Jenson Butler. They all knew they didn't have enough for an arrest or search warrant. No judge would sign off on it with his tenuous links to the crimes.

The task he'd been given had allowed him to immerse himself in work and push aside his fears about Jasper. He knew that Stacey and Alison thought he should loosen the reins a little bit, but that was harder than they could imagine. The text message from his brother had remained unanswered.

As the older brother it had always been Penn's job to protect Jasper from the cruel comments and curious looks. It was ingrained in him to shield the boy from anything that might hurt him. At Billy's he was safe, playing Xbox and eating pizza. Out in the big wide world he was vulnerable. Jasper loved everyone and felt that everyone loved him. He wouldn't understand if a gang of yobs decided to torment and abuse him. Just the thought of it made him sick to his stomach – Jasper's sweet, innocent nature having to accept that the world wasn't the bouncy castle he thought it was.

Their late mother had spent years preparing him how to take

care of his little brother. She just hadn't versed him on how and when to let him go.

Maybe Stacey was right about his own personal life. He'd set up two different dates to meet up with Lynne, just for a drink and a chat, and both times he'd had to cancel because of work. They hadn't spoken for a while, and he missed her.

'Is Butler too clean?' Alison asked, bringing him back into work mode.

Penn shrugged. 'Not even a hint of impropriety. He's been married for twenty-seven years, has two grown sons who appear to be responsible and respectable. One is training to be a geologist, and the other is finishing med school. His wife volunteers at a group for disadvantaged kids and, before you ask, there's no record of any involvement from Butler himself. No parking tickets, no speeding fines. Nothing.'

'He's in his fifties,' Alison observed. 'Surely there's something.'

Penn shook his head.

'Doesn't that make you think he's being extra careful so as not to attract any police attention to himself?' Alison asked.

'He's created one hell of a safety blanket,' Stacey said.

'Agreed, but it doesn't help us get a warrant,' Penn answered. 'Don't think any judge is going to accept "cos we think he's a bad egg" as justification for turning his life upside down.'

'I sure would like to get a look in Butler's computer to check for indecent images,' Stacey said as her phone rang.

'Hey, Paddy,' she said, putting him on speakerphone. She'd left a message for the lead cyber techie to give her a call.

'It's booby trapped,' he said, knowing exactly what she'd been calling about.

'He's booby trapped his phone?'

'Yep, we got around the facial recognition, but behind it was a password screen.'

'And you can't bypass it?' Stacey asked.

'Not come up with a way yet. There's some kind of app on

there that kicks in if you try to access the information through the back door. Wipes the whole bloody thing. There's no app this tight on the market.'

'He writes them,' Stacey offered.

'Aah, that explains it. I'll keep trying, but if I can't get that password, I risk losing everything.'

'Don't do that,' Penn called across the room. With the absence of any hard drive or computer, this could be the only link to Grace they had. His fierce guarding of the phone with the self-destruct app screamed that there was something on there to find.

'How many characters?' Penn asked.

'Eleven,' Paddy called out louder, realising he was talking to someone on the other side of the room.

'Okay, leave it with me,' Penn said.

'So, we done on the matching up or what?' Stacey asked Penn after ending the call from Paddy.

Penn passed over his printed sheets of Butler's projects.

'If you go any further before we get the results back from Wyley Court, we could have the boss digging up half the West Midlands before you know it.'

'Yeah, but—'

'No, you're right, Stace, but I need to get back to Harte's timeline. We're not gonna get Grace's location from the phone. I need to narrow it down.'

Harte's phone records had shown no activity on his phone from when he'd pinged a tower close to his home at 8 a.m. Monday, and then pinged another three miles away from the station ten minutes before he'd walked through the door.

He took a plain piece of paper and started making notes. His brain worked better if he could see it in black and white.

Grace Lennard had been abducted at 2.30 p.m.

'I've got a nine-year-old girl who went missing in 2002,' Stacey said to no one.

Harte had arrived at the station at 4.30 p.m.

'She's a perfect candidate for Harte's MO.'

Penn tried to block out his colleague's musings as he wrote down '30 mph' as the average speed. Now to try and convert speed and distance, taking into account both locations.

He heard his colleague's exclamations of 'oh shit' as he reached into his drawer for his headphones.

SIXTY-ONE

'They're here,' Kim said, impatiently jumping out of the car.

From the second Rory Duncan had understood her intention, his face had lost every ounce of colour.

He had reached for his phone and so had she. They had walked away from each other like duellists, her trying to action what needed to be done and him trying to stop it.

Her first call had been to Woody, where she'd warned him of the possibility of a complaint from a convicted sex offender.

'Always good to know when they're coming, Stone,' had been his response.

She'd explained her reasons and told him what she needed, and he had taken care of the rest. Her requests were starting to arrive right now.

The first vehicle contained racks of metal fencing.

Once Rory Duncan had understood that he couldn't stop what was happening, he had switched to damage control mode and they had reached a compromise. The inside part of the site could remain open to the public, but all outside access would be prohibited. A fence would be erected to stop members of the public wandering around the outside of the building.

Rory Duncan appeared beside her as the excavator came rolling into the car park. The man looked as though he was about to cry.

'If just one customer impedes the work, Mr Duncan, we will close the place down completely.'

'I understand,' he offered miserably.

She chose not to inform him that should they find anything looking remotely like human bones, the whole site would be shut down anyway. The poor guy had dealt with enough.

The excavator was followed by a loader and behind that were squad cars.

Bryant headed off to brief them.

Mr Duncan's hand went to his stomach. 'Oh dear, all this is really making me feel unwell.'

Kim didn't care to think how the discovery of human remains might affect his delicate constitution.

The vehicles continued to arrive and were attracting the attention of visitors both entering and exiting the site.

A man in jeans and T-shirt with a satchel had stopped to speak to Bryant.

'Is that your guy?'

'Yes, yes, that's Bradley,' he said, with relief, heading off to meet him.

Duncan had called the guy from some kind of historical integrity site, to oversee works and ensure that the least amount of damage was being done. She understood Duncan's concern for the fountain, but it didn't trump her concern for what may lie beneath it.

Duncan was headed back towards her with the man named Brad. She turned her back and walked away as her phone began to ring.

'Go ahead, Stace,' she said, covering her other ear against the sound of voices and machinery.

Other than the odd word, she was struggling to hear. She

ended the call and travelled towards the car, grabbing Bryant en route.

'What?' he said after excusing himself.

'Need to get somewhere quiet to call Stacey back.'

'Why, what did she want?' he asked, opening the car doors.

They both got in, closed the doors and blocked out the noise around them.

'Dunno – couldn't hear a bloody word,' she said, scrolling to the last caller. 'But I think she was trying to say something about finding another one.'

SIXTY-TWO

'Are you kidding me?' Kim asked as they drove through the Nimmings car park entrance to the Clent Hills.

'As I wasn't the one to give you the information, I'm guessing that's aimed at Stacey, and I suspect she wasn't kidding.'

'Do you know how many times I've bought coffee from here?'

'If you seriously want me to have a guess I will, but I'd say we're talking in the hundreds when you've brought the prince for a walk.'

Bryant always used her pet name for Barney because of her treatment of her four-legged friend.

Awful to think she could have been standing on remains every time she'd done so.

'So what did Stacey say?' Bryant asked, making no move to get out the car.

The café was standing room only, filled with dog walkers, ramblers and families. The queue stretched for twenty metres.

'Stacey said a seven-year-old girl went missing in 2002. She was named Helen Blunt, and she was taken from a summer fayre in Shrewsbury.'

'Why this particular girl?' Bryant asked.

'The news reports stated that the girl's mother had shouted at her for dawdling, and that little Helen had stormed off in a mood. The mother admitted to being quite worked up herself, with a toddler and a young baby and seven-year-old Helen, so she didn't calm down and go looking for her for a good twenty minutes.'

'What? In twenty minutes Harte could have travelled at least ten miles in any direction before the alarm was even raised.'

'It gets worse. Eyewitnesses say it was more than a good telling off. They saw the mother give Helen a good shaking and a slap around the face.'

'Oh, Jesus,' Bryant said.

'No leads. Never been found. In 2003, Harte funds the refurbishment of this place, and guess who he employs to do the work?'

'His mate Jenson Butler.'

'Correct.'

'Guv, you know this is problematic, don't you?'

'Nah, Bryant, I'm thinking they're just gonna let me tear their coffee shop down with my bare hands.'

'You know, sometimes you could just answer a question without hostility and sarcasm,' Bryant said as they approached the cabin.

'And where's the fun in that?'

The queue had reduced to no more than a handful of people as they approached the front of the line.

The kiosk was deceptively spacious and easily big enough for the two people cooking and serving inside.

Kim showed her ID.

They looked at each other and then back at her, as though doing their personal inventory of activities in case they'd done anything wrong.

'May I ask how long you ladies have worked here?'

'Too bloody long,' they said together and then laughed.

Kim waited.

'Nine years.'

No good.

'Fifteen full-time and four years part-time. Why?'

Perfect.

'Could we have a word, Brenda?' Kim asked, looking at the badge.

'Course yo con, me wench. What word would yer like?'

'Privately,' Kim said, glancing towards the queue.

Brenda shoved her head out.

'Yer gonna have to wait a minute, love. Abby cor manage this lot on her own.'

'It's kind of urgent,' she pushed, not too concerned about people having to wait an extra minute or two for a drink and a snack.

'Go on, Bren – I'll be fine,' Abby said, nudging her in the arm.

Brenda removed her apron and stepped out the side of the cabin. Seeing no seats available, she motioned for them to follow her round the back.

A small, round table and two wrought-iron chairs were nestled out of sight.

'Sorry,' Brenda said, taking one of the seats. 'Me feet are killing me.'

Bryant motioned for Kim to take the other seat.

She waited while Brenda removed a pack of cigarettes from her pocket and lit one.

'When opportunity knocks, eh?'

Kim was pleased they were the reason for her impromptu fag break.

'You were here when the works were carried out to the café?'

'Oh yeah, right bloody headache that was. Owners insisted we try and keep going while it was being done, over there with a marquee, some urns and a hotplate. We did it though.'

'And the work was instructed by a man named Steven Harte?'

'Dunno his name,' she said. 'Never spoke to me but he was a good-looking bloke. Tony couldn't believe his luck. He'd applied to the council for a grant. The shack was falling apart. He never expected to get the whole thing replaced for free.'

'Go on.'

'Well, that man you mentioned, he took it all very seriously. He spent time here, brought in his construction crew.'

'Jenson Butler?'

Brenda shrugged. 'Dunno – I kept away from all of 'em.'

'Why's that?'

'Cos of the trouble.'

'What trouble? Something happened with Jenson Butler?'

'Only if he's a really big guy with a tattoo on his neck.'

That wasn't Butler, but it sounded like one of his employees who she'd spoken to earlier in the week.

'What happened?'

'Got a bit too fresh with one of the other part-timers, Sasha – sixteen, I think she was. Started with wolf whistles and comments, which she ignored, but then that big bloke tried to corner her round the back of the toilets, tried to touch her. We told Tony, who wasn't having any of that. Anyway, your man was even here for all the drama when Tony kicked the crew off site.'

Kim felt her hopes of getting a yes from Woody dwindling. When Bryant had said it was problematic, he'd meant getting Woody to agree to a second excavation when they'd as yet got no results from the first. A second batch of complaints from business owners was not going to be tolerated. And persuading him otherwise, when Butler hadn't even completed the job, was going along the 'don't even waste your breath on a request' route.

'Your man came back after that bunch had gone. He couldn't apologise enough. It was late in the day but he still took the time.'

Late in the day rang all kinds of alarm bells, but Woody was not going to allow her to dig up this family-owned business because of her suspicion. Maybe if the Wyley Court dig produced something, Woody would hear her out.

'Thanks for your time, Brenda. You've been—'

'Thank goodness they did get thrown off site,' she said.

'Why's that?' Kim asked, retaking her seat.

'Well, the new construction manager suggested moving everything along by about fifty metres, so the seating area wouldn't be obscured by the trees. Better view, and cos the footings hadn't even been—'

'Hang on, are you saying that the café isn't sitting directly on top of the area that was dug by the first building crew?'

'Not even close,' she said, looking to her left. 'See where that bench is?'

Kim did and it was around fifty metres away.

'That's where the first bunch were digging out ready. New guys came and filled it in properly and started digging again.'

Kim felt a smile begin to creep onto her mouth.

Fifty metres wasn't far, but it might be far enough to get her a different answer from her boss.

SIXTY-THREE

It was almost three when Kim returned to the station, and it felt as though she'd been gone for days.

After her phone call to Woody, a second crew had arrived at the Clent Hills, and Brenda had moved into full-on organisation mode, clearing the public from the area. She'd taken on the task of informing Tony, the café owner, and Kim had completed a full handover with Inspector Tomkins before she'd left.

She'd been pleased to see that the board had been updated in her absence, offering clarity, though it did not make for easy reading.

Libby Turner 8, taken 1992. Returned 1993
Suzie Keene 9, taken 1994. Returned 1995
Melody Jones 7, taken 1996. ?
Lexi Walters 6, taken 1998. Hawne Park 1999
Paula Stiles 8, taken 2000. Wyley Court ?
Helen Blunt 7, taken 2002. Clent Hills?

'Where the hell did he bury Melody Jones?' Kim pondered out loud. She turned to the constable.

'Stace, stay on this. Melody has to be in there somewhere if we're right about the other two.'

'Okay, boss.'

'Anything on Harte's phone?'

'Encrypted, boss,' Penn answered. He nodded towards the screen. 'James Bond in there has put a self-destruct app on it. Paddy's still working on it.'

'The car?' she asked, after taking another sip of coffee.

'Nothing yet, but samples from all four tyres have been handed to the forensic botanist at Ridgepoint.'

Kim nodded and fixed her gaze on Penn, who combed his hand through his curls. That mannerism was rarely good news.

'Boss, whichever way I calculate it, we're looking at a search area with a radius of twenty-five miles.'

'Shit.'

'He had two hours between abducting Grace and turning up here. Taking off five or ten minutes to get her in the car and subdued, and another five or ten minutes to remove her at the other end, leaves us one hundred minutes of travelling time. At an average speed of thirty miles per hour, one mile every two minutes he could have covered fifty miles. Factoring in his return time from the location, we're looking at half that.'

'A twenty-five-mile radius?' Kim asked with disbelief.

'But he wouldn't be able to maintain thirty miles the whole time, with traffic lights and islands,' Bryant offered. 'It can sometimes take twenty minutes to crawl a couple of miles in bad traffic.'

'Yep, but he might also have driven on roads with a higher speed limit, so there's no way of knowing for sure.'

She could hear the frustration in his voice and see the sheets of paper with location points, lines and calculations. Penn hated nothing more than a puzzle he couldn't solve.

No matter how she looked at it, he was not going to get them any closer than that.

'Okay, step up the property searches and get those narrowed

down. Higher priority now we have a radius. Speak to Land Registry and see if they can help with reverse searches. She's got to be there somewhere.'

'Okay, boss.'

'And Bernadette should be calling through a list of movements for the last week for Claire and Grace. We need to see if we can find a link to Harte. He had to have seen her somewhere.'

'Got it, boss,' Penn and Stacey said together.

'Alison?'

'He's not playing anymore,' she said, tapping the keyboard. 'Look at this. The first clip is from Monday when he first arrived and was placed in the interview room. His posture is open and relaxed, sitting back in his chair. He's looking at his phone as though he's just scrolling through Facebook. No expression but no tension. Jack comes in, says something, and Harte is still relaxed as he starts tapping on his phone, but look at his face – he's smiling, he's enjoying himself. He wants the game to begin.'

Kim noted that everyone else had stopped work to listen.

'Now look at his posture the last time you spoke to him. He's hunched. His shoulders are tense. His face is pinched. He's trying to maintain that same composure, but his efforts are giving him away. He knows he's coming to the business end of the game, and he is no longer as happy to play it.'

'I don't understand. He came to us. He had to know how this was going to go.'

'He's conflicted. Imagine yourself at a funfair waiting in line for the fastest, highest ride in the place. You're excited and happy and full of expectation. And then you're sitting in the seat and you can see just how high this thing goes, and you begin to wonder if you've made a mistake. The excitement turns to fear, the anticipation to trepidation. Your entire body language changes, but it's too late. You're on the ride now.'

'You're saying that he no longer wants to tell the truth?'

'I'm saying that his body is having doubts, so you need to tread carefully and continue to appeal to the side of him that wants to let it out. Gently, gently, catchee monkey.'

'Is that a technical term?' Kim asked as the others resumed work.

'Think of it this way. He's like a turtle sticking its head out of his shell. The last thing you want is for him to pull it back in. Right now, you have nothing – no physical evidence to tie him to any crime. In the absence of that, you need his confession. The priority is finding Grace Lennard and, right now, the only source of information is him.'

Kim digested everything she'd said.

'Bryant, you ready?'

It was time to go catch them a tortoise.

SIXTY-FOUR

The meeting came to Alex sooner than expected.

Noelle Holten appeared in her doorway. 'What were you talking to that bitch about?'

Alex fixed surprise on her face at the question.

'You know who I mean? The murdering bitch.'

Alex ignored the irony that this woman was serving an eighteen-year stretch for murder herself.

'Emma, out,' Alex instructed.

'Oh, for fuck's sake, I just got to a really good bit,' she moaned, flouncing off her bed.

As Emma made her exit, Alex took a moment to appraise the woman before her. Noelle Holten was forty-nine years old. Her attractive face was framed by long blonde hair, and although few people looked like murderers, this lady couldn't have been further from the photofit, with her gentle features and studious, black-rimmed glasses.

From what Alex had learned, the woman hailed from Canada and had trained as a probation officer. Her diligence in her work had placed a drug dealer back inside to complete a four-year stretch. For payback he had waited for Noelle's fifteen-year-old daughter at the school gates. After injecting her with meth, he had raped and killed her less than a mile away from her home.

When asked who could have done this, Noelle had remained silent. She had known who it was and that there was nothing the police could do to him that would satisfy her need for vengeance. She already knew everything about him herself. She knew his family, his friends, his old haunts, his old habits.

She'd been wily and had waited a few months before getting together a kitchen knife, a balaclava and a pair of men's trainers a size too big. She found him, followed him, stabbed him and returned home. A drug deal gone wrong, the police had thought, until forensics found a couple of dog hairs on his coat. The detective remembered petting a brown Labrador named Buster when investigating the murder of Noelle's daughter.

When he'd explained the advances in DNA when it came to animal hair, Noelle Holten had broken down and admitted that she'd taken her dog for a walk shortly before.

The perfect crime – or it would have been if she hadn't been as bothered about her dog's ablutions and well-being before setting off to brutally murder someone.

The whole sorry tale had left her with a deep hatred of drug dealers and especially meth.

'You do know what she sells?' Noelle asked, stepping further into the room.

'Oh, Noelle, if I was to stop speaking to everyone in here who had done something foul, I'd never open my mouth again. We're in prison, after all. There are few paragons of virtue gracing these halls.'

'She kills kids.'

Alex sighed heavily. 'I understand that she cares nothing for the end user of her product, and no one wants to see children getting hurt, but I didn't voluntarily just strike up conversation with her. It's not like I want to be best friends with her.'

'So what did she want?' Noelle asked, taking a step closer.

Alex remained seated. She wasn't intimidated. Noelle was not a naturally violent person. Her frenzy during the murder had been driven by rage and grief.

Alex lowered her eyelids. 'She just wanted my help with something.'

'What could you possibly help her with?'

Alex remained silent for a minute to see if she would be able to make the leap herself.

Noelle waited.

Alex reached into her pocket and showed Noelle the top of the phone.

The woman's eyes widened in surprise. 'You've got a decent phone and you're gonna let that lowlife use it?'

'She has muscle,' Alex said, even though Titch would never touch her.

She forced fear onto her face. 'I can't say any more. If Titch finds out I've said anything...'

'But when and how is she getting the phone?'

'I can't say any more or...'

'Hang on. Don't you work alone in the library on a Thursday afternoon?'

Alex shifted her eyes to the door and back again. Just enough times for Noelle to think she'd worked it out all on her own. She bit her bottom lip for added effect.

'Okay, enough said,' Noelle offered with a smile on her face before she turned and walked out of the cell.

The smile wasn't as big as the one on Alex's face once she'd left. So far that was two for two and, right now, there was not one drop of blood on her very clean hands.

SIXTY-FIVE

Harte and his lawyer were sitting side by side in silence. Kate Swift was busy scribbling on a notepad. Whether she was writing notes about Harte's case or a shopping list for a trip to Sainsbury's, Kim had no idea.

'Thank you for joining us, Inspector,' Harte said.

'You've very welcome. We have been a little busy sightseeing some local beauty spots, but we'll come to that later. I'll hand over to Bryant for the formalities.'

She opened the folder she'd been carrying. It had been bolstered with plain sheets of paper to make it appear they had more information than they did.

'Thick folder you have there,' Harte commented with an amused glint in his eye, once Bryant was done.

'It's building, Mr Harte, it's building.'

She stopped at the page that had her notes and then leaned across them. Harte had controlled enough of this process.

'Mr Harte, did you know that Jenson Butler was a sex offender?'

He appeared unperturbed by the question.

'My client doesn't have to answer that,' Swift offered.

Kim waited to see if he would interject. He didn't.

'Did Mr Butler solicit your advice way back at university about a situation he found himself in?'

'My client doesn't have to answer that.'

Kim kept her gaze on Harte. 'Did Jenson Butler admit to you that he'd slept with a thirteen-year-old girl?'

'My client doesn't have to—'

'I know that, Ms Swift, but I do have a question that I really would like him to answer.'

'Go ahead,' Harte said.

'Why have you suddenly lost your voice since your solicitor arrived?'

'Is that a serious question, Inspector?' he asked.

'Actually, yes, Mr Harte. You came to us claiming to have all kinds of information, yet you've told us nothing, and now you don't seem able to answer the most basic question posed to you.'

'Do you have one, Inspector – a question that is?' asked Kate Swift.

'I do, Ms Swift. I'd like to know why Mr Harte did and continued to do business with a convicted sex offender.'

Swift deferred to her client.

'I feel that everyone deserves a second chance,' he answered.

'How can you know it was some kind of mistake and not a pattern of behaviour?'

'I don't delve into the personal lives of my associates to that degree.'

'We're not talking about their favourite takeaway or what football team they support. We're talking about whether they have sex with underage girls. Minors – children really.'

'It's my understanding that Mr Butler has no further convictions for any type of crime, which would lead me to believe it was a mistake.'

Kim wasn't buying it. 'Mr Harte, if you are to be believed that you admire and protect all things beautiful, how can you even tolerate the thought of doing business with a man who was convicted of—'

'In the absence of a question my client can answer, I suggest we move on to—'

'Mr Harte, did you abduct, kill and bury Lexi Walters at Hawne Park in Halesowen?'

'No comment,' he shot back.

'Okay,' Kim said, changing tack. Clearly, he was not going to answer any direct questions. 'You recall a great deal about the cases of missing girls. Do you remember reading about a six-year-old girl named Lexi Walters?'

'You've arrested me for her murder, so I'm assuming you feel I have some kind of connection to her?'

'Please answer the question. Do you remember reading anything about her?'

'I think something rings a bell. Pretty little thing if I remember correctly.'

Kim detected stiffening from his solicitor. She obviously disagreed with this line of questioning, but it had worked for her so far. Her perception was that his memory of the incident was his way of cryptically telling her that he was involved. So far he hadn't slipped up and given her anything she could charge him with, but while he was talking, there was hope. Direct questions were not going to trip him up.

Ms Swift appeared to be fearful of him talking at all.

'Please tell me what you remember about little Lexi.'

'If I remember correctly, little Lexi, as you call her, was removed from the care of her neglectful parent during the school summer holidays over twenty years ago.'

'Abducted,' Kim corrected. Steven Harte didn't seem to like the correct wording being used. Especially when it indicated the commission of a crime.

'Or liberated, some might say.'

'Liberated means freedom, Mr Harte. I'm not sure being taken by force and from her home and family to be imprisoned in a single room against her will could be called liberating by any stretch of the imagination.' Kim paused. 'You think she was kidnapped because her mother spent a little time taking a work call?'

'I'm sure I read that both her parents were career driven. They both worked exceptionally long hours.'

'How very awful of them both to try and make a decent life for their family.'

'I read that she spent more time with nannies and childminders than with her own parents. Such a shame.'

'It's a shame she's dead,' Kim snapped.

'It is, and she seemed like such a sweet little girl,' he said calmly.

Kim felt her fists clenching at his tone. She knew she had to rein in her anger. He was using it to control the course of the conversation.

Swift's tense expression told Kim she was eager to move on.

'Do you have any idea how she came to be buried at the site of a project worked on by both you and a convicted sex offender?'

'I have no idea,' he said easily.

'Okay, I'd like to talk to you about another little girl named—'

'My client is under arrest for the abduction and murder of Lexi Walters. Why would he know—?'

'Your client has demonstrated an impeccable memory when it comes to the historic accounts of missing girls, Ms Swift. He may remember something we missed.'

Harte held up his hand to his lawyer. 'It's okay. I'll certainly help if I can.'

Until they had results one way or another from Wyley Court or Clent, she could at least try and identify them using the cat-and-mouse game they'd been playing. Both she and Steven Harte knew the rules of the game, but his lawyer and, unfortunately, the video did not.

'Do you recall the case of a girl aged eight called Paula Stiles?'

He frowned, and Kim's breath caught in her chest. They were digging up Wyley Court fountain based on the timeline of her disappearance.

'Could you refresh my memory?'

'Eight-year-old Paula was on a day trip with other kids from the children's home where she lived.'

'Oh, dear, doesn't sound like she had the best start in life.'

'Indeed, Mr Harte,' Kim said, suspecting she didn't have the best end to her life either.

He made a show of thinking about it.

Kim held her breath.

'Wasn't she last seen in the Cotswolds somewhere.'

'The wildlife park,' she clarified, letting out a breath. His acknowledgement confirmed they were on track with the identification. She crossed her fingers that the location was just as accurate.

'Yes, I read somewhere that she was a lonely child, that her stints in and out of foster care had turned her into a secular girl, at ease in her own company.'

'And yet she never returned. I wonder why.'

'Perhaps she's still out there somewhere. Perhaps she ran away and made a good life for herself.'

'Or maybe she's buried beneath another project you and Butler worked on together.'

Swift leaned forward. 'Inspector, I suggest you keep your idle musings to—'

'Do you remember a little girl named Helen Blunt? She was seven years old when she was abducted from a summer fayre in Shrewsbury in 2002.'

'Not a town I know well, although I have visited it on occasion. They have a summer fayre?' he asked.

'They do indeed. Does anything spring to mind?'

He tapped his chin. 'You know, I do recall reading about a little girl who was taken. If I'm right, the witnesses recalled the event slightly differently to the mother. Wasn't there violence involved?'

'A slap.'

'Oh, I think the papers said it was a bit more than that. Didn't the mother take her time in reporting the disappearance of her daughter? Of course, if she'd been beating her—'

'Or it was an isolated incident of frustration from a frazzled mother dealing with three young children on her own.'

'You condone violence towards children, Inspector?' he asked, trying to twist her words.

'Absolutely not, but there is a distinction to be made between—'

Kim paused as her phone began to ring. It was Inspector Plant at Wyley Court.

She nodded towards Bryant, who terminated the interview as she headed into the corridor.

'You got something?' she asked, closing the door behind her.

'Nope, and that's the problem. This Brad guy with the satchel says that excavating any further beyond this point will mean permanent damage to the fountain's integrity.'

'Why?'

'One of the side walls that they've been trying to preserve is on the point of collapse.'

'How far down are they?'

'Almost four feet and both guys want it stopped. The machine operators are having a fag break but we've only got a couple of hours of good daylight left.'

Kim had to give herself a moment to think.

Never had she and the rest of her team worked a case where the apparent murderer had presented himself at the station.

After consideration, they had believed him and entered into the game he wanted to play. Every decision, every move had been based on that single fact. There would be repercussions for her next move if she'd called it wrong.

Did she have the courage of her convictions?

'Carry on digging,' she said before ending the call.

SIXTY-SIX

It was almost seven when Kim re-entered the squad room after briefing Woody about Harte and the dig at Wyley Court. He had commented that daylight was fading fast, which had done nothing to calm her nerves.

Her team had been at it for twelve hours straight, and their desks bore the evidence of meals taken while they continued to work. The search team had expanded by a further three square miles around the day-care centre, and crews were in place at both Wyley Court and Clent. Keats and Doctor A were on call for any developments, and Harte was off limits until he'd had his prescribed rest period.

'Okay, guys, I'm calling it,' she said, pouring the last coffee from the jug. 'Tidy up your mess and bugger off.'

'But, boss...'

'Nothing more we can do tonight. We can't have another crack at him until tomorrow. His lawyer has left the building, and we're all exhausted. We're not doing Grace any favours if we miss stuff because we can't see straight.'

The crinkling of packets came from all directions as they did as she'd asked.

'Not you, Alison. You can stay,' Kim said as jackets were lifted from chairs.

Penn offered a mock bow to Stacey.

'Your chariot awaits, milady, if you'd like a lift home. I would imagine a timely return home to your good wife is in order this fine evening.'

He held out his arm.

She took it. 'Why, thank you, kind sir. I would indeed benefit from a hasty retreat.'

Bryant groaned. 'It's like a low-budget *Downton Abbey*.'

Kim smiled as he followed them out, bidding them both good night.

She waited for a few seconds.

'Okay, Alison, with all due respect, that was a shit plan. You told me to go in there and appeal to the side that wanted to talk and, as you saw, that side of him has left the building.'

'It's not left. It's still there. He wants to talk. He wants to tell the truth, but something is holding him back.'

Alison turned back to her computer. 'Look at this,' she said, clicking on the footage of the last interview. 'He knows full well about Butler's past. There's not one element of surprise in his reaction, and check out his steepling fingers when you start talking about Butler and his past: there's a confidence, a superiority. But when you start talking about the girls, his micro-expressions and leakage go off the chart.

'Every time you mention a new name, there's a flash of wistfulness, tenderness because the name instantly conjures the memory, so he can't hide his first emotional reaction to it. There's a brief softness, a kindness around his eyes at the first mention of all the girls. He briefly relives his feelings for them.'

'He killed them.'

'He didn't want to.'

'What? Are you on drugs?'

'Sorry if you don't like what I'm telling you, cos I love how you demand my services to disagree with me, but hey ho. I'm telling you that the man is full of conflict, but not one time have I detected any anger or irritation or annoyance in his demeanour in relation to his feelings towards any of his victims.'

Alison sighed heavily. 'I don't know what changed with Melody Jones. I don't know why he killed her; I don't know where he buried her, but I can tell you that when he killed the girls, he got no pleasure from their deaths.'

Kim crossed her arms. This was not what she wanted to hear. 'Anything else?'

'What, you want more insights from me that you can disagree with?'

'It's nothing personal. I disagree with everyone.'

'I know, otherwise I wouldn't be here.'

'Give me your gut, Alison. You've studied the motivation and behaviour of some of the worst minds in the world. Take out the—' Kim stopped speaking as her phone rang.

Kim groaned before she answered it. Inspector Plant at Wyley Court.

'I know what you're going to say. The light has gone and digging has stopped because of visibility.'

'Digging has stopped but not because of the light. We've found something. Just another twelve inches or so down, and we found bones that look like a foot. A very small foot. Oh and the wall is still intact.'

'Fuck,' she said.

'Thought you'd be happy about the wall,' Plant offered in his second attempt at gallows humour. He was on site, he had seen the bones, and she could hear the emotion in his voice. He knew full well her reaction came from being right about something when you really wanted to be wrong.

Maybe a part of her was hoping that Paula Stiles had run away from the care home and was living a fantastic life somewhere.

For Lexi Walters, Kim had been able to console herself that a family was going to get closure. For Paula, it was a case of finding a care worker that still gave a shit after twenty years. In her experience, it was unlikely. Kim couldn't even put into words the depth of sadness that evoked in her.

'Make the calls. Get her out of there as soon as possible.'

'Her?' he queried, not privy to their investigation.

'We suspect so.'

Kim ended the call and growled. Inspector Plant would call Keats, who would call Doctor A, and the process for removal would commence. Both of them would treat her with dignity and respect.

'No need to explain,' Alison said sombrely.

'We have to nail him,' Kim said. 'This man has caused immeasurable pain to so many families. That's why I want your honesty. Take out all the finite details of micro-expression, leakage and squelching. When you watch him, what does your instinct tell you about the man?'

'Okay, I think he's highly intelligent, devious, with a healthy dose of ego thrown in. I do believe that he thinks he has you beaten and that you will only get the information through his confession. I absolutely believe that he kidnapped every one of these girls and has stashed Grace somewhere safe.'

'So he's an evil bastard?'

'Well, yes and no. I don't think it's as clear-cut as that.'

'So what are you saying?' Kim asked. It all seemed pretty clear-cut to her.

'I think even when you get to the truth he wants to share, he's still going to be hiding something.'

SIXTY-SEVEN

Kim pulled up outside Drake Hall as the sun was setting.

She'd spoken directly to the warden and arranged two meetings. She'd never met Warden Siviter, but she seemed to be a pleasant woman who had accommodated her requests.

She headed directly for the visitors' centre and was met by the same officer who had been present the day before.

Kim showed her ID despite the fact the woman's memory only had to stretch back twenty-four hours.

'Warden Siviter said no longer than fifteen minutes.'

'I'll take five and you can keep the rest.'

She headed towards the table in the centre that Alex had chosen. The same one they'd used the day before.

'Good evening, Kim. How lovely to see you again.'

'Cut the shit, Alex, you're not getting it,' she said, sitting down.

Her time with Alison was being spent wisely. Alex's facial expression was irritable but her first response had been blank, nothing.

'And you knew it,' Kim said, tipping her head.

'Oh, you do entertain me. I would have been pleasantly surprised if you'd given in to me. Perhaps a little disappointed but grateful none the less. A letter from you would certainly have been a feather in my cap. You really don't care about the identity of your father?' Alex asked as her fingers knitted together.

Less than two hours ago she'd been discussing this exact mannerism.

Superiority.

Kim's stomach began to swirl. She had just been told no but she was still feeling superior anyway.

Leakage.

'My thoughts about my father are not something I'd ever choose to share with you, Alex, but be sure that there is no information you could hold that would get my seal of approval on your release. You are the vilest, most despicable person I have ever had the misfortune to meet.'

Alex smiled. 'And yet you're here anyway. The absence of any letter from you would have given me your answer. Yet you chose to deliver your decision in person.'

'I wanted to see your face.'

'That's not true but I'll let it pass. And you're not even curious about who he is?'

Kim smiled. 'Thanks – that's the reason I came.'

Alex frowned. 'Excuse me?'

'You said *is* and not *was*. You've just told me he's still alive. That's pretty much all I wanted to know.'

Alex recovered quickly. 'You think I'm going to tell you anyway, don't you? You think I'll relent and give you his name because of our bond.'

Kim laughed. 'Oh, Alex, firstly there is no bond. I am nothing more than an unconquered challenge to you; a damaged mind that you failed to infiltrate and control. You've tried by using my brother, my mother, my father. Who's next? Cos I'm sure I have a half cousin twice removed somewhere if you fancy a crack at that one. And secondly, why would I think you'd give away anything for free, when having the knowledge and keeping it to yourself gives you way more enjoyment than anything I could offer?'

'Half an hour in your head and the information is yours.'

This time Kim's head rolled back as her laughter exploded. It was genuine and Kim had to wonder how it was that her best laugh of the day had come from Alexandra Thorne.

'That's like saying I have a stick of dynamite but I only want to blow up part of your house. The rest of it would be pretty useless afterwards.'

'You give me too much credit,' Alex offered with a smile.

'It wasn't a compliment. You've tried and failed, and I'd rather see you rot behind bars for as long as—'

'Not caught him yet then, your psychopath?' Alex asked, raising one eyebrow. 'Only you still seem to be a little stressed. Is he winning the game?'

'None of your fucking business,' she snapped.

'I could help if—'

'Alex, how many times do I have to say I want nothing from you, and if that's your way of trying to keep me here, it's not going to work.'

She stood. There was something she had to do. The unease in her stomach from Alex, given her refusal about the recommendation, meant only one thing.

'I'm leaving now. It's been just fabulous seeing you again but I'm bored.'

'Are you going to see her?' Alex asked.

'Fuck off.'

'You really should visit your mother. For your own sake.'

'Why do you do that?' Kim asked.

'What?'

'Act as though you care. We both know you don't, that you can't, so why bother with the pretence?'

'It's what friends do.' Alex shrugged.

The shrug came after the words. Forced. Not genuine. Leakage.

'We're not friends. I'm leaving, and I'd say take care of yourself but I'd really prefer you didn't.'

Kim strode towards the officer with only one thing on her mind.

'Pretty much,' Alex called out.

Kim stopped and turned. 'What?'

'You said that was pretty much all you wanted to know about your father, if he was dead or alive. You said pretty much but not all. There's more that you want to know but won't ask.'

Damn the woman. Yes, there was one more burning question in her mind that would never feel the outside of her lips.

'To prove to you that I do care as much as I'm capable of caring for anyone, I'm going to give you a gift.'

Kim met her gaze. The intensity sizzled between them. She couldn't look away, even though she suspected that Alex couldn't possibly know the question that haunted her.

'The answer is no. He never knew about you and Mikey.'

Damn the woman to hell and back. She saw the triumph in her eyes at knowing what her question was.

'Fuck you, Alex, and by the way you're... you're fucking leaking.'

She swallowed down the emotion in her throat as she approached the officer.

'I'd like to see Warden Siviter. Now.'

SIXTY-EIGHT

'Thank you for coming back,' Kim said as Warden Siviter got out of a blue Corolla in the external car park.

'I'd only been home long enough to shower and change but I was told it was urgent.'

The woman was dressed in jeans, a buttoned-up cardigan and trainers. She wore no make-up, and her curly black hair was still damp.

'I need to talk to you about Alexandra Thorne.'

'Is everything okay?' she asked, glancing towards the prison. 'Was she able to help with your enquiries?'

The story she'd told to get a late visit.

'Everything is fine and no, she was no help at all.'

'Oh, okay, then what can I help you with?'

'She mentioned something about a parole hearing,' Kim said, hoping she'd heard wrong.

'It's on Friday. Why, is that a problem?'

'It's not if you have no plan to recommend her release.'

'She has shown great improvement in—'

'She hasn't,' Kim shot out. This was exactly what she'd been afraid of. Alex never had only one plan. 'Please trust me in

knowing that she will never change. She can't. She is a true
sociopath. She is cold, calculating and ruthless. Every action is self-
serving and designed—'

'That's actually not true,' she said, holding up her hand. Kim's
unease was growing by the minute. She'd hoped the warden's first
response would have been the assurance that she knew Alex's
capabilities and that she would not be recommending her release,
now or ever. The fact they were still speaking about the subject
was of great concern. If the warden doubted that fact, even for a
minute, Alex would have found a way to exploit it.

'Only the other day she stopped a fight in the dinner hall at risk
to herself. I think she's changed.'

'Really, she hasn't. Who was fighting?'

'One of the seasoned prisoners assaulted a new inmate, and
Alexandra stepped in and broke it up.'

'You saw this?'

'Yes, she was nowhere near when Emma just decided to—'

'Emma?' Kim asked, remembering a girl with the same name
being a crony of Alex's from a previous visit.

'Is she friends with Alex?'

'They share a cell actually.'

Kim wanted to shake the woman into understanding.

'And this happened right in front of you, and you just
happened to see Alex play the hero?'

'I always nip to the hall before...'

Realisation dawned followed closely by suspicion. 'You think
she planned it for me to see?'

'I'd bet my dog on it, and if you knew me better, you'd understand the certainty I feel with that statement. I understand that
you stand firmly behind the process of rehabilitation. You have to
and so you should, but you should also acknowledge that for some
people it doesn't work. They can't change. They don't want to
change.

'I've known Alex for a few years now, and you have only seen the side of her that she wants you to see. If you recommend her release, innocent people will suffer.'

Siviter folded her arms. 'You know we can't make decisions based on that alone. We have to observe the behaviour, mark the changes, accept the truthfulness of the remorse shown for the crime. There are many things to consider.'

Kim fought the frustration that her plea of 'because I said so' was falling on deaf ears.

'Okay, read her file properly. Take the time to completely understand the type of person you're dealing with. Look at every situation and find the ulterior motive. Please just do these things before you make a final decision. You know your recommendation holds a lot of weight with the board.'

Siviter hesitated before nodding. 'I'll take a look.'

Kim thanked her and got into the car with the weight of uncertainty heavy on her shoulders.

She had done her best to keep the evil woman behind bars.

She just hoped it was enough.

SIXTY-NINE

'Everybody rested?' Kim asked. It was a minute after seven, the coffee was made, Penn's Tupperware box of Rocky Road pieces was open and a slab of it was already sitting on Alison's desk.

'Stace, she means you,' Penn said with a wink.

'Am I missing something?' Kim asked.

'Devon got home last night,' Alison offered.

'Aaaaah, got it.'

'Pack it in, you lot. There was sleep. Some.'

Kim smiled. The detective constable was certainly beaming this morning.

Her own night hadn't been as restful as she'd have liked. After walking Barney around midnight, she'd tried to spend an hour in the garage on the Vincent, but her mind had been completely besieged by thoughts of Alex, mingled with the fear for a little girl who had now been away from her family for almost seventy-two hours.

'I want her home today,' Kim blurted out.

No one needed clarification who she meant.

'Any luck with Land Registry?' she asked.

'Two thirds of our target area dismissed,' Penn answered. 'A

very helpful lady called Sophie has a linked database with algo-
rithms and grid references that can narrow down—'

'Fantastic, Penn,' Kim said, cutting him off with a half-smile.
'Stacey, I want you on the location, and Penn, keep working on the
password to the phone. If he has Grace on it, there may be some
clue as to where she is.'

'Will do, boss.'

'I've forwarded the list of places visited by Claire and Grace to
you all. Obvious front runners for me would be the Botanical
Gardens in Birmingham and the butterfly farm in Stratford-upon-
Avon. Given his love of all things beautiful I'd start there. Divide it
up between yourselves.'

Both Stacey and Penn nodded.

'Boss, I've sent all the dental records I've collected to Keats,'
Stacey said.

Kim nodded. She'd received a text that both Keats and Doctor
A would be at Wyley Court at six to begin the recovery. Stacey's
efforts in locating dental records could help speed up the process of
identification.

'Boss, I've found no other sizeable projects that Butler and
Harte worked together after the Clent project,' Penn said.

Kim glanced at Alison. 'You think Helen could have been his
last?'

Alison shrugged. 'It's hard to say. The change in his behaviour
came with Melody Jones, and until we know more about what
happened there, we can't possibly speculate.'

'And it's time to try and get some answers to that,' she said as a
sly smile worked its way onto her face.

Alison caught it first. 'What are you thinking?'

'I'm thinking that yesterday we did it your way and today we're
doing it mine.'

She looked around the room and her gaze rested on the detective constable.

'Okay, Stace, listen carefully: here's what I want you to do.'

SEVENTY

Alex couldn't help the satisfied smile that was playing around her lips as she combed her hair. She knew that she was literally days away from doing this once again in her own home.

She had already decided that she would spend her first few nights in the most expensive hotel she could find. It would have a beauty salon, a spa, a pool, a gym and a restaurant that cooked decent food.

She smiled at the irony that she'd be in one room having her meals cooked for her. But it would be a luxurious room and the food would be of her choosing. As would the option to go shopping or go see a show, read any book she wanted instead of the slim pickings in the prison library, surf hundreds of channels for educational viewing instead of being forced by the rest of the inmates to watch every soap on the box. Most of them wouldn't know a decent documentary if it slapped them around the face.

She would arrange to have her home cleaned from top to bottom and her car taken out of storage. As her wealth was not tied to any of the crimes she was alleged to have committed, it was all there waiting for her.

After a couple of weeks cleansing her body and mind and recuperating from the ordeal of the last few years, she would start working again. She already planned to apply for reinstatement to the medical register.

The medical board was indeed fickle and inconsistent. She knew of a recent case of a psychiatrist struck off for having sexual relations with one of his female clients. Because he admitted it, he'd been allowed to wind up his business and retire. Another doctor, convicted over the death of a six-year-old boy, had been allowed reinstatement to the medical register.

She had no doubt she would be reinstated and then she intended to get paying clients back through her door. She needed to be back in that circle of people coming to her for help, being able to use her skills. She'd used them in the last few years to get what she wanted only she hadn't been getting paid for it.

She classed today as her last full day before the process for her release began.

She had a six o'clock meeting with Warden Siviter to talk through the parole hearing process and for the warden to share her recommendation. If everything went to plan, Alex had no doubt as to the outcome of that meeting.

She had the sudden feeling of being on holiday. She felt as though she'd been stuck in a seedy caravan with torrential rain for the whole week, and then on the last day the sun had come out, and it was time to make the most of the time left.

She was going to enjoy it and have the most fun possible.

'I think you should probably start preparing for a new cellmate, Emma,' she said, tying her hair into a ponytail.

She was gratified to see the woman's face fall.

'You might not get it, you know,' Emma warned with concern in her voice. Oh, how touching.

'I will,' Alex said confidently.

'It's your first parole hearing. Folks don't always get—'

'I will, Emma – I can promise you.'

'But how can you be sure?'

'Careful – anyone would think you don't want me to go back to my normal life, just so I can stay here with you.'

'Well, we do make a good team.'

Alex sat on the bed and regarded her cellmate for a minute.

'The word team indicates members of equal standing. Individuals working together with one common goal. Ours has been more of a master and puppet situation.'

Emma's expression was puzzled. Oh dear, she was going to have to spell it out. Fine, she had time to kill and today was about enjoying herself.

Emma tipped her head. 'Why has your voice changed?'

'This is my normal voice. Like everything else, I have adapted it for my audience. I have paused my outstanding conversational skills. I have lowered my superior intelligence. I have downgraded every part of myself for the benefit of the people around me.'

Emma began to shake her head in disbelief.

'Do you remember when you were first moved into this cell?' Alex asked.

Emma nodded eagerly, as though waiting for something to make that one hurtful comment go away.

'Do you remember how I let you talk and talk about yourself and your kids and how much you love them and all your regrets blah, blah, blah?'

'Yes, you were listening to support me.'

Alex laughed. 'I was listening for your pressure points. I was looking for your vulnerabilities, your skills, your asset value, your worth. I was listening to see how you would benefit me.'

Emma's mouth dropped open. 'But you were interested. You cared.'

Alex laughed. Oh dear, the woman's delusion as to the nature of their relationship was worse than she'd thought. It would be a frivolous diversion to set her straight.

'I could not care less about you, Emma. I am not the slightest bit interested in your mundane life, annoying kids, husband or your next-door neighbour's cat. I lied, I deceived and pretended to like you so I could see your value and, to your credit, I found some useful qualities I could use.

'It was immediately clear to me that you were easily led and eager to serve. You are so used to looking after people on the outside. A fine quality in your home life and a totally exploitable trait for me. You wanted someone to follow around, to help, and so I did you a favour by being that person. I gave you a purpose. You were happy to run off and do all the little errands. It's no bad thing. It's your personality type.'

'But I thought we were friends.'

Again, Alex laughed. 'I don't have friends. I don't want them or need them. I need assets, tools, grunts that are useful to help me get what I want. And to be fair, you have been useful. Your invisibility amongst these women has meant that I've found out much more information than I ever could have gained on my own. Your need to gossip has brought me knowledge on other assets that I've been able to exploit. Do you see how this works now?'

Emma's crestfallen expression told her that the woman was waiting for the punchline, that she was still hoping that it was some kind of joke.

Alex sighed. You tried to be honest with people and it wasn't worth it. Some people didn't want the truth if it wasn't a truth they liked.

Yes, Alex could have left Emma thinking they were good friends. The woman would have been none the wiser, but where would have been the fun in that?

Alex could see Emma's lower lip trembling. *Oh, Jesus, save me from the frailties of human emotion.*

Alex stood and saw there was still hope in Emma's eyes.

She shook her head and carried on down to breakfast.

SEVENTY-ONE

'What exactly are you hoping to achieve?' Alison asked as they gathered around the computer screen.

'Let's watch and find out,' Kim said as Stacey entered the interview room.

Kate Swift had arrived ten minutes earlier, and both she and her client were seated in silence.

Harte eyed Stacey suspiciously.

'I'm Detective Constable Stacey Wood and you've already met Detective Sergeant Bryant.'

'Where is Det—'

'Please wait one minute,' Stacey said, holding up her hand.

Kim watched as Stacey stared at the tape recorder for a second as though remembering how to use it. She then pressed the wrong button, realised her mistake, began the tape recording and reminded him of the reason for the interview.

'Okay, Mr Harte, you have a question.'

'Where is Detective Inspector Stone?'

'I'm sorry but she had to be somewhere more imp... er... urgent so I will be leading the questioning this morning.'

'His lawyer is pleased about that,' Alison observed.

'Of course she is. With one hour to go before charge or release, she's already singing Christmas songs.'

'I have another question. May I have a cup of tea?'

Stacey appeared puzzled. 'Were you not served a beverage of your choice with breakfast this morning?'

'I was but I'd like—'

'In that case, I think we'll press on.'

Kim silently congratulated the young officer on her acting ability.

Stacey opened up her folder.

The first page was an official police statement. On it were words that were typed in 8-point font. He had no way in hell of reading it upside down.

Stacey made a show of reading it word for word.

Harte watched her closely, continually looking down at the page and then at Stacey.

'Oh, he's getting annoyed now,' Alison said. 'You see his right fist clenching? He thinks it's buried in his other arm but look at the crease of the material. By constantly looking from Stacey to the page, he is trying to exert control. He wants to catch her eye. He wants to begin.'

Yet it was Kate Swift who leaned forward.

'Constable, do you intend asking my client a question any time soon?'

'Why, does your client have somewhere else to be?'

Kim felt a jolt of pride. Stacey was under instruction to annoy the hell out of the man, and she was doing a damn good job.

She continued to watch.

'Mr Harte, I'd like to talk to you about your memories of Paula Stiles. You recall a great deal of detail about her abduction in... Hang on...'

'My client is here to talk about Lexi Walters only,' Swift interjected.

'And I've already been over this in detail with Inspector Stone.'

Stacey made a show of looking through her folder.

'My apologies. I must have somehow missed...' Stacey's words trailed away as Harte and Swift looked at each other.

'Okay, maybe we should move on. Your relationship with Jenson Butler started at school, is that right?'

'No, it bloody well isn't. I met him at university. Have you even read the file?' he asked, stabbing the table.

'Well, yes, I am familiar with the case,' Stacey said, leafing through all the paperwork, as though she was looking for something in particular. She was doing it quickly, adding panic into her movements.

'Have you done this before, Detective Constable?' Harte asked.

Kim didn't need to read his body language. The contempt was dripping from his words.

'Yes, I once interviewed...'

'Once?' he exploded.

Kim couldn't help but laugh.

They had decided to play on every weakness they knew of him. His self-importance, his attachment to her and his need for a cup of tea.

She wanted him annoyed; she wanted him agitated. She wanted him bursting with negative emotion.

Stacey had primed him brilliantly, and now it was her turn to go in for the kill.

SEVENTY-TWO

'You not gonna come and watch this, Penn?' Alison asked him as the boss left the room.

'Not right now,' he said without looking up. He'd heard enough to know his colleague had knocked it out of the park.

'You okay?' she asked.

'Fine.'

Alison tipped her head. 'Did Jasper stay at Billy's last night?'

'No, I decided it was a bit much for Billy's mum.'

Alison opened her mouth to speak but changed her mind and returned her attention to the screen. He was glad because he didn't want to admit to her that he had made a terrible mistake.

He'd known it as soon as he'd walked in the door.

Jasper didn't do sullen. He wasn't a moody teen, but he did do quiet. And the quiet broke Penn's heart.

Jasper had been at home for at least two hours before he'd got back from work. Hours he'd been waiting for Penn to come home when he could have been having a laugh at his friend's house.

Penn had acted out of fear of Jasper pulling away from him and being vulnerable when all he was trying to do was dip his toe in the outside world and find his place.

Penn had realised too late that he had no right to stop him. He saw a long, honest heart-to-heart in their future, but right now he was just angry at himself for depriving his brother due to his own fears. He didn't need to share his failure with anyone else.

He realised he'd been short with his colleague. 'Sorry, Alison, just trying to crack this bloody password.'

He'd had the phone since 8.15 a.m., and he was no closer to getting into the front screen.

Eleven characters.

He'd tried hundreds of variations of dates, names, places and he was only grateful that the phone didn't have a limited number of attempts. Trouble was, even with the information he had, there were quadrillions of possible permutations.

He sat back and closed his eyes, blocking out everything around him. He needed to think more about the man himself. He liked to play games, he was arrogant, he thought he could do whatever he wanted. He liked to play with people. He liked people to get close but not quite get him. He did things to amuse himself, acted purely for his own entertainment.

'Alison, can you ping me that footage of Harte on his phone?' he asked, having a sudden thought.

'Yeah, sure,' she said, pressing a few keys. 'On its way.'

He opened the clip and watched it, then scrolled to the point where Harte was on his phone. He was smiling as he did whatever he was doing. His fingers worked busily. He finished and then glanced at the camera. He already knew the camera was there so that glance was unnecessary. It was almost an unconscious message to them. A bit like 'there you go'. Or 'that one's for you'.

Penn felt an excitement in his stomach. Was this another game? Was he playing with them and had mistakenly given himself away?

He returned to the beginning of the footage and watched carefully.

Harte walks in.

Harte looks around as he heads towards the seat.

Harte sits down, relaxes, looks up at the camera.

Jack enters.

'Can I get you a drink?'

'Tea one sugar would be great.'

Jack nods and walks out.

Harte smiles and reaches for his phone.

Penn found himself at the beginning of what he'd already watched.

He pulled the cursor back to the start.

Harte walks in.

Looks around.

Takes a seat.

Looks at camera.

Jack enters.

'Can I get you a drink?'

'Tea one sugar would be great.'

Jack leaves.

Harte reaches for his phone.

Penn pulled the cursor back one more time.

Jack enters.

'Can I get you a drink?'

'Tea one sugar would be great.'

Jack leaves.

Penn reached for Harte's phone and pressed the screen. The login page appeared as it had done a hundred times.

He typed in the words in lower case. Eleven characters.

teaonesugar

Alison was watching as the screen sprang into life.

'Bloody hell, I'm in.'

SEVENTY-THREE

'Where the hell have you been, Inspector?' Harte asked as she walked in the door, Bryant following her.

She ignored him.

'For the purpose of the tape, Detective Inspector Stone has entered the room and will continue questioning the suspect.'

She nodded at Stacey who rose and left the room.

Harte didn't even wait for the door to close.

'Where were you that was so important you sent me a low-ranking, incompetent—'

'DS Wood is neither low-ranking nor incompetent. I was dealing with the discovery of bones beneath the fountain of Wyley Court. Another project completed by yourself and Jenson Butler.'

'Inspector, my client is not under arrest for anything other than—'

'Your client asked me a question, Ms Swift, and I'm answering it, so settle down.' She paused. 'In addition, I checked on the progress of an excavation we're carrying out at Clent.'

'Inspector, I must—'

'Still answering the question, Ms Swift. I was unaware of the detail required by your client, whether he wanted a brief summary or a blow-by-blow account of my day so far.'

She was not allowed to question him about other crimes while only being under arrest for the first, but she could make him aware that she had followed the crumbs and these were the sites she'd found. There was a blink that lasted longer than normal. Almost an acknowledgement.

'Is that enough detail for you, Mr Harte?'

'Yes, thank you.'

She took a breath and expelled it slowly. This was her only chance. He was under arrest for the abduction and murder of Lexi Walters, for which he'd been in custody for twenty-four hours. She had twenty minutes to go.

'The time for games is over, Mr Harte. We're not prepared to play anymore.'

She leaned forward, as close to his personal space as she could get.

He leaned back.

'What did you do to Lexi Walters?'

'I didn't do anything.'

'She crawled into that hole by herself?'

Kim could feel the set expression of her own face. His gaze met hers, and there was just the two of them in the room.

'Did she try to escape before you'd finished ogling her? Had you not had your fill of voyeurism before she tried to get out of the prison you'd made for her?'

Harte's eyes were burning into hers.

'Was it an accident? Did you accidentally kill her while trying to subdue her?'

No answer and Kim hadn't expected one. He was rattled. She could see that, but he wasn't angry enough.

'Did you sexually assault six-year-old Lexi Walters, Mr Harte?'

Nothing.

'Did you allow Jenson Butler to sexually assault her? Was this some kind of sick, perverted partnership where you got to watch while he raped a child?'

Colour was flooding into his face.

'Were you and Butler a tag team, taking it in turns to rape her? Is that why you're both involved in the disposal? You had a deal, a pact that neither of you could break because you both are guilty? Are you covering for each other's sick and disgusting games?'

Kim opened the file and pushed a photo of a smiling Lexi towards him. Next she pushed a photo of the skeleton as it had been arranged in the morgue.

Kate Swift looked away but not before Kim saw the horror on her face.

'What did you do to take Lexi Walters from this to this?'

Harte's muscles were jumping all over the place.

Kim hated the pictures in her head but she had to keep at him. The whole idea of baiting him was to lead him to say something that would incriminate him. She had to take away his control.

'Did you and Butler allow other men to come and rape her? Did you all do it together? Was Lexi passed around like a toy? Was that beautiful little girl raped by a bunch of your paedophile friends as well as—?'

'I never fucking raped her. I loved her,' he shouted in Kim's face.

The room fell into silence as everyone realised what he'd just said.

Kate Swift looked about ready to explode.

It was enough.

That comment alone was enough to get her the twelve-hour extension she wanted and would give Woody the opportunity to begin the process for charging with the CPS.

Harte was still looking shell-shocked, and Swift's expression was grim.

Kim pushed back her chair, ensuring that the relief she was feeling did not show on her face.

She stood and reached for the folder. 'Well, after that little admission I would think maybe you two need to have a chat.'

Bryant formally ended the interview as she hurried out of the room.

SEVENTY-FOUR

Kim stepped back into the squad room with Bryant following closely behind.

'Okay, guys, we need to— What the hell is that?'

'We got her, boss,' Penn said, handing her the phone.

Any thought of what had just occurred went straight out of her mind as her eyes rested on a small figure sitting on the edge of a bed, her legs together and her head bowed.

It was Grace Lennard, and she was alive.

'Is this live?'

Penn nodded.

Kim felt a rush of mixed emotions gather in her throat.

There she was: the little girl abducted almost four days ago, looking so small and vulnerable. Kim wanted to reach in there and grab her, pull her out of the screen and tell her everything was going to be okay.

She looked to the detective sergeant responsible for giving them this link.

'He sure does like his tea.'

'Bloody good work, Penn,' she said, still holding on to the phone. She raised an eyebrow at Stacey. 'And who knew you could be that annoying?'

'My mum.'

'You primed him well, Stace. Well done.'

'We saw, kind of,' Penn said.

Kim understood. Their focus had been on Grace and looking for clues.

'Anything?' she asked, taking another look at the screen.

She took a good look around the room. Although she'd never seen it before, it appeared familiar to her. She knew she'd visited somewhere that looked similar. The daisy bedspread and matching curtains, the desk, the lamp, the positioning of the television on the wall. Only the desk she'd seen hadn't been filled with crisps and biscuits, fruit and bottles of water.

She stared harder. 'Bryant?'

'Suzie Keene's bedroom – or rather her daughter's room.'

'Of course,' Kim said. They'd spoken to Harte's first victim as she'd folded washing. The only difference was the size of the bed.

'Why would Suzie Keene have decorated her own home so similarly?' she asked Alison.

'Safety. Suzie has recreated for her daughter her own illusion of safety, and it's a memory prompt for herself. When she goes in there it's a happy, contented feeling.'

'That's not right. It's weird, and I dare him to tell me again that the experience had no long-lasting effects on Suzie and Libby.'

'But it's no different to the rest of us,' Alison argued. 'We all surround ourselves with things that comfort us and make us feel safe. The colours we choose, the furniture, layout, pictures, ornaments – everything is for comfort and pleasure. Yes, she's recreated a scene from her past that should have been a traumatic experience, but for her it wasn't.'

'You don't think there's anything wrong with that?' Kim asked, unable to see Alison's view.

'Would you find it more palatable if she'd been so traumatised that she'd retreated into herself out of stress; maybe started self-harming or later turned to drink or drugs? Would that have been normal enough? I know how you feel about him, but we've got two grown women who don't agree with you at all.'

'And I've potentially got four dead girls that do.'

Alison nodded, conceding her point.

'Get her in here,' Kim instructed Stacey. 'I want Suzie Keene brought to the station to identify this room. I want to know if it's exactly the same room where she was held. It might jog her memory and help with the location.'

'On it, boss,' she said, reaching for the phone.

'I've been looking into something else,' Alison continued. 'I've not come across it before but I know it exists. Mr Harte may be a candidate for Lima syndrome.'

'What syndrome?' Kim asked, taking a last glance at Grace before handing the phone back to Penn. He placed it gently on his desk, as though not wanting to hurt the little girl, before returning to his view of Google Earth on the screen.

'Lima. You have Stockholm syndrome, where the captive becomes emotionally attached to the captor, but it can also work the other way around, where the captor can become attached to his subject. There's not much known about it but it was a term developed after 1997 when members of the Túpac Amaru Revolutionary Movement took high-level diplomats and government officials hostage, to demand the release of MTRA members from prison.

'The captors were interviewed afterwards, and the characteristics of Lima syndrome suit Harte down to a tee.'

'Go on,' Kim said.

'The captor feels empathy for a captive's situation; he becomes more attentive to their needs and wants, and develops feelings of attachment, fondness or affection. When talking of Lexi, he's just cried out that he loved her and that may well be true.'

Kim knew the doubt was clear on her face.

'I know that look,' Alison said with an eye-roll. 'Okay, let me give you an example. Have you seen *Beauty and the Beast*?'

'Alison, are you taking the piss or...?'

'Beast imprisons Belle in exchange for her father. Over time he feels empathy for her plight of being imprisoned, as he himself is imprisoned. Empathy turns to affection which turns to love. It happens.'

'It's a fairy tale.'

'It's an example,' Alison persisted.

'So why is Lexi dead?' Kim asked. There was no escaping that fact.

Alison shrugged. 'I really wish I could answer that.'

'You and me both,' Kim said, turning back to the room. 'Okay, guys, I'd best go and brief Woody while Harte confers with his solicitor. The only focus right now is finding out where Grace is. Don't take your eyes off her for one minute,' she said as Bryant picked up the phone.

His expression was puzzled as he turned the screen to landscape.

'You okay?'

'Yeah, it's just that bed.'

'What about it?'

'It's smaller than the one at Suzie's house. Suzie mentioned a nice big bed all to herself.'

'Libby said the same,' Penn said, leaning over to take another look.

'That's a small bed,' Bryant insisted.

'I really don't think it's—'

'I mean it's smaller than a normal single bed.'

'And?'

'This is more the size of a bunk bed.'

Damn. Now she understood what he was saying.

Bunk beds came as a pair.

SEVENTY-FIVE

As she headed to her target destination, Alex savoured the experience, safe in the knowledge that she wouldn't be trudging these soulless hallways for much longer.

Her plan was coming together nicely – just a couple more hours to wait and one more thing to do.

'Hey, Lisa,' she said, stepping into the cell of the young woman she'd spoken with a couple of days earlier. This time there was no attempt to force a cheerful expression onto her face. This time she aimed for a mixture of sadness and concern.

'How are you doing?' she asked, sitting on the other bed. She could see for herself that the girl wasn't doing well. She appeared even thinner than the last time. She hadn't showered, and her eyes were red-rimmed and heavy.

'Shit, Alex. I don't think I can take much more.'

'Hey, you're stronger than you think,' she said, reaching into her pocket for the item she'd been hiding for weeks. The one that had cost her more than a meal at The Ivy. 'I brought you this to cheer you up.'

She took the disposable razor and placed it next to Lisa on the bed. 'Smooth legs always make you feel better.'

Lisa closed her hand around it. 'Where did you get this?'

Alex shrugged as Lisa placed it under her pillow. 'Someone owed me a favour, and I thought you'd appreciate it.'

'Thanks,' she said, trying to be upbeat. She failed miserably. That was good.

'That man of yours been in yet?' Alex asked.

Lisa shook her head.

'How long is that now?'

'Three weeks but he's been working a lot.'

'Even at weekends?' Alex asked doubtfully. 'Some bosses are bastards, aren't they? Does he work at some kind of twenty-four-hour place or something?'

'He's a landscaper, self-employed.'

'Oh,' Alex said. She was pretty sure they didn't work all week-end, and if he was the boss, he could certainly give himself a couple of hours off here and there, but there was no need to state it. She'd done enough to put the thought there.

'Is he coming this weekend?' Alex asked brightly.

'Can't get him to ask him. He's not answering his phone.'

'I'm sure there's an innocent reason for that.'

Just one word. Subtle. Put the word out there, plant the thought. Give it time to grow.

'Good gardeners are always busy. I had a really good one. Couldn't do enough for his customers. Used to come to trim the hedges but ended up mowing the lawn and jet washing the slabs. Sometimes he'd be there all day.' She smiled and rolled her eyes. 'I didn't half learn a lot about his home life: cheating missus, rebellious kids, the lot. Gardeners are good guys,' she said with a smile.

'He could be up to anything while I'm in here,' Lisa said, scratching at the skin between her thumb and her forefinger.

'Of course he could.' She paused. 'But you can't think like that. You've got to trust him. It's not like he's cheated on you before.'

Her face fell further. 'He did once, about a year ago. He got drunk and had a one-night stand.'

'Well, at least he told you about it,' Alex said.

'His mate told me,' she said, raking at that small area of skin.

'Oh, okay,' Alex said, appearing to be at a loss for words. 'But that's not to say he's going to do it again. It was obviously just sex because you were—'

'But I'm not there, am I? He doesn't have me to come home to,' she said as the tears sprang once more into her eyes. 'For all I know he's already met someone, and I'm not talking about just sex. What if he meets someone at work and it's more than sex? What if he has another woman around my child? Another woman putting my baby to bed at night, singing to her, feeding her, rocking her back to sleep, calling her mum?'

Alex knew that picture had been playing over and over in her mind. It was her worst fear.

'You can't think like that. He'll wait for you. A lot, I mean, some men are stronger than—'

'But not all. He's already done it once and now I'm not even there. I can't bear these thoughts, these pictures in my head of other women around my child. It's driving me insane, and the warden hasn't come back to me about recommending early release.'

Alex knew Lisa had put everything into her extenuating circumstances appeal. She'd had a meeting with Warden Siviter a week ago. It was her final bullet.

'Oh, you haven't been told yet?' she asked innocently.

'You know something?' Lisa asked as the scratching paused for just a second.

'No... I mean... not... It's just something.'

'Tell me, Alex.'

'No, I might have got it wrong.'

'Just tell me what you know.'

Alex sighed heavily and hesitated while she saddled up the wild horses to drag it out of her mouth.

Remove all hope.

'I just overheard a conversation. That's why I came to see if you were okay with the news.'

'What news?'

'Oh, Lisa, I don't want to—'

'What news?'

'The warden isn't putting you forward. She thinks you'll be refused.'

Alex hid her delight as she watched any hope fade away and the realisation that there was no escape. There would be no early release; her boyfriend would be out there all alone; her baby would be without her for years. Her boyfriend wouldn't visit, and her child would forget all about her.

'Lisa, I'm sorry. I thought you knew.'

She shook her head. 'Doesn't really matter, does it? Nothing really matters anymore.'

Alex pushed herself up off the bed. Her work here was done. All that remained for her to do now was lay low and wait.

She reached the door and turned. Just a reminder.

'I'll try and get you another one of those shavers. That'll cheer you up.'

SEVENTY-SIX

Suzie Keene had been placed in interview room number two. Right next door to where Steven Harte sat with his lawyer.

Kim took a seat opposite. 'Thank you for coming in.'

'I didn't feel I had much of a choice when a squad car rolled up to my place of work.'

'My apologies, but due to the urgent nature of our enquiries, it was the quickest way to get you here.'

'I'm not sure why. I've already told you I can't remember anything that will—'

'Is this the room where you were held captive?' Kim asked, taking out the mobile phone.

Suzie hesitated before looking at the still photo Penn had taken of the empty room while Grace had visited the bathroom.

She stared at it for a full minute before uttering a word.

Kim watched her closely as a multitude of emotions flitted across her face. Recognition, sadness and realisation. Perhaps the penny had dropped about how she'd furnished, arranged and decorated her own daughter's room.

'I... I think so. It looks the same, exactly the same, except...'

'Except what?' Kim asked.

Suzie tipped her head and studied it for another minute. 'The bed. It's smaller than I remember it.'

'This one looks bunk-bed size,' Kim agreed.

'It definitely wasn't a bunk bed. I'd slept in one of those at a friend's house. It was definitely bigger than that bed. My own at home was a normal single, and the bed was bigger than that.'

'Suzie, is there anything else you remember?' Kim asked, placing the phone between them.

She shook her head. 'Nothing since you asked me a few days ago.'

'Anything at all about the location?' Kim pushed.

'I've told you. I didn't look around as I got into the van. I don't remember any sounds or smells or anything. It was so long ago.'

'You were asked at the time and you didn't remember anything then,' Kim said, trying to keep the accusation out of her voice.

Suzie met her gaze but said nothing.

Kim picked up the phone. Penn had shown her how to revert back to the live feed.

She turned the phone around. 'Look again.'

'I've already confirmed... Is that... Oh my... There's a little girl in there.'

'There is, Suzie, and do you see what she's doing? She's crying. She's alone and frightened. She wants to be back—'

'It'll pass after a few days. She'll be fine,' Suzie said dismissively.

'But that's where she is right now. In the first few days, so you know exactly how she's feeling, don't you?'

'Look, it doesn't matter what you show me. If I can't remember... wait a minute,' she said as realisation dawned on her face. 'How did you get this? Is this his mobile phone?'

Kim remained silent.

Suzie pushed her chair back. 'Is he here? Can I speak to him?'

She stood as though she was about to go looking for him.

'Where is he? Let me see him.'

'For what reason?' Kim asked, surprised at her reaction.

'I've just always wanted to meet him, ask him some questions.'

'I'm sorry but he's being held in connection with a serious—'

'Just two minutes, maybe five. That's all I want.' She paused. 'And you never know if it'll help to break something free,' she said, tapping her head.

Kim weighed up her options as she moved the phone back from the centre of the table.

Steven Harte was not a plaything while under their remit. They couldn't just foist upon him people that wanted to meet him. Even if he agreed to meet with Suzie, what exactly was he going to reveal?

It was an unorthodox request which she could see playing out badly in court.

Her only hope was that the meeting would indeed shake something free in Suzie's memory, but if the image of a vulnerable child crying with fear and loneliness hadn't nudged a memory free then nothing would.

For Kim there was a lot more to lose than gain.

'I'm sorry, Suzie, but I don't think that's a very good idea.'

Kim was surprised to see the hardness that formed on her face on hearing the finality in her tone.

'Have it your own way, Inspector, but I think it's a decision you may live to regret.'

SEVENTY-SEVEN

It was almost twelve by the time Kim was given the all-clear to continue questioning Harte, and Suzie's words were still ringing in her ears. She firmly believed that there would have been no benefit in orchestrating the meeting between the two of them, but something in Suzie's tone had left an echo on her nerves. Woody had agreed, and after he'd reviewed the evidence and the CCTV with the CPS, both had been satisfied with the charges of kidnap and murder in relation to Lexi Walters.

'So, Mr Harte, you've been charged with kidnapping and murdering Lexi Walters. Would you like to talk to us about your relationship with the little girl?'

Kim held her breath. Everything inside her said that he was ready, that she had passed every test and she would finally get the truth. But he'd had the chance for a good chat with his lawyer in the time since he'd admitted that he'd loved Lexi.

'It wasn't sexual,' he said, opening his palms. 'I didn't view her that way at all. When I saw her I just wanted to look at her. She was beautiful, innocent, unspoiled. I never wanted to keep her. I wanted to just borrow a moment of her life, that particular moment.'

'It wasn't just a moment though, was it, Mr Harte?'

He shook his head. 'No, I wanted to keep her for as long as I could.'

Kim had already decided on the direction of the interview. She wanted confirmation of identities before details of any other murders.

'Mr Harte, you already know that we've found remains beneath the fountain at Wyley Court. Is there anything you'd like to tell me?'

She couldn't question him directly about a crime for which he had not been arrested or charged, and without identities she couldn't charge him anyway. She had to hope that she'd played the game he'd wanted, and he was now ready and willing to confess.

'That is Paula Stiles.'

'Steven,' Swift warned. Until now she had been sitting in stony silence beside him.

He held up his hand to silence his solicitor.

'I saw her at the wildlife park. It had been a year since Lexi had gone. I'd swore I wouldn't do it again, but there she was. She looked so lonely, a shining, beautiful star glowing brighter than anything around her. I fought it but it was no use. I had to take her.'

Kim worked hard to control the rage she felt at his nonchalance at simply plucking people from their lives, as though everything was there for the taking. For him, for his benefit, for his entertainment, his enjoyment.

'And Clent?' she asked, although no remains had been found there yet.

'Helen Blunt,' he said as Swift sighed deeply. Kim was pretty sure she'd got more than she'd bargained for when she'd agreed to represent him.

'It was that slap from her mother. I can still see it now. She bravely fought back the tears as her mother just walked away after hitting her. She was lost, alone, ignored and then left on her own. That mother didn't deserve her.'

Kim ignored his justification. At times, it sounded as though he was the victim.

'But you won't find her exactly where you think you will.'

'At the site of the old coffee shop where Butler was digging before the company was thrown off site?' Kim clarified.

He shook his head. 'About twenty metres east of that spot along the treeline was another hole. A rubbish hole.'

'A what?' she asked, feeling her heckles rise. 'A bloody rubbish hole?' Kim worked hard to push her rage back down, but the pictures going through her mind were tapping directly into the forced calm that she needed to conduct the interview.

'A hole for rubbish. It can be hard to get a skip to some areas, so some builders dig a hole ready for crap that's coming out of the main excavation like stone and tree roots. The soil can always be dispersed easier.'

'You put her in that?'

He nodded and had the grace to look ashamed.

She waited.

He shook his head. 'Helen was the last.'

'What about Melody Jones?'

'Have you found her?' he asked.

'Not yet.'

'Then I have nothing to say.'

She put down her pen, safe in the knowledge that her team had heard his admission about the Clent Hills, and that the information was being passed on to the search and excavation team.

'You appear to have grown fond of all the girls you've mentioned,' she said. Kim desperately wanted to ask about Grace, but Alison had advised her to keep him in the past until she had all the information. Now she needed to know how they'd died.

'So why did you kill them?'

Harte shifted uncomfortably.

'What happened with Lexi?'

He took a deep breath.

'She saw me. One night while I was delivering the food she woke up. She was watching me for a while. I knew she'd be able to identify me. I knew then that I could never let her go.'

'Did you have to kill her?' Kim asked.

'Of course. She knew what I looked like.'

'How did you kill her?'

'I strangled her. It wasn't hard, and she didn't suffer.'

Of course it wasn't hard. He was a grown man and she'd been six years old. She begged to differ on the suffering. Having your body scream out for breath wouldn't have been a pleasant experience.

'And the disposal of her body?'

'I was already distantly involved in the project at Hawne Park. I'd donated a small amount. I brought in Butler as I knew he'd think nothing of me turning up last thing to inspect the work. His guys left, and I put her body into the hole and covered it over.'

'And how did that feel, Mr Harte?'

'Fucking awful, Inspector, but I didn't have a lot of choice, did I?'

Every fibre of her being wanted to scream at him about choice. Of course he'd had a choice. He could have chosen not to steal little girls from their families in the first place. He could have chosen to let Lexi go and take his chances. He could have chosen to come clean and admit what he'd done so that no other little girl got hurt. He could have chosen to get help for his compulsion and saved the lives of Lexi and the rest of the girls. He wasn't the one who'd had no choice.

'And what happened with Paula Stiles?' she asked calmly.

'Same. She saw me, and I had to let her go.'

'And you killed her the same way?'

'Yes, I strangled her and buried her beneath the fountain.'

Kim noted that she was getting less and less detail. She figured he wasn't enjoying reliving these memories. Shame. She was pretty sure the girls hadn't particularly enjoyed their experience either.

'Would you like to elaborate, Mr Harte?'

'What more do you need, Inspector? I'm telling you who they were and admitting to their murders. The CPS will need no more information to bring further charges against me. I refuse to relive every single detail.'

'And Helen Blunt?'

'She managed to get out. I found her, brought her back and then I had to let her go.'

'And after that?'

He shook his head. 'There were no more.'

She waited.

'I swear. Helen was the last. I couldn't face the thought of any more girls getting hurt because of me. All I ever wanted to do was look at them, enjoy their beauty. I couldn't do it again.'

She had enough to charge him with the murder of three young girls. She'd got him. He'd confessed, and he would spend the rest of his life in prison.

She had everything she needed to put him away and yet, some-how, she'd expected something more.

SEVENTY-EIGHT

'I've bloody got him,' Penn cried out, beckoning Stacey over. The detail of dates and times formulated by Claire Lennard had enabled him to request specific snatches of CCTV from both the butterfly farm and the Botanical Gardens. Given that the butterfly farm had only two cameras, theirs had come through first.

Stacey rolled her chair out from behind her desk, navigated the aisle between the four desks and landed beside him.

'I'm just going to play the section, and you tell me when you see him.'

He took the recording back to 11.27 a.m., exactly one week earlier.

The camera view opened up in the entrance foyer and gift shop of the Stratford Butterfly Farm. Third from the front of the queue were Claire and Grace Lennard, waiting to pay for entry.

Grace pointed at a poster on the wall.

'Jesus, he's right there,' Stacey exclaimed.

'Yep,' Penn said. Steven Harte was standing to the left of the shot, talking to one of the girls about something in one of the display cabinets.

'It's that movement she just made,' Stacey said in wonder.

Penn nodded. 'Grace's left arm pointing to that poster got his attention. Just watch.'

Penn said nothing as Stacey's mouth fell open. Harte's gaze fell on Grace's arm and stayed there, even though the member of staff carried on talking to him. He continued to watch as Claire and Grace moved towards the desk, paid and entered the heavy plastic ribbon doors into the butterfly farm.

'Now watch this,' he said, clicking on the next piece of footage.

The camera moved to the exit just an hour or so later, where Claire and Grace exited through a different set of plastic ribbons. Steven Harte was exactly ten seconds behind. He'd already timed it.

'Bloody hell, Penn,' Stacey said, sitting back. 'We've just watched his entire selection process.'

Penn nodded as the screen went blank. 'Pretty sure he would then have followed them home to find out their address.'

Stacey was still shaking her head as she wheeled herself back to her own desk.

He glanced at the phone and felt his heart lurch at seeing her on one camera so innocent, happy and excited to be visiting the butterflies, and on another screen curled up tightly on a bed in a strange room.

'Do you think he was just going to let her die?' he said to no one in particular.

Alison glanced over. 'There's one sandwich, an apple, some cheese strings and two bottles of water left on the desk. It's going to run out soon, so how was he going to refresh the supply? He knew what he was coming here for. He knew he might not get back to her.'

'Then why leave her food at all?' he asked.

'You've just heard him admit to the boss how he callously strangled three girls, so you really think he was bothered about one more starving to death? With Grace, he doesn't even need to go hands-on.'

Penn was not convinced. Since he'd walked in the door, Steven Harte had been giving clues either consciously or unconsciously.

Was there anything at all he was giving away without realising it?

Penn accessed the live feed on his computer but rewound to the beginning.

They already knew that Harte's default comfort gesture was to make circles around the rim of his cup of tea. He hadn't been allowed that comfort, so what had he been doing with his hands? How was he comforting himself right now?

He watched closely as the boss asked him about Lexi Walters. His right hand started making circles on the table.

From his focused expression, he appeared to be completely unaware of the action.

Penn kept watching.

He talked about Paula, and the circles began again.

The boss moved on to Helen. More circles on the table.

Penn watched again and noticed something new. The circles were in different places on the table. He felt the excitement churn his stomach. It probably meant nothing, he thought as he grabbed a plain sheet of paper.

He drew a circle on the page and pictured that same circle on the desk in front of Harte.

Lexi Walters. The circles were at ten o'clock.

Helen Blunt. The circles moved to six o'clock.

'Stace, get a map up and plot the burial sites of the victims,' he said, checking the movements again, and then a third time.

'Done,' she said.

'You got all three on the screen?'

'Yep.'

'Put an imaginary clock around it and put Lexi Walters at ten o'clock.'

'Er... okay.'

'Where would you put Paula in relation to Lexi?'

'I'd go north-east.'

'Give me a number.'

'Twelvish.'

'And where would you place Helen in relation to Paula.'

'South. Sorry, six o'clock.'

'Jesus, I think the table is a map in his head.'

Alison rolled towards him.

He played the footage and showed her his drawing.

She took another look and began to nod. 'Penn, I think you might be on to something. He's thinking of the last place he left them. He needs to be asked about Grace.'

'Someone needs to tell the boss.'

SEVENTY-NINE

Kim sat back at the table and resumed the interview. Both Harte and his lawyer looked at her questioningly. What could possibly be urgent enough to remove her from the room while a suspect was in the process of confessing to the abduction and murder of three little girls? She'd wondered the same thing until she'd heard what Penn had to say.

'My apologies for the interruption, Mr Harte, but it was important. We have gained access to your phone.' She paused. 'We understand you like your tea with one sugar,' she said so that he knew she wasn't bluffing.

Kate Swift frowned. She appeared to be irritated that she wasn't in on the joke.

Harte hid his surprise with a resigned nod of the head.

'We can see her. She's safe and well, just as you intended.'

Swift was looking from her to Harte, as though waiting for someone to tell her what was going on.

'Let's finish this, Mr Harte. Why don't you tell us where you've put Grace Lennard?'

His lawyer appeared stunned.

'Who the hell is Grace Lennard?' Swift asked as Harte's hand rested on the table.

Kim met Harte's intense stare and waited.

Swift watched the silent exchange for a full minute.

'Inspector, I'd like to pause the interview. I need to confer with my client.'

Kim held his gaze for a few more seconds before pausing the interview.

Swift had cut them off quickly, and Kim just hoped her team had got what they needed.

She stepped outside, and Bryant followed, closing the door behind him.

'What the hell was all that about?'

Bryant didn't know why she'd been called out of the interview.

'Something to do with circles on the table. The guys think he's giving away the locations of the girls unconsciously.'

Bryant looked doubtful. 'We stopped the questioning because—'

Bryant stopped speaking as the door opened.

Kate Swift exited the interview room and closed the door behind her.

'I'm sorry, Inspector, but I can no longer represent Mr Harte. He refuses to tell me the truth or listen to my advice; therefore, my presence here is pointless. I've recommended alternative legal counsel, but as far as I'm concerned, Mr Harte is now on his own.'

Without giving them a chance to respond, the woman strode towards the doors to the foyer.

Bryant's stunned expression matched her own feelings, which then turned to irritation. Without legal counsel, they could no longer talk to Steven Harte. Even if they were to appoint a solicitor on his behalf, he was now off limits for hours.

EIGHTY

It was three minutes past two when Alex heard the alarm in the distance as she sat on her bed. Perfectly timed. The sound was coming from the siren just outside the library. They all knew what it meant. *Go back to your cell and await lock-up.* Some would go quickly and others would try to linger and find out what the incident was about.

'What's going on?' she asked Emma innocently as she bustled into the cell.

'Dunno,' Emma said, throwing herself onto her bed and reaching for her book.

Oh dear, it looked as though the woman still had the hump from their earlier chat. Never mind – Alex would enjoy the peace anyway.

And she knew exactly what was going on. Noelle had made it to the library in time to find Stella grabbing the phone from where she'd stashed it. Without Titch nearby, she was pretty sure Noelle was giving her the hiding she deserved. When the guards searched Stella, they'd find the phone, and as she'd restored it to factory settings, it would never be traced back to her. Just a little bonus.

She could hear the sound of rubber soles heading her way at

speed. Any second now an officer would appear to lock them down. Standard practice during an incident.

If her plan had worked how she'd expected it to work, there should be a surprise waiting for them three cells down.

She heard raised, firm voices at the end of the corridor as a couple of prisoners refused to do as they were told. Other inmates were shouting to each other, trying to find out what was going on.

It was music to her ears when the second siren sounded, much closer this time.

She popped her head out of the door and, sure enough, guards were rushing into Lisa's cell.

She heard frantic calls to each other, movement, panic, urgency and then silence.

Oh dear, what could possibly have happened? she wondered.

A guard appeared in the hallway, smears of blood over her crisp white shirt.

'Back inside, Thorne,' she ordered.

'Of course, Officer,' she said, returning to her bed.

She would get an update soon enough. But it looked as though her plan had worked.

Two major incidents in one day. And where was the warden during the chaos?

Same place she always went at 2 p.m. on a Thursday afternoon.

EIGHTY-ONE

'Okay, guys, did he give you what you wanted?' Kim asked, rushing back into the squad room.

'Three o'clock,' Penn said.

'What the...?'

'In relation to Paula, Grace is north-east and she's south-east of Helen. So we've narrowed it down to this five-mile-square area from Belbroughton down to Bromsgrove to Alvechurch back up to Rednal.'

That was still a chunk of area.

Kim looked at Stacey who appeared to be on the phone with Sophie from Land Registry.

She covered the mouthpiece. 'Doing a reverse search right now.'

The square around the area Penn had drawn on the map was approximately twenty per cent residential, with the balance being rural. There were more than a hundred wooded areas within the scope, and any one of them could have properties hiding within them.

'Get the forensic botanist on the phone,' she said to Penn.

He called Ridgepoint as Stacey continued talking and Alison watched something on the playback.

'Sharon Bairden, how can I help?' said a pleasant voice on loudspeaker.

Penn gave the background of the case.

'I've not had a chance to carry out a full analysis of the sample but there's everything you would expect to find: road dirt, soil, oil deposits, petrol, cigarette ends, gravel.'

'Is there anything you can tell us about the soil? Anything that would help us pinpoint a location?'

'Well, there is one thing. I've found a tree seed, and there may be more. It's distinctive because it lives on a catkin which looks like a caterpillar. This particular seed comes from the *Betula pendula* tree which—'

'English name, Sharon,' Kim said.

'Sorry, to you guys that's the silver birch tree.'

Penn was scanning the aerial view of the search area. 'What am I looking for?'

'The silver birch grows anywhere from fifteen to twenty-five metres, with a slender trunk. The tree has an open canopy which lets light through, allowing mosses, grasses and flowering plants to grow beneath them. It needs plenty of light and does best in dry acid soils.'

'Sharon, anything you can—'

'Look for white trunks. They're easily visible through the light leafage.'

Penn zoomed in on something that looked promising, but there was no property anywhere nearby.

'We're struggling here, Sharon. Can you give us anything more?'

'So far I've only found one of them. If I don't find many more, then it's not the actual trees you're looking for.'

'Come again,' Kim said.

'If the tyres had been amongst the trees themselves, I'd expect to find at least another dozen. If not we're looking at a deposit.'

'Of what?'

'Not of what. By what. Birds.'

Kim and Penn looked at each other.

'Birds will use almost anything to make nests. There's every chance a seed could have been attached to a particularly good twig.'

'But how does that help us?' Kim asked.

'Birds will travel up to one mile with bedding.'

'So you're saying find the right silver birch tree and our location will be no more than a mile away from where the seed was picked up.'

'Stands a very good chance, Inspector.'

'Thanks, Sharon,' Kim said, ending the call.

'Three specific areas, boss,' Penn said. 'Two quite close to Alvechurch, the other one around Belbroughton.'

'Stace, what have we got around Alvechurch?'

Alvechurch was a village under the Bromsgrove district of Worcestershire. With a population of just over five thousand, it was located in the valley of the River Arrow. The village was steeped in history, and had much to be proud of, but was probably most well known for being the home of Tracie Andrews, who infamously killed her boyfriend, Lee Harvey, in 1996, and then tried to blame it on a road-rage incident.

'Give me one sec. Just one more minute. The report is coming through from Sophie right now.'

'Stace.'

'Got it. Harte owns thirty-seven acres of the valley between the village and the Lickey Hills.'

'Properties?'

'Looks like two, boss,' Stacey said. 'A barn and a small farmhouse. The rest is fields.'

'Show me.'

Stacey enlarged it on the screen. The barn was only seventy metres away from the road into the village. The house was at the end of a half-mile lane.

'No footpaths or bridle paths this side of the hills, boss,' Stacey said. 'No passing ramblers or vehicles anywhere near the farmhouse.'

Kim turned to Penn. 'Is this inside your travel radius for the timeline on Monday?'

'Just about, boss.'

'Does it work with your clock theory?'

'It does, boss,' Penn said.

'Okay, Bryant, looks like we're going to Alvechurch.'

His phone tinged with the address and postcode for the property. Kim found herself praying that they were on the right track, and that Grace would sleep in her own bed tonight.

She reached for her coat. 'Great work, guys, and—'

'He's lying,' Alison said to her computer screen.

Kim's head snapped round. 'About what?'

'The murders.'

'Go on,' Kim said, even though this was not something she wanted to hear.

'There's something not right. He's happy to give as much detail as you like about the abduction. Believe it or not he shows micro-expressions of regret, but there is no detail and no emotion when it comes to the murder of any of the girls.'

'Maybe he's not up for reliving it in the same detail. It's one thing to borrow a life, but it's another thing to extinguish it completely,' Kim offered.

'But it doesn't match. His demeanour when talking about the murders is much tighter. There's a tension creeping into his jaw. His left fist has clenched twice. He's rubbed at his nose more than any other time.'

'Are you trying to say he didn't kill them?' Kim asked.

'I'm not saying that for sure. I'm saying that it didn't happen in the way he described.'

Kim felt the dread forming in the pit of her stomach. 'What about sexual assault?'

'Harte didn't do that.'

'But someone else might have?'

Alison shrugged. 'It's possible.'

'Boss,' Penn said. 'What if Harte and Butler really were in it together? Maybe Harte abducted them and once he'd had his fill of looking at them, he allowed Butler to abuse them and then kill them.'

'Given Harte's reasons for taking the girls in the first place, that doesn't add up. I know he's just admitted to killing them but in a very quick, clean way. I'm just not sure about him allowing anyone to defile their beauty.'

'But it would explain why he's not giving a very convincing account of the murders,' Alison argued.

Kim's own sense of his warped integrity did not agree with the evidence, and she didn't like where that thought led.

'Shit. You know what this means, don't you, guys?' she asked, grabbing her jacket.

'Boss?' Stacey asked.

'It means that Grace Lennard isn't as safe as we thought.'

EIGHTY-TWO

'Is she okay?' Penn asked, overtaking a bus that had pulled in to pick up passengers.

The boss had asked them to keep Grace on screen while he and Stacey headed over to Butler's builders. The boss and Bryant were heading straight for the property.

'She's pacing at the moment,' Stacey said. 'I wish I could reach in and reassure her that everything is going to be okay, that she's being watched by the good guys now.'

He nodded. He felt the same way.

'I just have this awful feeling that we've missed him, that he's on his way and—'

'Stace, stop it. Just focus on the fact that right now we can see her and she's safe.'

He had the same feeling, and although he kept telling himself that by using the M5 and M42 Alvechurch was only about twenty-five minutes away, it felt a long way the boss was travelling right about now.

'What happened when you called his phone?' Penn asked.

Before they'd left, Stacey had tried to make contact with

Butler, to ask him a couple more questions to gauge if he was in the car or somewhere other than the office.

'The first time it rang out until it cut off, and second time it went straight to voicemail.'

He really didn't want to speak to them right now.

'What about the landline to the business?'

'Answerphone.'

'Bloody hell,' Penn said, wishing the car would eat up the miles to Quinton a bit quicker.

Stacey put Grace on her lap as she reached for her own ringing phone.

'Go ahead, boss,' she said after putting it on loudspeaker.

'You got him yet?'

'Not quite, boss – we're just a mile or two away.'

'Is Grace okay?'

'Fine at the minute, boss. How far out are you?'

'About ten minutes. Less if Bryant would—'

'Hang on, boss,' Stacey said urgently.

'What?'

'Let me just refresh the link to Grace.'

'What?' Penn asked, looking to his left.

'Stace, what's going on?' the boss asked.

'The camera. The link to Grace. It's gone. I'm reloading the link but it's gone. Network coverage is fine but it's like...'

'Like what, Stace?'

'It's like someone has cut the power.'

'Shit. Okay, get Butler's location as soon as possible.'

'Just pulling up now, boss,' Penn said.

'Call me as quickly as you can,' she said before ending the call.

'Bugger, it's totally gone,' Stacey said, trying again to access the link to the camera.

'Stace, we can't do anything right now,' he said, getting out of the car. 'Come on – let's go and find out where he is.'

Penn opened the door to the reception.

Both he and Stacey showed their identification. 'We need to speak to Mr Butler. Right now.'

The woman looked stunned by their urgency but recovered quickly.

'I'm sorry but Mr Butler isn't available to—'

'Okay, thank you,' Penn said, walking around to her side of the desk to access the archway behind. 'But it's imperative that we speak to him.'

Stacey had followed and was now between them.

'You can't just—'

'What I can't do is stand here and argue,' he said, moving out of the reception and into the inner workings of the property.

He continued forward and passed a glass box that appeared to be a conference room. It was empty.

He moved forward into a general office area. Seven or eight pairs of eyes were upon him.

'Mr Butler's office please?' he called out.

Three hands pointed over to the corner.

He took a breath and entered, unprepared for what he was about to see.

EIGHTY-THREE

Kim tapped her phone as they turned into the lane that led to the farmhouse at the end.

'National speed limit, Bryant – step on it,' she said.

He growled in response as he positioned the tyres either side of the grass column that had grown in the middle of the road. The increase in speed caught every pothole on the poorly maintained strip of tarmac that was more like a dirt road, but she didn't mind being bounced from pillar to post. Every second counted.

Her heart rate had been steadily rising ever since they'd lost visual contact with Grace.

She was praying desperately that her colleagues had Butler and that there had been some kind of rural power cut in this neck of the woods.

'Bryant, I swear, if you don't—'

'There's bends, guv,' he argued. 'Trust me, I want to get that little girl safely home more than anyone, but who's coming to get her if we get hit by something coming the other way?'

'And anyone we might meet will be coming from the farmhouse, so feel free to speed it up a bit.'

He did as she asked.

'Come on, Penn. Come on.'

As if on cue the phone rang, just as they approached the farmhouse.

A blue Jaguar XF was already parked.

'Oh shit. He's already here,' she said by way of a greeting to Penn as she got out of the car.

'He really isn't,' Penn said. 'He's here in his office. I'm looking right at him.'

'What the...?'

Kim stopped speaking as everything she'd learned throughout the week stormed into her head. Removing Butler from the equation had cleared her mind like a sliding door to reveal the truth standing behind it. Everything fell into place as she finally understood who and what they were dealing with.

How the hell had she missed what had been staring her in the face all week?

'Oh shit,' she said again as she ran towards the door.

EIGHTY-FOUR

The door was flung open, and for a second Kim was disoriented by entering the physical area of a space she'd been watching virtually.

Surveying the scene before her, she had no time to waste. Adult hands were clamped around Grace's throat.

She threw herself forward and grabbed the woman by the hair.

'Loose her, Kate,' Kim screamed as the lawyer's hands released from around Grace's neck.

They landed in a heap on the ground.

'Or should I call you Melody?' she asked, pinning the woman with her legs.

'Get off me,' Swift cried out, but Kim wasn't going anywhere.

She turned to see Bryant comforting a coughing, spluttering Grace, who looked terrified, but she was alive.

'It's okay, Grace – we've got you now,' he said gently.

Just another couple of minutes and they would have been too late.

Swift writhed beneath her. Kim tensed her thigh muscles to hold her still.

'Bryant, get Grace out of here and lock the door,' Kim instructed.

'Guv...'

'Just do it.'

Grace was crying hysterically. The tears were rolling over her cheeks. The child didn't need to see any more.

'It's okay, Grace. We're the police,' she heard Bryant say. 'We're not going to let anyone hurt you.'

The girl sobbed loudly.

'Get Claire on the phone. Let Grace speak to her mother,' she called over her shoulder as the door closed and locked.

Swift took the opportunity of Kim's shift in weight to turn on her side and dislodge her thighs. She pushed up and managed to topple her to the ground.

Swift was on her in a second. The first blow landed on the side of her face. As the second one came down, Kim managed to move her head out of the way. Swift's fist landed on the ground.

'You fucking bitch. How dare you stop me.'

Kim continued to dodge the blows, but the woman was stronger than she looked, and Kim's bucking was not shifting her. Swift had her in the exact same position that she'd used. All she could do was hold up her arms to defend herself.

'Get the fuck off me,' she cried as a left hook caught her cheekbone.

'She didn't deserve to live,' Swift spat as another blow made it through. Swift's knuckle made a direct hit on the side of Kim's nose. Her vision blurred as the pain shot into her head.

Her arms couldn't keep up with the blows reigning down from the woman whose eyes had glazed over. Hair had broken free from her ponytail, and spittle was flying out of her mouth.

This woman bore no resemblance to the controlled, professional solicitor who had sat opposite her for the last couple of days. And she had a good idea why. She was no longer Kate Swift. She was Melody, the little girl who was prepared to kill to get what she wanted.

Kim had to find a way to break free. Swift's rage was fuelling her energy. Just one of these blows could render her unconscious.

She tried catching one of Swift's wrists, but she broke free easily. Her centre of gravity from above gave her every advantage.

Another punch to the head brought the nausea to her stomach.

She continued to hold her hands above her head as she counted. There was a pattern to the blows. Right, right, left. Right, right, left. Right, right left. Right, right and Kim grabbed the left wrist with both hands.

She twisted it until Swift howled, then bucked her body with every ounce of strength she had left and sent her tumbling to the ground. Swift rolled once before jumping up and banging on the door.

'Let me at the little bitch.'

'It's over, Kate. You're not going to hurt another one,' Kim said, wiping a trail of blood from her nose.

'She has to die. I'm the special one, not her.'

The woman's eyes blazed.

'She is special, and so were the others: Lexi, Paula and Helen.'

Every name was like a bullet going into her body, but not because she was sorry for what she'd done, but because Harte had loved them too.

Swift continued to bang on the door. 'Let me out,' she screamed.

How had Steven Harte warped her to this degree?

'Not happening. You're getting nowhere near her,' Kim said as her breathing began to return to normal. The danger was over. She ignored the pounding in her head and all over her face. She needed to get some answers.

It had all come to her outside. Alison's observation that Harte was lying about the murders. His cryptic clues that he would lead them to Melody, but never once had he stated she was dead. They had assumed that from day one. The bunk bed in the room instead of the bigger bed described by Suzie and Libby indicated that, at times, there had been more than one girl in the room. Swift's reaction when he had talked about the other girls. She hadn't been annoyed that he was going against her advice. She had been upset at the very mention of their names. When Kim had shown them the old photo of Lexi, Swift had been horrified. Not because of the fate of the little girl, but because it was a reminder of having to share Harte. Her rage when Harte had declared that he'd loved Lexi was not because he was going against her instruction, but because she was jealous of his feelings for her first victim. And finally, her sharp exit from the station at the mention of Grace's name. That's when she'd learned there was another one, and she'd known exactly where to come.

'What was different about you, Kate? Why didn't Harte let you go like the others?'

'I didn't want to leave,' she said, turning around.

'What?'

'Oh, wake up, Stone. Have you met my family?'

'I have but still...'

'But still what?' she asked, sliding down the door and landing on the floor. 'Look around you. My own bedroom, television, bathroom, new clothes, occasional toys, games. No fear. Why would I want to leave?'

'You didn't miss anybody?' Kim asked, trying to understand.

'Stone, I don't know what your childhood was like. You probably come from two loving, well-adjusted parents who prioritised you and made you feel loved, cared for, treasured.'

'Not quite.'

'Well then perhaps you'll understand that it's hard to miss people to whom you meant nothing. How do you miss people who feel like strangers? I was the youngest, the runt, the invisible, the forgotten. I detest them and I don't feel bad. They've made enough money over the years.'

Kim heard the bitterness in her voice, and she could understand why. 'You said you'd escaped the fear – of what?'

Swift tipped her head and raised an eyebrow.

'Your brother?'

She nodded. 'Most nights.'

'You couldn't tell your mum?'

'I did. She told me he'd soon get bored if I just lay there and took it.'

Kim felt the nausea rise in her throat.

'So I wake up here,' she said, sweeping one arm around the space. 'Everything I ever needed or could have dreamed of. It was all mine. And no one wanted anything in return.'

'You were being watched the whole time,' Kim said, nodding towards the camera.

Swift shrugged. 'Didn't care. I wasn't being touched, mauled, raped. I was away from all that. I was safe and protected.'

'What happened?'

'One day, after about a year or so, the door opened. I was confused. I didn't know what to do. I didn't know what I was supposed to do. I waited but no one came. I didn't want to leave.'

'So?'

'I closed the door and carried on as normal.'

Kim couldn't help but wonder what Steven Harte had made of that. 'And then what happened?'

Kim had a pretty good idea but she wanted Swift to walk her through it.

'Some months later, I woke up to find myself in a smaller bed, up high with another bed below.'

'Did you understand what that meant?'

'I think I did and I didn't. I guessed that another girl was coming, and I didn't mind until Lexi actually arrived. Jesus, she did nothing but moan and cry.'

'Is that why you killed her?'

Swift looked as though she was going to argue the point, but as a lawyer especially, she must have understood the futility of denial. Only moments ago, Kim had entered the room to find her with her hands around the throat of a little girl, doing exactly what Steven Harte had tried to admit to doing.

'No, it wasn't that I was angry. Once she stopped crying she was sweet and nice and...'

'You were jealous?'

'She was trying to take my place. I was the special one. I was the one he took care of, and I didn't want to share.'

'Did you strangle her?'

'Yep,' she said with not one ounce of emotion. 'I waited for her to go to sleep, and I knew what to do. Robbie had done the same to me when I threatened to tell my teacher what he was doing to me. When he put his hands around my throat and squeezed, I felt as though I was going to die, so that's how I did it.'

Despite the lack of emotion in Swift's voice, Kim's mind recoiled at the scene. A child on top of another child, squeezing the life out of her.

'What happened next?'

'Steven came and took her away. He didn't speak to me, and it was the first time I saw him.'

'He just disappeared with her body?'

Swift nodded.

'And then there was Paula?'

'Yeah, I didn't like her for even a minute. She climbed up on to my bed. I told her I didn't like to share. She said it was better than some of the foster homes she'd been in. I did her after three days.'

There was no remorse in her tone.

'Kate, you were a child.'

She shrugged. 'I wanted them gone.'

'Was Helen the last?'

Swift nodded. 'She fought me harder. I actually got a bruise on my arm from her fingers, and I had to use a pillow to finish her off.'

The emotionless recital of the facts was chilling Kim to the bone. Whatever had been instilled in Swift over the years hadn't included a conscience.

'When Steven came to get her, I told him I wasn't going to stop doing it.'

'And what happened?'

'A couple of weeks later he came and got me and took me home.'

'Home?' Kim asked. Her home had been on the Hollytree Estate.

'My new home, his house, and if I thought this was heaven, you should have seen my new room.' Her eyes lit up. 'A four-poster bed, all matching furniture, bigger television, games and toys and books.'

Kim realised that it was almost like the murders hadn't happened.

'That's when Melody died and I became Kate.'

Kim wondered if she really had disassociated herself completely from the person who had killed three girls, or if she truly had no regrets for what she'd done.

'Steven formally changed my name and sent me to private school as his orphaned niece.'

Now Kim understood why there was no trace of the Black Country accent. 'And no one suspected anything?'

'Why would they?' Swift asked, genuinely perplexed, as though she really was Steven Harte's orphaned niece.

'Did no part of you want to return home? To tell the truth?'

Swift looked at her as though she was mad. 'Why the hell would I want to do that?'

'To be yourself. To get your identity back.'

'Melody's life was shit. She was miserable, scared. She was a coward. She was a nobody. They exploited Melody's disappearance for every penny they could get. How much do you think they'd have tried to make from Melody's reappearance after all these years?'

Kim noted again how she referred to Melody almost as a totally separate person.

'And the truth is overrated anyway. Just like this conversation. It was truthful, but it was private, and no one else heard a word.'

As though a switch had been flicked, she stood and dusted herself down.

'I wasn't cautioned, I wasn't arrested and I'll never repeat what I just said. Your colleague didn't see a thing. I was here to help Grace and you got the wrong idea. Steven will never testify against me. That confession counts for nothing. You have someone at the station that has confessed to three murders. It's on video. I know which option the CPS is going to go for.'

She smiled widely, an open and genuine smile that held no remorse for the young lives she'd taken.

There wasn't one word she'd said that wasn't true. In her mind, Swift had committed the perfect crimes and was now going to return to her perfect life, as though nothing had happened, while the man she professed to love as a father would serve the time.

'So if you'd like to ask your colleague to open the door and let me out, I'll be on—'

'Kate Swift, I am arresting you for the murders of Lexi Walters, Paula Stiles and Helen Blunt. You do not have to say anything but it may harm your defence if you do not mention when questioned something which you later rely on in court. Anything you do say may be given in evidence. Do you understand?'

Swift laughed. 'I'm a lawyer – of course I understand. I also know I'll be free and clear in twenty-four hours.'

Kim knew she had no evidence to charge. She knew she had to get it.

And it could only come from one source.

EIGHTY-FIVE

It was almost seven when Alex was shown into the office of Warden Siviter.

The woman looked pale and drawn. Tendrils of hair had escaped from her ponytail and small perspiration marks peeped out from the armpits of her pink shirt.

The woman hadn't had a good day.

Shame.

'Alexandra, we'll need to keep this short. I have urgent matters to attend to and—'

'How is Lisa?' Alex asked, feigning concern.

'On life support at the moment. They're not hopeful.'

Alex wasn't bothered either way. A nice clean death would have been preferable, but whether she died today or in a few days, it made no difference to her.

Warden Siviter shook her head. 'Her suicide attempt was unexpected, especially as she was being recommended for early release. I was going to tell her that today.'

'Shame,' Alex said, already bored with talking about other people. She already knew that Noelle had beaten Stella to within an inch of her life and that she'd be in the hospital for at least a few days.

Alex waited expectantly, eager to move on. This meeting was about her.

Warden Siviter cleared her throat. 'As you're fully aware, you have a parole hearing tomorrow, and I have yet to formalise my recommendation. I think you've made great strides here with your rehabilitation. I see you interacting well with others. I see you even stepping in to protect the vulnerable. Many of your fellow inmates appear to respect you, and you've never been involved in any episodes of violence. In fact, you've earned yourself an impeccably clean record over the last few years.'

Alex relaxed back in her chair. She liked the direction this was going.

'However, I have reservations.'

Alex didn't care for that word very much. 'Which are?'

'The opinions of other people that have known you for much longer than I have. I've known you only a couple of years, but my predecessor noted in your file that you should serve no less than your full sentence.'

'But surely...'

'And then there are people in responsible positions who have made their feelings known.'

Fucking Stone, Alex thought, still smarting from being inter-rupted by this woman who thought she was controlling both the conversation and the situation.

'So, on balance, I'm sorry to say that I am not going to recom-mend your early release to the probation board, as I think you would benefit from further—'

'Is that your final decision?' Alex asked.

Siviter appeared surprised at her curt tone but continued anyway. 'I understand your disappointment but I have to do what I feel is in the best interest of—'

'I think you might want to reconsider,' Alex said, unwilling to listen to concerns of the interests of anyone other than herself.

'Excuse me?' she asked, narrowing her gaze.

'For your own sake,' Alex explained.

'Are you threatening me?'

'Absolutely not,' Alex said, offering a half-smile. She was in control now. 'I am merely forewarning you of what is about to happen next.'

Alex took a breath. 'There is no doubt that you are a firm and fair warden. You are professional, objective and approachable. You have the respect of your team as well as the inmates. You're here early and you leave late. You actually do care about the people in your prison, and I can understand why.'

Alex sighed heavily and forced sympathy into her eyes.

'What's that supposed to mean?'

'Every one of these ladies could be the child you gave away. They could even be the child you lost.'

The colour drained from her face.

Alex continued. 'You put every ounce of love and affection into these prisoners as if they were your own—'

'How did you find out...?' Her words trailed away as she remembered one particular woman being held in her care.

'Of course, if you'd been lucky enough to have your own children now you wouldn't be so focused on the women under your care, but that's no bad thing for these prisoners. I mean it when I say that your absence would be a huge loss to this prison.'

'I'm not going anywhere,' she said as the sadness in her eyes grew hard.

'Well, maybe not by choice. It's been a very busy day here today. There was a serious assault and a suicide attempt. The guards did their best, but they were floundering, lacking direction, leadership, prioritisation from the person in charge. You weren't here and things got missed. Decisions were delayed.'

'My time off on Thursday is completely authorised. I wasn't here because I was visiting my mother in residential care.'

'There will be an enquiry, obviously, and your performance will be questioned – more so if Lisa dies.'

'I was visiting my sick mother,' Siviter spat.

'Well, yes, you were at first.' Alex paused. 'Until 1.30ish and then you walked fifty metres down the road to the betting shop. You would have left at around half past two if you hadn't received the emergency call. So let's be clear: at two o'clock, when everything kicked off here, you were betting on horses and playing fruit machines. That's a headline that's going to—'

'You can't prove that,' she said, reddening. Alex would swear the stain beneath her armpits was growing.

'I don't need to. I only have to contact a couple of reporters who will establish within half an hour of my call that there is CCTV from both inside the betting shop and across the road. You'll be the juicy headline instead of the events that occurred. The bad press will be too much for your employers, and you will be forced to resign.'

Alex could see the rage filling Siviter's eyes. That was good. That meant the woman felt trapped, that she'd been beaten.

Alex stood. 'I look forward to your recommendation for my release.'

EIGHTY-SIX

Kim took a breath before entering the room.

It was almost seven, and the last couple of hours had been hectic. Kate Swift had been returned to the station, re-cautioned by Jack and then placed in a cell awaiting her representation.

She was sticking to the story of having remembered where she'd been kept and returning to help free Grace and bring her to safety. When asked, Bryant had admitted that he hadn't seen Swift's hands around Grace's throat before Kim had rushed her to the ground.

If Steven Harte stuck to his story, Kate Swift would walk free in less than twelve hours.

Kim entered and sat, saying nothing as Bryant took care of the formalities.

'Mr Harte, you have agreed to speak with us without legal representation. Is that correct?'

'I have nothing further to add to my previous confession.'

Kim met his gaze. There were no inflated folders, no cups of tea, no games.

'The jig is up, Mr Harte. I mean, make no mistake, you're never going to see free daylight again, but it won't be for murder. Five charges of kidnap and imprisonment will keep you behind bars for the rest of your life.'

'Five counts?'

'Yes, five. We found Melody. And we also found Grace.'

He held her gaze but said nothing.

'The farmhouse in Alvechurch is a lovely spot. But why did you take Grace in the first place? You knew what you were going to do. You knew you weren't going to be able to watch her, so why did she have to suffer any of this?'

'To get your attention. Had I come to you and admitted to the kidnap and murder of three girls, you would never have listened and you would have pegged me as a crackpot and sent me on my way. Even if I'd told you where they were buried, you still wouldn't have gone and excavated the historic fountain on my say-so alone. There had to be the threat of a live, missing girl for you to believe my involvement.'

'She could have died.'

'Grace had enough food and water to last her for seven days. A cleaning company has been booked for 9 a.m. on Monday morning. They have a key. Grace was never going to die.'

'Why not just tell us?' Kim asked, trying to keep the incredulity from her tone.

He shrugged. 'Where's the fun in that?'

Kim bit her tongue. She had to remember that although not a killer, the man before her was a twisted, ruthless individual who had enjoyed playing games with them from day one.

'We know you didn't murder the girls, Mr Harte, but we'll come to that in a minute. First, what made Melody different to the others?'

He regarded her silently.

'Mr Harte, she is sitting in a cell down the hall, so feel free to be honest about the circumstances of her abduction. Was it the Hollytree connection?'

He hesitated and then nodded.

'I opened the door to return her to the police station like the others, but she refused to leave. She closed the door. She carried on as though it had never opened. She didn't want to return to that life, to that family, to that place, and I couldn't blame her.'

He paused and met her gaze. 'It's hard for others to understand. I've been to many places but rarely have I seen anywhere as soulless as Hollytree. It is the place where everything goes to die. It's like a landfill site for hopes and dreams, kindness and conscience. Everywhere you look there's filth, despair and ugliness. It kills your hope that there's anything better. And you know exactly what I'm talking about.'

'Is that why you came to me?' she asked.

He nodded. 'I saw you on the telly a couple of years back when your past was being targeted. I was surprised when I learned of the Hollytree connection. No, not surprised – I was impressed. For some reason I was proud that you'd done okay for yourself. It made me smile and it stuck with me. You were the obvious choice.'

'But what exactly did you think I'd understand, Mr Harte? Did you think I'd excuse what you'd done?'

He smiled. 'No, because then you wouldn't be the police officer I think you are. I hoped you'd understand that you can take the person out of Hollytree but you can't take Hollytree out of the person.'

'You wanted me to understand that the place damages everyone in some way or another?'

'I suppose so.'

'And did you want me to understand that for Melody or for you?'

'I couldn't send her back when she had no wish to return,' he said, not answering the question. 'I'd removed her. I'd given her a taste of life away from the ugliness, and I couldn't force her to go back.'

'You developed feelings for her?'

'Yes, but not...'

'I know it wasn't sexual, Mr Harte. It's called Lima syndrome.'

He shook his head.

'Just as your victims developed Stockholm syndrome in relation to you, their captor, it is also known that the reverse can happen and the captor can develop feelings for the captive. You stopped seeing her as your butterfly, pinned in the cage of your making, and began to see her as an individual, a little girl with feelings and needs.

'And yet you still blamed yourself for taking her away from all she knew. You couldn't stop yourself from bringing back another girl. You couldn't have known how Melody would react, that she would be so overcome with jealousy that she would actually take Lexi's life.'

'I've told you. I killed—'

'I know what you said, Mr Harte, but you were lying, so now I'm telling you what I think happened. You brought in three more innocent girls who all lost their lives because you couldn't help your fascination, and Melody couldn't help herself in killing them. Somehow the relationship between the two of you had become so twisted and warped. At that point, you took Melody into your home, and that's when she became Kate. I think the name change enabled you to see her differently and allowed you to put the deaths to the back of your mind. It was Melody who did it, not Kate.'

He shook his head in denial.

'I think you did everything you could to turn her into Kate. You took care of her, you educated her, you became some kind of twisted father figure to her and I think, eventually, you saw her as though she'd always been Kate. I think it's the only way you could forgive her for what she'd done.'

'She didn't do anything. It was me who—'

'I think you blamed yourself not only for the deaths of Lexi, Paula and Helen but also for the fact that your actions had turned Melody into a killer. You buried the bodies where Butler was working because you knew he had a predilection for young girls. You knew that if the bodies were ever found, he'd be a definite suspect.'

'This is all just preposterous.'

'Please hear me out, Mr Harte. I think you started to panic when the works began at Hawne Park; you actually instructed the work because you wanted this to be over, but you were worried that there might be some kind of DNA or evidence that would link back to Melody, so you decided to confess to the crimes to save her. If we had a culprit, we wouldn't waste unnecessary funds on all the lab work.'

'Really, Inspector, I expected better than this flight of fancy.'

'No, actually, this is exactly what you expected, Mr Harte, and that's the reason for all the games.'

His eyebrows drew together.

'You came in here on Monday. You could have just told us everything without the drama. We may have believed you without the abduction of Grace to get our attention. Right now, you'd be in prison and we'd already be building our court case, but that's not what you really wanted, is it?'

Alison had told her he'd been conflicted, and now Kim knew why.

'There's a part of you that's still angry with Melody for what she did. You never did anything to hurt Suzie or Libby. You watched them and let them go. You never touched them. You took the girls because you were fascinated and in some ways entranced by their beauty. You wanted to cherish them. Melody took that from you.'

She paused and let out a long breath. 'I think despite your loyalty and love for Melody, despite your conscious wish to protect her, I think you wanted us to get to the truth. I think deep down you wanted us to know what Melody had done. I think you want us to punish her because you never could.'

She saw the emotion and truth of what she'd said register in his eyes.

'And there's one more thing you should know before deciding if your guilt and loyalty have been misplaced. You've dressed Melody up as Kate for the last twenty-five years. You see a different person now, but she's still the same Melody she was back then.'

He shook his head. 'Kate is—'

'Kate was found with her hands around Grace's throat. She hasn't changed a bit. She was perfectly happy to try to kill another girl just so she could remain your number one.'

Kim paused to allow him to form the vision of Kate Swift's adult body towering over Grace's small frame.

'It's time to come clean properly, Mr Harte.'

His head fell into his hands. The palms rubbed hard at his forehead. She was unsure what part of the things she'd said he was trying to rub away.

He sighed heavily before raising his head to reveal reddened, haunted eyes.

'May I trouble you for a cup of tea?'

'One sugar?' she asked with a raised eyebrow.

'Yes please. And then I'll tell you the truth.'

EIGHTY-SEVEN

Kim parked the car outside The Dog in Tipton and took a breath.

It looked quieter than when she'd visited earlier in the week. And boy had it been some kind of week.

The office was still in chaos.

After her conversation with Steven Harte, Kim had left her team hard at it while she took half an hour to try and give a man his life back. It was important to her that Gum didn't hear the news from anyone else.

It wasn't hard to spot the ex-police officer who had tortured himself for a quarter of a century. He was warming his usual spot in the corner and looking dolefully at the empty glasses on the table.

She knew better than to go empty-handed so got him a pint on her way.

'What the...?' he asked, looking at the colour of the liquid and then at her.

'Hey, Gum,' she said, taking a seat.

His eyes moved back to the offending glass that she'd put on the table.

'You need to know something before it hits the news at ten and the internet in about five minutes.'

'Whatever you've got to say, I don't want...'

'She didn't die, Gum. Melody Jones wasn't killed.'

'Wh... What?' he asked, putting down his glass before it slipped out of his hand.

One revelation at a time.

'She was abducted by a man who liked to watch little girls. He let the first two go after a year, but he kept Melody. She had a great life. All these years you've punished yourself for not bringing her home, and she didn't even want to return.'

He rubbed at his forehead as though trying to make the information stick.

How much had this man lost through this one case? Kim wondered. His marriage. His friends. A career that had stagnated because he couldn't get beyond his own failure or guilt.

'You didn't let anyone down, Gum. I've seen the files. You worked that case as hard as you possibly could have. Her abductor didn't show up on your radar, and there's no reason why he would have. It wasn't your fault.'

He shook his head, and Kim understood his mind's refusal to accept her words. It was like having a wart that bothered you every single day for twenty-five years and then suddenly having it removed.

'Sh-She's still alive?' he asked, blinking away the emotion. She could hear the thickening in his throat.

'Those pictures that were in your head all this time weren't real. She didn't suffer. She wasn't raped; she wasn't beaten.'

A tear slid over his cheek which he quickly wiped away.

She gave him a moment before continuing. 'There's more, Gum. You can read all the gory details when it comes out, but Melody was responsible for the deaths of three little girls.'

'The ones you're digging up half of the Midlands for?' he asked.

She nodded. 'I'm saying no more until all the charges are in place, but I didn't want you hearing this on the news. You deserve better than that.'

He wiped at his eyes and opened his mouth to let out one of the hundreds of questions that must have been on his mind, but he closed it again. He knew she was going to say no more.

He took a deep breath. 'Thank you. I appreciate the courtesy. Now, what the fuck is in that glass?'

'Lemonade.'

'Why the bloody hell would you—?'

'You know, Gum, there are times when we need to know shit. I mean, we need answers that we as police officers can't get. I'm talking stuff that only a seasoned, experienced, gifted ex-police officer can find out. One that's sober, has an excellent memory, impeccable contacts and a nose for getting to the truth. It doesn't come with a title but most likely expenses, a few quid for your time and a chance to do what we all know you do best.'

Interest lit his eyes as she glanced at the glass of lemonade.

'Your choice, Gum. I'll leave it with you, okay?' she said, pushing herself away from the table.

She turned at the door to see him staring at the glass of lemonade as though it would give him the answer; he hadn't yet touched his other drink. His brain had a lot to process.

If he wanted to turn his life around, she had given him a reason.

She could offer him no more than that.

EIGHTY-EIGHT

Kim leaned against the seat of the Ninja with her ankles crossed and her hands balled in her pockets.

Her day had been the equivalent of a three-ringed circus. After speaking to Gum last night, she had sent the whole team home for some much-needed rest.

Overnight the news had come in that bones had been located at the Clent site. No one doubted they would be formally identified as belonging to Helen Blunt, Melody's third and final victim.

The whole team had returned this morning, fresh and alert, ready to sort out all the charges for both Steven Harte and Melody Jones.

The CPS hadn't been best pleased but had agreed that with Steven's testimony they were happy that convictions of Kate Swift for the murders of Lexi, Paula and Helen would be achieved. And for his part, Steven Harte would never walk free again.

A couple of hours ago the press had exploded both locally and nationally. Every outlet and media were carrying the story; initially, that Melody Jones was alive after all this time, and then that she'd been charged with murder. Kim was sure that documentary makers were lining up talking heads already.

It was one of those stories that had captured the public's interest. They wanted to feast on an oddity. To try to understand how the relationship had formed and then twisted between Harte and Melody.

She was pretty sure the Jones family would be considering how to milk this new development for everything it was worth. Not one of them had phoned the station to see how Swift was doing. Melody Jones was truly dead to them, and they would try and find some way to profit from her crimes.

Except a local reporter had been given a tip-off about certain eBay accounts, and Kim felt sure a juicy article about the family's profiteering ways would be appearing imminently. The offers would soon dry up after that. They had made enough money out of Melody. It was time for it to stop.

Grace had been reunited with her mother at the police station. They had held each other as though they would never let go. The gratitude in Claire Lennard's eyes had said more than any words she could have spoken.

So much pain, so much anguish caused by the twisted relationship of two people that never should have even met.

Two people had been responsible for the fact that three little girls had died, and yet she couldn't find it in herself to hate either one of them.

Hollytree had been her home once too. Her own six-year hell had happened against the backdrop of a place that was devoid of humanity and hope. There was an ugliness there that consumed everything that lived within it.

Steven Harte had been imprisoned there for years, desperate to find hope, life, beauty. He had found that beauty in the faces of little girls.

He had admired them as one would admire a piece of art, a sculpture, except he'd allowed his fascination to drive him, to control him. He had not harmed any of the girls and had tried to justify his actions in relation to their backgrounds. In his own misguided way, he felt that he'd taken care of them.

During his confession he had admitted that he was repulsed by what Jenson Butler had done all those years ago, and he had used him only for the purpose of directing suspicion towards the man in the event that any of the bodies were found sometime in the future.

And then there was Melody – unloved, unwanted and abused. She had found a life with Steven Harte. She had become so attached to the ghost that protected her that she couldn't bear the thought of sharing him with anyone else.

Her experience had turned her into a child killer. Would anything like that have happened if she'd never been taken? They would never know. Harte had been the only father figure she had ever known, and she had wanted to remain an only child.

It wasn't the only time the subject of father had come up this week. Her arch nemesis had not only informed her that her mother was close to death, she also now held the only missing part of Kim's childhood. Kim had been offered the piece of the puzzle and had turned it down. The price had been too high. There was no way her conscience would have allowed her to make any kind of trade with Alexandra Thorne.

And yet her refusal had all been for nothing, she thought as the prison doors opened.

Kim's breath caught as the woman herself stepped out of the facility. The guard handed her a small holdall like a bellboy at a top hotel.

The afternoon sun glinted off her blonde hair as she closed her eyes and took a deep breath, savouring the taste of freedom. A slow smile that Kim knew well turned up the corners of her mouth. It was the smile of victory.

Kim had no idea how she'd managed to swing it but it made no difference now. She was out and there was nothing she could do about it.

She waited for the woman's searching glance to fall upon her, as she knew it would.

She was ready. Their eyes met, and Kim saw the expression soften. After what seemed like an eternity Alex lowered her eyes and laughed at some private joke, as though she had known that Kim would not look away first.

'Too right, bitch,' she said as Alex got into a waiting car.

Kim watched it leave and wondered how long she had before Alex re-entered her life. It wouldn't be for a while yet. Alex's priority would be to get her life back in order, rebuild her business and re-establish her standing in society. She would come at her from a position of strength. The woman had been dangerous enough before her years in prison, and she could only wonder at the tricks she'd learned since.

She didn't know how and she didn't know when, but she did know that at some stage Alexandra Thorne would come for her again.

A LETTER FROM ANGELA

First of all, I want to say a huge thank you for choosing to read *Stolen Ones*, the fifteenth instalment of the Kim Stone series, and to many of you for sticking with Kim Stone and her team since the very beginning.

I loved writing *Stolen Ones,* and if you enjoyed it, I would be forever grateful if you'd write a review. I'd love to hear what you think, and it can also help other readers discover one of my books for the first time. Or maybe you can recommend it to your friends and family...

And if you'd like to keep up to date with all my latest releases, just sign up at the website link below.

www.bookouture.com/angela-marsons

Many readers of the Kim Stone series will know that when dreaming up plots for the books, I like to present Kim with a situation she hasn't been faced with before, just because I want to see how she reacts to it. In *Stolen Ones* I wanted to see how Kim would react when the killer appears to present himself right at the beginning of the case.

Like many others, I've recently been enthralled by the TV series *Criminal*, which focused on interviewing techniques and interrogation. From the very first episode I wanted to present a similar situation for Kim where along with the normal criminal processes followed by the team, she was reliant on reading and deciphering the suspect.

I thoroughly enjoyed researching CIA interrogation and questioning techniques as well as body language, and it gave me a great opportunity to bring back Kim's favourite behaviourist, Alison Lowe.

In addition, it was interesting to catch up with Alexandra Thorne and continue to explore the strange dynamic that exists between her and Kim. I know that Alex is like Marmite and you either love or hate her, but from a writer's point of view she is an intriguing character to write.

I'd love to hear from you – so please get in touch on my Facebook or Goodreads page, Twitter or through my website.

Thank you so much for your support, it is hugely appreciated.

Angela Marsons

www.angelamarsons-books.com

facebook.com/angelamarsonsauthor

twitter.com/WriteAngie

ACKNOWLEDGEMENTS

As ever my first and foremost thanks go to my partner, Julie. There is no idea that she doesn't encourage me to explore. She is there to listen to the enthusiastic early ideas. She is there to appease the 20K-word doubt monsters. She is there to reinvigorate me through the soggy middle, and she's right there to push me over the finish line. She has always been and continues to be my partner in crime.

Thank you to my mum and dad who continue to spread the word proudly to anyone who will listen. And to my sister Lyn, her husband Clive and my nephews Matthew and Christopher for their support too.

Thank you to Amanda and Steve Nicol who support us in so many ways and to Kyle Nicol for book spotting my books everywhere he goes.

I would like to thank the growing team at Bookouture for their continued enthusiasm for Kim Stone and her stories.

Special thanks to my editor, Claire Bord, who gives me the liberty to explore new ideas and supports me in taking Kim in a slightly different direction now and again. Her trust in me and the process allows me the luxury of creative freedom to dream up new experiences and challenges for the team. I know that if I jump off a cliff with no wings, she will be there to catch me.

To Kim Nash (Mama Bear) who works tirelessly to promote our books and protect us from the world. To Noelle Holten who has limitless enthusiasm and passion for our work and Sarah Hardy who also champions our books at every opportunity.

A special thanks must go to Janette Currie who has copy-edited the Kim Stone books from the very beginning. Her knowledge of the stories has ensured a continuity for which I'm extremely grateful. Also need a special mention for Henry Steadman who is responsible for the fabulous book covers which I absolutely love.

Thank you to the fantastic Kim Slater who has been an incredible support and friend to me for many years now who, despite writing outstanding novels herself, always finds time for a chat. Massive thanks to Emma Tallon who keeps me going with funny stories and endless support. Also to the fabulous Renita D'Silva and Caroline Mitchell, both writers that I follow and read voraciously and without whom this journey would be impossible. Huge thanks to the growing family of Bookouture authors who continue to amuse, encourage and inspire me on a daily basis.

My eternal gratitude goes to all the wonderful bloggers and reviewers who have taken the time to get to know Kim Stone and follow her story. These wonderful people shout loudly and share generously not because it is their job but because it is their passion. I will never tire of thanking this community for their support of both myself and my books. Thank you all so much.

Massive thanks to all my fabulous readers, especially the ones that have taken time out of their busy day to visit me on my website, Facebook page, Goodreads or Twitter.

Printed in Great Britain
by Amazon